BERSERKER BOYS

BEAR. WOLF. BOAR.

LULU M. SYLVIAN

MOONTAN
PRESS

ISBN: 979-8-9885533-0-4

Edited by: Michelle Cooper
Cover: MedeirosCreative.com

 Formatted with Vellum

This one is for the hot, nerdy, geek boys, and himbos.

BEAR

Cosplay takes on a whole new meaning when Viking gamers have the power to shape shift.

Vik had already chosen to follow the path of the Norse Heathen, and embraced his Viking persona for game play when magic forced the shift on him.

Using the power of online video gaming, magical forces have started opening portals between worlds. That same magic causes Vik to shift into a bear when he is called to do battle against invading hordes of orcs and goblins.

After challenging him on the true meaning of his Viking marks, he invites the feisty Aaliyah to come see what his tattoos really mean, only realizing too late, that he may have put her in danger.

You don't choose the berserker life.
The berserker life chooses you.

CHAPTER

ONE

"Don't look now, but these guys behind you think they're Vikings or something," Aaliyah said.

Maisie twisted in her seat. Her eyes were wide, and she practically vibrated with excitement when Aaliyah could see Maisie's face again.

"I thought I told you not to look."

Yeardley leaned back in her chair and quickly glanced in the direction Aaliyah had indicated. "What the fuck?"

Aaliyah shrugged. "Who knows, maybe it's the latest fashion?"

Aaliyah wasn't bothered by fashion. Having grown up without access to the current trends, she had developed a sense of style free from the influence of fashion magazines or influencers. Her denim jacket was an odd green color, not kelly green, and not olive, but some bastard child in the middle. Her mother had bought it Aaliyah's senior year of high school. She had spent four years begging for a denim jacket with visions of looking like a badass in denim. It had taken her months to get over the disappointment she had felt, but in the end, she loved the uniqueness of it.

Most of her clothes were thrift-store finds or modifications, a habit that stuck with her from her youth. Case in point, the light cardigan she wore as a blouse was navy with gold stars she had embroidered on herself. She wore a color block skirt with a designer label, another thrifting score. Anything she didn't understand was always 'the latest fashion.'

"Are you okay?" Aaliyah asked Maisie.

Maisie was visibly shaking and looked like she was going to start crying at any second. Her lower lip quivered.

Yeardley leaned forward and rested her hand on Maisie's arm. "Maisie?"

Maisie fanned her face, her hand moved so rapidly it was more of a hand flapping than anything else.

"That's Scottie," Maisie squeaked out.

Aaliyah looked from her friend to the group of men dressed in leathers and furs like post-Iron Age warriors, and back.

"Who is Scottie?" She was ready to march over to them no matter how intimidating they looked and give this Scottie a piece of her mind if he had wronged Maisie in their mutual past.

Yeardley cast her glance to the group and back to Aaliyah. "Why is that name familiar? You didn't date him, I'd remember if you had gone out with—"

"Oh my god, no. He's on MinVid. I've shown you his video clips. He's really cute." She was talking through clenched teeth. Panic written all over her face.

"Oh, him. That's why he looks so familiar," Yeardley said.

"I still have no idea which one you're talking about," Aaliyah admitted.

Maisie sighed long and deep. "The ginger one. He's so cute." She fell forward and face-planted against the table.

Without Maisie's head in the way, Aaliyah had a clear view of the Viking men. Two white guys, one with flaming orange hair, the kind that Aaliyah always thought of as nature's warning label, and a Black guy with long locs. It was hard to see what Maisie found appealing about the redhead. It was hard to find anything about them appealing, they were all rather ragged looking with varying colors of makeup smeared across their faces.

She rolled her eyes and looked away when the other white guy winked at her. He did have pretty blue eyes, though.

Yeardley was patting Maisie on the back. "Why don't you just get up and go say hi?"

Maisie bolted upright, her twin long braids swinging. "Oh my god, I couldn't. What if he..." she pressed her hands to her face, covering her eyes.

After a moment, she uncovered her eyes and waved her hands down her front, blowing air out of pursed lips. "They're probably in town for a con or something. I don't know what's around. But, yeah."

"Maisie you are avoiding getting up and going over there and saying hi," Yeardley chastised. "What's the worst that could happen? You'll say, 'Hi, I like your videos,' he'll say, 'thanks.' And that's it."

"That's not the worst thing that could happen. And I just don't want to have to deal with that ever again."

"I know exactly what you're talking about, and Maisie, that guy was a douche with a capital D. No self-respecting, sober artist is going to be that disgustingly rude."

"No, they'll just lie to me, and the entire time I'm only going to be thinking about what they aren't saying."

"He was drunk."

"He just didn't have his filters in place, so I got his truth," Maisie said. Her excitement that Scottie was at the table behind her visibly melted away. She frowned.

"Just because Dave Bacca, a known drunk and asshole, said those things doesn't make them true," Yeardley said.

Maisie stared down at her hands, her fingers twisted together in a show of nerves.

"Who is Dave Bacca?" Aaliyah asked.

"Dave Bacca used to be a voice actor. He did some big sci-fi animes. I met him at a meet and greet for fans, and he said... he said some crappy things to me about cosplaying characters I shouldn't because I was fat," Maisie confessed.

"He also got hit by cancel culture hard because he was a fucking drunk and kept hitting on teenagers that were part of the show's fandom. It's why she hasn't been back to a con in a while. She used to go do all that cosplay stuff," Yeardley said.

"What a fucking dick," Aaliyah commented.

"We should all go sometime," Yeardley suggested. "Aaliyah, have you ever been? You'd love it. They have these things called artist allies. Local artists display and sell their work. You can meet comic book artists, people who do fan art like you do."

"I doubt it's the same kind of fan art," Aaliyah said dismissively.

"No, we should. Maisie could get back on her cosplay bike, it would be fun. Besides, the guys there can be really hot."

"Or super douchey," Maisie added.

"I doubt this Scottie guy is going to be anything like

that. He's not super famous, so maybe he doesn't have an ego?" Aaliyah asked.

"He has over a million followers. Oh, no I can't." Maisie blushed.

Aaliyah pushed up to her feet. "You are going to meet him. I'm going to go over there and ask him to come say hi. I will screen his little attitude and if I think he's gonna be a dick, I'll save you from having your MinVid crush disappoint you."

"Aaliyah, you can't."

But she was already crossing the patio to stand in front of the Vikings' table.

"Apparently your name is Scottie?" she said to the redhead. Up close he was kind of cute. He had high cheekbones and a strong rounded chin. His hair was cut in a shaggy mullet, and the orange strands curled a bit on the ends. His dark blue eyes were rimmed in copious amounts of black liner.

"Yeah, that's me. What'd I do?" he smirked. Oh yeah, Aaliyah could see exactly why Maisie thought he was cute, he was totally her type.

The man he sat next to reached out and backhanded him on the shoulder. Aaliyah didn't want to stare, but it appeared that he had claws. It must be part of the costume.

"What's your name?" the other white guy asked. He pointed to his friends, "Scottie, Wolf"— his finger landed on his chest— "Vik."

Aaliyah was temporarily stunned into silence. Vik's eyes seemed to pin her in place. They were simultaneously beautiful and eerie, a piercing vivid clear blue. They didn't look real. She swallowed.

"I'm Aaliyah. My friend over there," she pointed over her shoulder and then froze as she stared at Vik's scalp. His dirty blond hair was shaved into a wide mohawk. Messy braids and strands decorated with gold beads were twisted into a larger messy braid that followed the contour of his head before splaying out into hair that needed to be combed. Tattooed on his scalp along the shaved edge were a series of symbols.

Her vision turned red. She twisted her pointed finger to Wolf, the Black man sitting between the two white guys.

"What the hell are you doing with someone like him?" She practically yelled as she pointed an accusatory finger in Vik's direction. And to think she had thought that he was hot for a split second.

Wolf's hands went up, and Scottie leaned forward aggressively. Wolf clamped a hand with— yep he had claws — long fingernails over Scottie's arm.

"What do you mean, with someone like him?"

"You're Black, and he's a fucking white supremacist."

Aaliyah's eyes blazed with the fury of a goddess of wrath.

Vik shook his head, he couldn't have her thinking the wrong thing, "My lady, I assure you I am not a white supremacist or anything of the like."

"You have Nazi hate symbols tattooed on your head, so, I'm not convinced." She turned her attention back to Wolf, and then to Scottie. "You should be ashamed. I can't believe Maisie was nervous about meeting you, thinking you were going to end up some kind of asshole. She is going to be crushed."

"Aaliyah it's not what you think." Wolf held up an amulet from around his neck. It was his Mjölnir, Thor's hammer, worn around his neck the way a catholic might wear a cross. "We're pagans. Norse Heathen specifically, and these are the symbols of our gods."

"And we claim them back from hate groups. Please, let me explain." Vik moved a chair out from the table for Aaliyah and gestured for her to take a seat.

"We don't do Nazis here," Scottie said, holding up his messenger bag, it was covered in patches. He pointed to a stylized Mjölnir design with the words, 'No Nazis in Valhalla.' Vik had a similar sticker on his laptop.

"I can't believe I'm doing this. You don't deserve my time." She sat hard and crossed her arms.

Vik stood, before he towered over her, he dropped to his knees in front of her.

"I am a follower of Odin the Allfather."

"By Allfather, we do mean all. Odin doesn't discriminate," Wolf added.

Vik ran his fingers over the markings. "These runes represent a prayer of protection. Calling on the god Tyr for protection and strength in battle, take me to Valhalla should I die, tiwaz, othalla, ansur."

He pointed to the first one shaped like an arrow. "This is a symbol of victory and making the right choices. It represents the god of battle directly. Now, this one"— he pointed to the one shaped like a squared-off ribbon loop— "If you ever see it with feet, that's a bastardization used by hate groups. I will never use that version of the rune. Othalla is home. And this one breathes life into the previous two"— he pointed to the rune shaped like a stylized F— "basically means make it so. It gives these a power boost."

"If those marks are being used by neo-Nazis why do you keep using them? Why tattoo them on your body?"

"Because we will not let those bastards win and poison the symbols of our gods," Vik said with conviction. "They kept me protected when I was younger and stupid. They protect me now. I am sorry my markings have caused you distress. "

He wrapped his hands around hers and lowered his head until his forehead touched her hands clasped in her lap.

"And I thought you were just dressing up for fun." Aaliyah sounded confused, but she stayed.

"We are dressed up for fun," Scottie said.

Vik felt an uncomfortable pang when he realized Aaliyah was looking at Wolf.

"Vikings though?" Her brow scrunched up with her question. She pointed at Scottie and then back to Vik. "They make sense, they're..."

"They're white?" Wolf asked. "Viking is a job description, not a cultural designation. They recruited from other places. Vikings traveled as far as China and into the Middle East. There are runestones at the Black Sea. Vikings were more interested in your ability to fight, if you were clean, and if you looked good. Besides, it's fun."

"What the hell is going on over here?"

Vik looked past the beautiful Aaliyah. As a tall blonde, shield maiden stormed over.

"Oh, hi." Her tone and demeanor changed dramatically when she looked at Wolf.

He had that effect on women. Someone had once said it was his puppy dog eyes. Vik had no idea what they meant. It didn't matter, it took the wind right out of her indignant sails.

"This is Vik," Aaliyah said as she took one of her hands away from his. He noticed she continued to let him hold her hand. "And that's Wolf and Scottie."

"Okay, you can't abandon me over there all by myself.

Hi Scottie," their third friend said. All he could see of her earlier were her long dark braids. She was cute and round, and blushed furiously as she waved awkwardly at Scottie. "I follow you on MinVid. What are you guys all dressed up for?" She bit her lip and shrugged.

"Have you ladies ordered yet?" Vik asked.

Aaliyah shook her head. "I haven't even looked at the menu."

"Why don't you join us? We can drag another table over." Scottie was on his feet and wrangling an additional table.

The waiter came out and helped Scottie move chairs, and then helped to carry menus over to the now larger table.

"I see that you are all dressed normally, what are you up to today?" Scottie asked.

Maisie melted into a blushing fit of giggles. "Nothing, just hanging out. Getting lunch."

"I think that's supposed to be what one of us asks you," Yeardley said. "And don't say nothing, cause fur, and chain maille isn't nothing."

"Apparently they are on some kind of Viking education outreach mission," Aaliyah said.

"Oh yeah?" Yeardley asked. "Okay, hit me with everything I ever wanted to know about Vikings but was afraid to ask."

"I'm more interested in why you guys are all dressed up. Are you doing a photoshoot or something?" Maisie asked without stammering.

"Vikings knew about the American continent, had settlements, and probably harvested wood for their ships hundreds of years before Christopher Colombus sailed," Wolf answered Yeardley directly.

"Please," Maisie cut in. "Lots of people knew about the Americas before Columbus and his lot. It's almost as if the Spanish and Italians were the only ones who didn't know about the Americas. There's plenty of evidence supporting that Asians had landed on the west coast, and even African traders interacted with South America."

"Vikings were raging feminists." Wolf crossed his arms with a smug expression.

"Excuse me, raping and pillaging and invading lands to take their women?" Aaliyah commented.

Vik sighed. "We're really going to have to work on what you know about Vikings, aren't we?"

He smirked at Aaliyah, and she smiled back. The idea of working with Vik on anything was kind of thrilling. She wanted to know more about this man who hadn't gotten angry, only sad when she misjudged him, and then he calmly explained while she all but screamed in his face. She lifted her hand, palm up, giving him the floor, as it were.

"Remember Viking is a job description, but in the Norse societies these men lived in, the women had rights. They worked the settlements, they tended the safety of their villages when the men were away. Women had their own money, they were allowed to divorce. They were allowed to train and fight."

"So you're saying that Vikings liked strong women?" Yeardley asked. Her eyes hadn't drifted from Wolf since they sat down.

"Absolutely," Wolf drawled.

"So how do you know all of this?" Aaliyah asked.

"Reading, online research. It came to me as a spin-off of my following Odin," Vik answered.

"I wanted to know more about Vikings if I was going to

cosplay one, I figured I should know more about them than what gets put in video games," Wolf said.

"Yeah, what they said," Scottie answered.

"So, you read a Wikipedia page?" Maisie asked.

Aaliyah was impressed. Her friend had gone from blushing fan-girl to snarky with no more fucks to give.

"You are a feisty one, aren't you?" Scottie smirked.

"Can we take a selfie?" Maisie blurted out.

Okay, maybe she still had plenty of fucks to give.

"Sure," Scottie said.

Maisie handed him her phone. "You have longer arms."

Scottie reached out and Maisie leaned in, making crossed-finger hearts, K-pop style. They held still and smiled at her phone.

"Oh we should take a group picture," Maisie cooed.

Aaliyah felt a shiver run down her spine when Vik placed his arm over her shoulder and leaned in close as Maisie posed in front to take a group selfie.

"Can I help you with that?" The waiter showed up in time to help out.

Vik kept his arm over the back of her chair, even after the waiter handed Maisie her phone back.

"The point is, if someone is dressing up like a Viking, claiming any kind of connection to them, they should know their history, and the mythos surrounding the Norse deities," Vik said.

"So you're saying there is more to Thor than long blond hair and a flying hammer?" Maisie asked.

"Yes, and Loki was supposed to be a redhead when he wasn't a horse," Scottie said.

"There is a story there, but, um, no, I can't wait. What?" Aaliyah asked.

Vik laughed. "The Loki and Thor stories are great. They

did a lot of crazy things. A lot of the gods did. And yes, Loki turned into a female horse to cause a bit of a distraction."

"Okay, why did you emphasize female horse? Isn't a horse a horse?" Yeardley asked.

"Yes, well, only female horses can have babies," Wolf answered.

Aaliyah closed her eyes for a long moment to process the conversation around her. Of course, female horses are the ones that had babies. Why the hell did that matter? "Wait. Are you saying Loki had a horse baby?"

"Yeah," Vik said. "Loki is a mother. There's a lot of stuff like that in Norse mythology. That's why it's important to know what you're getting into if you want to represent Vikings, or even get into the religion."

"It sounds like a lot," Aaliyah said.

"It is a lot. But it's cool shit."

"Okay, so Viking lessons one-oh-one aside, why are you guys walking around all decked out. Unless it's the newest trend, what gives?" Aaliyah asked.

Vik's handsome face narrowed into a glare that he directed at Scottie. Aaliyah noticed that Wolf had also cut a glare in Scottie's direction.

"Okay, okay, fuck. How long are you going to hold it against me?" Scottie held up his hands and leaned away from the onslaught of glares.

"Oh, hold what?" Maisie perked right up.

"We were attending a LARP," Vik started.

"A what?" Aaliyah asked.

"Are you familiar with gaming? D and D? Role play tabletop games, video games? All of that?" Wolf asked.

Aaliyah smiled. "Yes, I know about gaming. Oh my god, I don't live in a cave. I'm just not big into geek culture or

Vikings." She quickly turned to Vik. "But I'm willing to learn."

"LARP, Live Action Role Play. It's a lot like playing any role-playing game where you roll the dice to determine the outcome of any given scenario. But you dress up, and get into it a bit more," Vik explained.

"So you are all headed out to play games dressed up like Vikings?"

"Exactly," Scottie answered with a huge grin on his face. "It's so much fun. We're going to battle."

Aaliyah looked at Vik, hoping he would provide a more in-depth answer.

"There is an all-day regional LARP battle. People come from all over, dressed up in their favorite cosplay and—"

"And we beat the crap out of each other with foam and duct tape swords." Scottie finished.

"Foam and duct tape?" Aaliyah asked.

Vik shrugged. "No one wants to get hurt, they want to have fun. There will be people there dressed up from their favorite video games, and they'll have crazy unrealistic weapons."

"And then there will be others like us," Wolf started. "With safe, harmless mock-ups of real weapons."

"Like what? Oh, can you show me?" Maisie asked enthusiastically.

"Why don't you come with us after lunch? You can check out what it's all about," Wolf offered.

"If it's all day, why are you here?" Yeardley asked.

Scottie let out a long dejected sign. "I left the cooler with all of our food in the driveway at my house. I forgot to put it in the car, and I was in charge of food. So, I'm buying the guys lunch."

TWO

"That's their car, hurry up or we're going to lose them again," Maisie squealed.

Ever since she got in the car after having met Scottie she was bouncing off the walls.

"This would be easier if that Scottie guy didn't drive like a maniac," Yeardley grumbled.

She was doing a pretty good job of keeping up, but it certainly felt like they were in some kind of a car chase weaving in and out of traffic. Aaliyah braced herself with one hand pressed up into the ceiling and another on the window just to keep from being thrown all over the back seat. Maisie's manic panic over losing the guys was not helping her fraying nerves.

She had made a complete ass of herself in front of Vik, calling him a white supremacist. Talk about jumping to conclusions, but she ran with the information she had. Even he admitted it was confusing. But she understood why they were holding onto their symbols fiercely. People had to take a stand where they could, and if that meant not giving away what was theirs while the real assholes tried to use them, well, she understood why Vik and his friends were digging in their heels and holding tight.

"How far away is this LARP thing?" she asked. Not that she was prone to car sickness, but the ride was getting to be a lot too much.

"Scottie said it wasn't far," Maisie answered.

"Yeah, he also didn't say where it was. 'Follow us!'" Yeardley mocked Scottie's battle call when she asked for an address to put in her GPS.

"Oh, look, a sign. World LARP this way," Maisie said.

The car noticeably slowed and stopped weaving about. Aaliyah sighed.

"You okay back there? You aren't going to be sick are you?" Yeardley asked.

"We're going to lose them," Maisie panicked.

"Watch for more of those World LARP signs. They should get us there. If Scottie loses us, it's on him. Aaliyah is about to puke, she's turning green."

"Oh like an orc?" Maisie turned around to look at Aaliyah from the front seat. "Ah, you look fine. You're not going to puke are you?"

"If I do puke, I'm saving it so I can hurl on Scottie's shoes."

Maisie turned and huffed back into her seat. "What do you have against Scottie?"

"He drives like a fucking maniac, that's what. He's driving like he wants to lose us."

"You're just mad you didn't get Wolf's number."

"Well you didn't get Scottie's," Yeardley snapped back.

"No," Maisie pouted. "But I did get a selfie."

Aaliyah closed her eyes and focused on breathing and not puking the rest of the ride.

"Turn right up ahead," Maisie announced.

The car bounced on uneven ground. When Aaliyah opened her eyes, they were following a line of cars and being directed to park in a field. Just beyond the cars were a row of tents with flags of different colors and symbols.

"Okay, kids, we're here. Remember to hold hands with your partner and don't wander away from the group," Yeardley said with the perfect inflection of someone who had been a camp counselor and taken plenty of kids on field trips.

"This is so exciting," Maisie practically jumped up and down as soon as she was out of the car.

Aaliyah rolled out of the back seat and felt like kissing the ground. Everything was blessedly still.

"Let's go find the guys."

Aaliyah wished Maisie's enthusiasm was infectious. After that ride, she wasn't feeling particularly eager to check out this event.

Yeardley put her arm around Aaliyah's shoulder. "You were looking pretty peeked there, you up for this?"

"I'm out of the car, and the fresh air is helping. Besides, I really kind of want to see them in action."

"You mean Vik," Yeardley chuckled.

Aaliyah pointed from herself to Yeardley to Maisie. "Vik, Wolf, Scottie, I mean... yeah totally. He's fucking hot, I'm not gonna lie."

"I know right?"

"There they are!" Maisie squealed again.

Aaliyah really wanted to give her friend a little chill gummy. She had never seen this level of enthusiasm from Maisie before. It was taking a modicum of acclimation. Aaliyah followed Maisie's gesture.

The guys were there all right, but they looked like they

were about to fight. Vik was squaring up to Scottie, and Wolf stood glowering with his arms crossed.

Damn, they were all freaking tall. Scottie was wiry in comparison, so he didn't appear as big, but he was just as tall as Vik. It was hard to gauge with Wolf, seeing how he wasn't right up in the middle of the two of them.

"Scottie!" Maisie called as she quickened her step.

Vik shoved Scottie and strode in their direction. Aaliyah didn't want to smile, he looked like a fierce warrior coming toward her. Like some scene out of a movie, only better. When he made eye contact with her, he visibly relaxed and his step quickened.

"I thought that asshole lost you. Shit, are you okay?" he said as soon as he reached her and Yeardley.

"He's lucky I grew up on Speed Racer and the Fast and the Furious franchise. I could probably take him on Pole Position any day," Yeardley said with a grunt. "It's a video game." She shook her head and continued walking.

"I got a little car sick. Yeardley may be able to drive like that, but her car is not made for it. I am definitely not made for it. But we made it."

"You did." His smile made Aaliyah feel a little weak in the knees.

They walked slowly back to the car where Scottie and Wolf were pulling swords and battle axes and more furs from the car.

If Aaliyah had thought the guys had looked like Vikings before, she had clearly been mistaken. Wolf adjusted a large fur across his shoulders. His long locs blended in and he looked as if he were wearing even more fur.

Scottie hefted two large broad sword replicas. The way he twirled them around made Aaliyah think they had to be pretty light, after all, hadn't one of them said something about the swords being all foam and duct tape?

"You fight in all of this?" Aaliyah asked as she fingered a fur Vik draped over his shoulders. It was rough, not soft like she expected.

When he turned she noticed it had a bear head hanging down, like some kind of extreme hood. She pulled her hand away before slowly reaching back out to touch the fur.

"A bear head? Is this real?"

Vik rubbed the fur at his shoulder and twisted as if he could see the head that hung down behind him.

"A bear is my symbolic animal. Why are you smiling?"

Aaliyah bit her lip. "You didn't use a culturally appropriative term. Like, you didn't even have to think about it. And I was such a bitch earlier. And I'm a dork."

Vik leaned in close. "You make a cute dork. Since I think it would matter to you, Björn here was ethically sourced."

"It has a name?"

"He has a name, he gives me his spirit in battle, he deserves a name," Vik said with all seriousness.

"Björn is a good name. You get into these things, don't you?"

"It's better than tagging freight trains. Keeps me out of trouble and from getting bored."

"How do you find out about these things?" she asked as they crossed the field turned parking lot, and headed toward the tents.

"Once you get into it, it's kind of hard not to know about them. You join one list-serve, one social media group, and the next thing you know you're following LARPs and cons on every freaking platform. And joining others just to stay in the loop."

"I get it, it's like listening to K-pop. You follow one band

and go in search of the fans, and then you're following all the bands, and all of your friends seem to be into it."

"Is that how you all know each other?"

"Isn't it obvious?" Aaliyah laughed. "That's exactly what happened. I met Yeardley online, and she already knew Maisie from college. And we all met up with some others at a concert last year. It was so much fun."

"And now fandoms collide," Vik said.

They had reached the tents, slightly behind the rest of their group.

"Are you fighting? You need to check-in." Aaliyah couldn't decide if the girl directing them where to go was dressed up, or if she just had an extreme sense of style with platform boots and a PVC vinyl mini skirt.

"Oh, um, I'm just here to observe," Aaliyah stammered.

"Okay, you get one of these." The girl wrapped a red Tyvek wristband around Aaliyah's wrist. "Remember to stay behind the white chalked line on the field for your safety."

"I'm fighting," Vik said.

"You need to check-in at the booth with the blue Federation flags." She pointed along the row of tents.

Aaliyah felt as if she had been plunged from reality into a sci-fi movie's version of the outdoor bazaar crossed with a Ren Fair. There were characters from different movies that she recognized, and general characters from fantasy that she could identify but didn't know if they were from a game or what. A wizard tended to look like a wizard. And orcs had a definite look about them from a variety of sources. But there were so many more characters. She saw pirates, both the scourge of the Spanish Main and the space kind. There were skinny kids in long black coats walking around with swords that looked like giant blades from wind turbines.

She gasped when she saw people dressed up in the long flowing robes of her favorite genre of Chinese magic martial arts costume dramas.

"Did you see the guys dressed up like Lan Xiao and Lan Ying?" It was Aaliyah's turn to gush.

"Who?" Yeardley asked.

"Wait, those are the hot guys in that Masters of Discipline show from China, right?" Maisie asked.

"Yeah, and they did a beautiful job on their costumes."

"Those guys are so hot," Maisie said. She made an expression like her face was melting from their hotness. "That show is so gay, I love it so much. I can't believe they manage to get away with so much homoerotic subcontext." Maisie sighed. "So many men, so little time."

"I thought you just said they were gay?" Yeardley asked.

"I would beard so hard for them. I can still look and admire," Maisie said.

"Right? I mean, it's not fair those men are prettier than I am, but damn it, at least let me admire and revel in their relationship. I swear the sexual tension in that show is off the charts hot. There are episodes when I just yell at the TV 'kiss already.'" Aaliyah laughed.

"You two are wack," Yeardley said.

"Wack-a-molé," Maisie confirmed.

VIK WATCHED AS AALIYAH AND HER FRIENDS WALKED AWAY IN THE opposite direction. Maybe this had been a bad idea, but he had wanted her to see what he and the symbols on his scalp meant. He had almost given away too much when she started asking about the bear on his back.

"I get it, you're a fucking prick, but do you have to act like one all the time?" Wolf growled at Scottie.

They shuffled back and forth waiting to fill out the waivers so they could go out on the field and wail away on anyone and everyone. It was a video game battle raid brought to life. And that was one of the main reasons they were there, things were coming to these events that shouldn't be.

"You're lucky Yeardley isn't afraid to drive like a drag racer," Wolf continued.

"Yeah, man," Vik started. "Aaliyah got car sick."

"Are you two going to be up my ass about that all day? So I drove a little fast? Your girls caught up no problem," Scottie complained.

"What's your problem man?" Vik asked. Scottie had something up his ass alright, he had just better chill out before it was Vik's boot.

"Nothing," Scottie huffed. "Why did you suggest they come?"

"I thought you liked fangirls."

"I do, but she's a bit too much fangirl, if you know what I mean?" Scottie shrugged and wiggled his eyebrows.

"Jesus Scottie, do you have to be such a fucking pig?" Wolf snarled.

"But I am," Scottie exclaimed.

"That's no excuse to act like one. And no, I don't know what you mean. That Maisie chick is cute. Explain yourself," Vik said as he readjusted the battle axes he wore on his belt. So what if Maisie was a big girl? So was Aaliyah. Hell, all three of the women they had met were not dainty little things.

Scottie's tastes tended toward the barbarian-Viking fantasy chicks who went for the fur bikini aesthetic but didn't look like they could lift an axe. Vik admired a good Frazetta barbarian babe himself, but that didn't preclude him from admiring or being attracted to different body types. That Yeardley chick, now she could probably carry that barbarian look off. Maybe that was Scottie's problem, Yeardley only saw Wolf and wasn't fawning appropriately over Scottie. It was still no excuse to be a dick to his friends, or rude about Maisie.

Scottie closed his eyes and sighed. "Why does it matter? You're getting what you want. Hot girl, socially-oriented. I mean did you spring a boner when she started yelling and you were gonna have a chance to show off, or after when it was clear she accepted your apology and explanation and was into you again?"

Vik started to laugh, it was sarcastic and bitter. "Stay away from me out there. Something has crawled up your ass and is riding you hard. And I don't think I care for your company right now. Also, fuck you."

Vik stepped out of line and let a pair of cosplaying fighters from the popular anime Sword Craft Streaming take his spot in line. Scottie was his friend, and if he throat punched the asshole before they filled out any waivers, or ran into Scottie out on that field today, they might not be friends much longer.

Yes, he had found Aaliyah attractive when she went into protective warrior mode when she thought Wolf was hanging out with fascists. It meant they saw things in parallel, it meant he knew a lot about her from a few moments of righteous indignation. For him, it was just a preview of everything about her he wanted to know. He knew she was adorably sexy.

Her hair looked soft, like a dark cloud. Her smile illuminated her entire face. And those glasses were straight out of the sexy smart girl playbook. She looked like she would be soft and feel good in his arms, and be a responsible recycler.

He stewed in his anger as he walked back to the end of the line. Scottie could be a prick, but he typically wasn't this much of an asshole. Maybe inviting Aaliyah to come see the LARP battle wasn't the best idea. But it hadn't scared her off. How many times had he gotten a cute girl to act interested only to run away when he suggested they do something remotely geeky, or obviously pagan? So far Aaliyah hadn't seemed discouraged by either.

There was a nagging at the back of his brain. What if this was all a bad idea? The LARP seemed innocuous enough. So far no one tripped any red flags for him. And neither Wolf nor Scottie mentioned having encountered any energy surges.

They walked the field before lunch and participated in an earlier battle. Everything had stayed normal. Facsimile weapons stayed fake. The only characters from magical realms were people in costume and make-up. They could participate for fun.

Maybe that lack of anything bad happening lulled him into a false sense that nothing bad would continue to be the standard for the afternoon's battles. A shiver rolled down his spine, a sensation that was unfamiliar. He didn't like it.

"You okay?" Wolf asked.

"Yeah, I just need to cool off. Something got me on edge."

"I feel ya. I don't like it. There are enough gamers here with mobile setups, something could be brewing," he said.

"Was inviting Aaliyah here the wrong thing to do? Did I put those women in danger?" Vik asked.

Wolf clapped him on the shoulder. "The fact that you are even asking me that tells me two things. The first is that you really like this girl, even though you just met her. And two, you think this morning's battle was too easy."

"Hey man." Scottie rubbed the back of his neck and looked sheepish. "When I said Maisie was too much, I meant her enthusiasm, not her ass. Fill out the forms, I'll be over there." He nodded indicating he would be in the same direction as the women.

Fuck. If Vik hadn't stepped out of line, he could be hanging with Aaliyah right now, and not waiting behind a winged demon from Edgeland who smelled as if they had not learned the importance of airing out one's cosplay between events.

Aaliyah was startled and jumped when an air horn blared. Her heart raced and she had to catch her breath.

"Clear the field. That was the first warning. All players must clear the field."

"What's that all about?" Yeardley asked.

Aaliyah shrugged.

"They want everyone off the field so they can confirm wrist bands before the battle starts," Wolf seemed to sneak up on them and was answering before she even realized he was there.

The band on his wrist was bright neon green.

"Oh that's bright," Aaliyah said.

"I like it, it's fun. It's more fun than ours," Maisie said pointing to her red wrist band.

"It's so that it's visible from a distance. They don't want anyone on the field who hasn't signed a waiver."

It made perfect sense to Aaliyah. The field was designated by a series of barriers that started a good twenty yards away from the tents. The first barrier was a chalk line in the dirt. The next was a make-shift fence of sorts using orange safety cones with strings of plastic pennant flags between them. Only the side of the field closest to the tents was roped off. Aaliyah assumed the rest of the field on the other side was fair game.

"This is so cool," Maisie said with her typical enthusiasm. "The costumes and battle gear are insane. I haven't seen this much cosplay in one place since I went to a con."

"You say that like you haven't been to one in a while," Wolf said.

"I haven't."

"Why not?" Scottie asked as he joined their little group.

Maisie looked him dead in the eye, all of her exuberance gone. "I had a bad experience with a minor celebrity. It kind of put me off."

"You need to come with us. We'll make sure you have a good time, and if anyone bothers you, I'll gut them for you."

Maisie looked like she was going to explode as a fierce blush grew on her cheeks.

"That sounds like fun. I miss the vendor's rooms. So much cool stuff," Maisie sighed.

"Vendor rooms are great. I'm partial to the panels," Wolf said.

"Those can be fun."

"You mean a panel discussion?" Aaliyah asked. "What kind of panels do they have?"

"Sometimes TV shows will send promotion tours out, and you'll get actors from something popular," Maisie started.

"Or something old. The old sci-fi show actors are always making the rounds at smaller cons," Scottie added.

"They have panels on anything, costuming, 3D modeling, gaming, programming," Wolf said.

"Programming?" Yeardley asked. "You mean coding?"

"Yeah, especially coding for games. Those are big. People want to know how to get into the business, or how long it takes to do a build. The testing process, what kind of influence we have on game design," Wolf said.

"We? You?" Yeardley asked.

Wolf chuckled. "Yeah, I'm a programmer for Edgeland. So I tend to be on a lot of panels."

"Really?" Yeardley seemed to lean in closer. "I do programming too, but not for games. I do logistics software. I'd like to see one of your panels."

"There is a con in a few weeks."

"Oh, we should go," Maisie said.

"Where are you going?" Vik asked as he slid into the space next to Aaliyah.

"There is a convention coming up. It looks like we're all gonna go, and meet up there."

Vik smiled, and Aaliyah felt it like butterflies in her midsection.

"Okay, so Wolf and Yeardley are both programmers. I work retail. What do you do?" Maisie asked Vik.

"I'm a Viking," he answered.

"I mean, what do you do to pay the bills?"

"I sell my services to the highest bidder," Vik smirked.

Aaliyah squinted at him, he was either claiming to be an escort or a mercenary. Vik looked at her and gave her another knee-weakening smile. "I'm a contractor for game testing. I worked on Edgeland for a bit, and now I'm with Planet Games."

"I've heard of Edgeland, I mean it's big and I actually don't live under a rock, but Planet Games?" Aaliyah asked.

"They make games for phones. So what do you do?"

"I'm an admin," Aaliyah said.

"She's an artist," Maisie added, "She does these amazing watercolors."

"I'd like to see them sometime," Vik said.

Aaliyah smiled. She wanted to show him, and she didn't typically want others to see her work.

Another air horn blared. "Final call to clear field, final call to clear field."

"Damn that thing is loud," Aaliyah said after wincing at the noise.

"It's got to be loud enough to be heard in the midst of battle."

"It works. So, Scottie, what do you do? Are you in video games as well?" Aaliyah asked, distracting herself from overtly flirting with Vik.

"I make MinVids."

"Right, but for work," Yeardley pointed out.

"I make MinVids."

"You can make money doing that?" Yeardley asked.

"With enough followers, you end up getting added to the creator fund, and based on views and followers, yeah. I get paid to make MinVids."

"Oh shit," Maisie exclaimed.

"What?"

Maisie sighed. "I have to go. I totally forgot I'm babysitting my nephews tonight." She looked at Yeardley. "I'm sorry."

"Oh, I was looking forward to this," Aaliyah said mournfully.

"You don't have to go too, do you?" Vik asked.

"I drove," Yeardley said. "If I'm leaving…" She shrugged in defeat.

"I can give you a ride home," Vik volunteered.

"But didn't you ride with Scottie? Is there even room in the car with all the weapons and costumes and stuff?"

"That was just for lunch. My car is out there in the parking lot."

"Oh, are you sure?" Aaliyah asked.

Vik nodded.

She looked over at her friends. "I think I'll stay."

"You'll be okay?" Yeardley asked.

"Yeah, I can text you a blow-by-blow recount of what's happening."

The horrendous air horn sounded again. "The field will open in five minutes. Battle starts in fifteen, all players must be on the field."

"Sounds like that's our call, Ladies." Wolf gave everyone a regal bow and turned to leave.

"DM me," Scottie told Maisie, pointing back and forth between them. "We'll work out deets for the con."

Maisie nodded her head in tight little movements. She had to be too stunned to reply.

"You sure you'll be fine?" Yeardley asked.

"I'll take good care of her," Vik said as he slid an arm around Aaliyah's shoulders and started walking toward the battlefield.

THREE

"I'm glad you decided to stay," Vik said.

Aaliyah shook her head. "I don't know what I'm getting myself into."

"I promise it will be worth your while."

They walked to an area near a stand of trees. The field was in front, the tents and parking lot behind. A fallen tree had been cut into stumps and logs so that observers had a place to sit. It wasn't exactly observation stands, but in a way it was.

"I'll come find you here between battles."

"How many battles are there going to be?" Aaliyah asked.

"They had two this morning. We got here late for the second one, so we watched that one. It gave us a chance to check out what kind of fighters are out there. There are three scheduled for after lunch. They last about twenty to forty minutes. With breaks in between. Each new battle starts fifteen after the hour."

"Sounds like someone put a lot of effort into coordinating this," Aaliyah said.

"Exactly. I wouldn't want to be on the organization committee. It's a lot of work, and it's all volunteer-run. They literally couldn't pay me enough to do it."

"But you come and fight. You enjoy the fruit of their efforts."

"Hell yeah. I paid my entry fee."

"You pay to do this? But I got in for free," Aaliyah pointed out.

"That's because you aren't fighting. If you had to pay to come watch, odds are you wouldn't. But people will pay to get whacked by other people's fake weapons. We're all kind of nuts if I'm honest."

She laughed. It was worth every penny of attending this LARP to have met her and hear her laughter.

"You be here"— Vik pointed to the seating area— "and I'll be out there."

"I'll be watching." Aaliyah leaned in and gave him a quick kiss on the cheek. "For luck."

Vik placed a hand over her kiss. He was still rubbing his cheek when he joined the cattle drive through the orange cones and onto the battlefield. There were three "armies" crowded on the field. Vik spotted Wolf and Scottie across the field and strode over to join them.

The mass of gathered participants looked more like the starting gate of a costume-themed 5k run with people stretching and running in place to warm up.

"So far so good," Scottie announced when he arrived.

"I thought I got a tickle of something earlier, but, I don't know, maybe it was just a random shiver. I haven't felt anything since," Vik added.

"I strolled over to the gamer's area earlier, just to see if I could pick anything up, and I didn't get anything either.

There's no signal out here, so the guys were stuck playing what they had downloaded."

"Tell me again why you would come to a LARP and bring your gaming setup?" Scottie asked.

"So you can game between battles," Wolf answered. "So you can meet up with your raiding party in person."

"So you can participate even if you physically can't participate," Vik added. "Don't you have your laptop in the car? You never know what happens if you get side-lined after one battle."

"It's a gamer's paradise here today, let them have their fun," Wolf smirked. "Because I'm about to have mine." He crouched down and held his battle-axe high.

Scottie twirled his double swords like batons.

The air horn sounded. If there was an announcement, no one on the field heard it, because all at once everyone roared their battle cries and the three army groups rushed together.

Vik ran into the horde with his own intimidating scream that sounded more like the roar of an angry bear. He swept his battle-axe up, blocking the downward sweep of a claymore from a man wearing a kilt and covered in blue body paint. He spun and got the guy in the solar plexus with a back jab of the axe handle. The blue Scot doubled over gasping for breath.

Vik spun and hooked the ankles of another assailant, bringing them crashing down. He worked swiftly and efficiently vanquishing his foe at every turn. That was until he came across the type of LARPer he objected to fighting with, Kawaii Battle Princess. She was the main character from a popular game. Its online community of gamers were rabid and vicious, and not all girls. He could go head to head with anyone dressed like the small fluffy little princess with her oversized mallet, as long as they weren't actually the size of the game character.

The character was a five-year-old princess who wore all the fluff and ruffles, with curly blue hair, and a temper that could scare off the grouchiest of silverbacks.

Vik froze when he was confronted with a petite fighter dressed in all the pink and blue fluff of the character, who just about topped off at four feet tall, wig included. Legally she had to be over eighteen to participate, but she barely looked older than ten.

She raised her spiked mallet and swung it on a perfect trajectory to bean him on the top of his head.

"For fuck's sake," he grumbled and fell forward into a roll.

The hammer missed his foot by a breath of air. He swung around and scooped her up by the waist. She struggled and screamed like a banshee. He set her down out of his way and kept on moving through the battle. The next opponent he had no qualms about hitting. The man was dressed like an orc. Built like one too with shoulders as wide as a pickup truck and arms as thick as tree trunks.

He came at Vik with an unholy roar. Vik slid to his knees, his velocity carried him past the orc. He swung his axe into the back of his assailant's knees. The axe stuck against the other guy's boots. Vik wrenched it away convinced he had just broken his favorite toy.

"Fuck!"

Black ooze dripped from the axe head.

That's when he felt the magic slam into him. He watched it roll over the battlefield like a blast of light. Suddenly the nature of the sounds of the play battle around him changed. The screams took on a terrifying pitch as fake weapons became real ones, and blows that should have only left bruises cut into flesh.

"Oh my god. Help, I'm bleeding!"

"Medic!"

Cries of pain and panic rippled across the battlefield.

Vik spun and delivered a killing blow into the orc's back, severing its spine.

He saw Scottie arch back, screaming into the sky. Tusks already protruded from his lips. He fell out of Vik's line of sight. He would be fully changed by the time he landed.

A blur of fur that was Wolf already in his battle form cut past Vik's vision. He followed the direction of the running wolf to see the portal.

Sparking flames in blue and gold hues swirled around an opening in the middle of the field. Orcs, tall muscular, and green, covered in thick spiny armor ran into the middle of their game. Gray and purple-hided goblins moved along the ground like creatures who had more limbs than they did and didn't know how to stand upright. They snuck up on their victims by staying low and out of their field of vision.

He felt the change coming, but he still had time to act. He ran, grabbing the Kawaii Battle Princess and spinning her to face him.

"Get out of here, run!"

"Fuck you," she yelled in his face before they were both hit with a splatter of blood from the fighters next to them. She screamed.

"Go!" He yelled.

The change was close. He pulled his bear hood over his head, and suddenly those were now the eyes he saw through. He grew taller, his muscles multiplied. He managed to still grasp his battle-axe in one paw, but he didn't need it now, not with the claws that grew from his large paws.

"What the fuck is happening?" a shout from somewhere behind him.

He lumbered at speed to the front line of the invading orcs. Now as tall as the creatures who did not belong in this dimension, he swatted them aside with barely any effort. The orcs were tough. The resilience of the LARP fighters impressed Vik. A band of humans in orc cosplay and over-the-top paladin armor from several games fought back. They formed a line protecting fallen comrades.

Goblin screams and falling bodies let him know that Scottie was tearing through the creatures as they hovered closer to the ground. They needed to press the invasion back through the portal, and get it shut.

Vik tore the limb from an advancing attacker as he continued to rip through his adversaries. He flanked the humans, together they could put the squeeze on the invasion and press them back.

"Holy shit there's a bear!"

Ignoring the screams that didn't directly impact his actions, Vik charged into the thick of the raiding party. He no longer cared if he got them back on the other side of the portal, as long as they could no longer injure the people on this side of the portal.

Aaliyah sat and watched the battle. It looked like the fever dream of a fantasy film, only they didn't have a budget for matching costumes. Also, it wasn't nearly as well choreographed.

Everyone had their own fighting style. She eyed the two

in the cosplay from Masters of Discipline. She left the seating area to walk along the barrier, following them. They did their very best to fight as if they were in a kung-fu movie. Only without the wires and aerial flips, it wasn't nearly as mesmerizing. They were impressive with their rolling spins. And she loved the way their sleeves and robes flowed.

She cast her gaze about, not certain if it would be acceptable to take photos. She wanted reference material for her art, and this battle was full of inspiration. She pulled her phone out and began taking pictures. She lost sight of the men in the beautiful robes with the beautiful long black wigs.

She saw a group that stood in a small group and hit each other one after the other in their small circle. They seemed to be trying to knock each other over, but not very hard. They spent most of their time laughing. They were having a good time.

That's what this was all about, having fun. There were a few fighters out there that seemed to be in it to unleash their aggression. They slammed their homemade weapons with force. A few participants, who had enough, staggered off the field. She jumped out of the way as an elf in rough spun with pointy ears helped a vinyl-clad character in dark sunglasses limp off to the medic tent.

She caught a glimpse of Vik and Wolf, they moved like they had practiced a dance, block, thrust, spin, flip, hit, only to repeat it all over again. They moved through the battle knocking their opponents to the ground as they moved. If this was a last-man-standing competition, they were taking out opponents left and right. Scottie wasn't quite as fluid. His approach was more hurling and beating. The three of them together were an army all their own.

She took picture after picture. Mesmerized by the way they moved and flowed with the battle, she stopped snapping pictures and let her arms fall. She wanted to experience everything with her own eyes and not through the tiny lens and screen of her cell phone.

Something slammed into her. It wasn't physical, but it certainly felt as if it could have been. Her skin tingled and she looked around to see if there had been a lightning strike or some kind of power surge. But where would something like that have come from? She tried to shake off the weird feeling that crept up her spine.

The battle in front of her was loud, but suddenly it grew louder. And the screams seemed real. She fell back as the smell of blood assaulted her senses. What was happening?

She frantically looked for Vik. Surely he would come off the field soon. They had to call an end to the battle if people were getting hurt. Wouldn't they?

She caught sight of Vik. Before she could wave and try to get his attention she watched with disbelieving eyes as he pulled the bear cloak over his head and face. At first, she thought he was wrapping Björn around him for protection, but that's not what happened. He pulled the bear on, and he became the bear.

A scream froze in her throat as she scrambled away from the edge of the battlefield and landed on her ass. She couldn't seem to get her arms and legs to move, to get her way from the horror she watched as what had started as fun and people in costumes seemed to turn into a real bloody battle with... holy shit, were those goblins and orcs?

AALIYAH WAS FROZEN IN PLACE AS A VERITABLE GIANT OF A MAN, not a man, an orc, an actual green-skinned, tusked monster from the realms of fantasy and video games stomped toward her. The ground shook with every booted footfall.

She fumbled with her phone and began recording everything. Her brain seemed to fracture with one part continuing to panic and scream, while the other part was fascinated and studying the details. And the details were amazing. Top to bottom the creature stalking toward her wore the most interesting armor. Plates of giant scales of heavily textured hide formed the base layer of his protective wear. His chest was mostly exposed with his arms covered in the scales and his shoulders, neck, and head with a second layer of articulated armor made from spiny bones. As if he wore the spiked spines and ribs of several small dragons. Dragons? If he was an orc, why wouldn't there be dragons too?

All of this was fastened across his chest with a double row of belts and buckles. The muscles of his chest and abdomen looked more like a mountain range. He was so jacked. Around his hips, more belts and buckles. A kilt of plate-sized scales hung to mid-thigh, and his legs were wrapped in more of that articulated bone armor. It made no sense that his vital organs were exposed while his limbs were protected. Then again, he looked exactly like so many video game designs.

Aaliyah snapped photos. There were real orcs and goblins crawling around. She wanted to get as much reference material as she could.

The two parts of her brain ignored each other and continued doing their thing— one side taking notes on the way the monsters moved and dressed, the other side screaming in abject fear— as both sides realized she was in very real danger, her ability to scream stopped. She forced herself to scramble backward and try to gain her feet.

Suddenly, with a roar, a grizzly bear was between her and the orc. He skidded to a stop in front of her, she could barely see over its furry shoulder. The orc paused, smirked, and began laughing. Aaliyah got her feet under her. She backed away, but not too far. The fighting had spilled out of the roped-off area.

Goblins that moved more like spiders crawled over everything.

"Take that!" A Kawaii Battle Princess smashed one with her oversized mallet. It lay squished, much like the bug it moved like.

Aaliyah placed her hand on the bear's back, as it stepped back into her space. A detail she would remember later as her fingers sank into the thick pale brown fur, this fur was soft unlike the fur on Vik's bear-headed cloak. The fracture in her brain that was half fascinated, half terrified had merged back into a cohesive unit, and she knew that the bear was safety, protection. She gasped when he reared onto his hind legs. He went up, and up, and up. No longer able to see the expression on the orc's face, she could only imagine that nasty smirk getting wiped off with a swipe of the bear's claws.

She took another step back with the animal in front of her. The bear launched himself at the orc. The green monster raised its massive arm, cudgel in hand. And then it disappeared under the onslaught of angry fur and muscle that was the bear.

As the bear and orc did battle, Aaliyah turned to run. There seemed to be a line at the tents none of the monsters could cross. Goblins clawed at an invisible barrier as if there was a glass wall between them and the humans cowering on the other side.

There was a loud rumble, the distinct sound of a modified engine. A tricked-out truck barreled in from the parking lot, past the tents, and bowled into a rush of oncoming orcs. They scattered like bowling pins. The driver spun his truck in a circle, letting the back end take out a cohort of goblins.

He was making a good-sized dent in the invading party until he sped toward the wrong monster.

The orc in front of the truck looked like what Aaliyah knew gamers liked to call a boss. This motherfucker was the biggest, ugliest, meanest looking orc out there. He wasn't green so much as he was a gray-blue color. The spikes and spines of his armor seemed to grow directly from his hide. And he wore a very dramatic cloak over it all. The cloak seemed to ripple and flow on a breeze that wasn't there. He was epic looking.

As the truck raced toward him, he stood his ground and raised a fist. His fist came down with enough speed that even Aaliyah could hear it boom through the sound barrier. It slammed into the hood of the truck. The truck folded, its front end bent down as it was forced into the ground. The rear wheels lifted and the truck flipped up and over the boss orc.

The air horn sounded. It seemed so out of place in this very real melee of costumed humans and monsters. It may have been set on a timer to announce the end of the battle, but the fighters who were still out there ignored it and continued to attempt to force back the hoard of creatures.

A second sound filled the air. It sounded like shattering glass. It pierced Aaliyah's ears to the point of pain. She covered her head and fell to her knees. Oh god, what was that? It needed to stop. If people were screaming from the pain of the sound, Aaliyah couldn't hear any of it.

She was vaguely aware of fur surrounding her as she curled up into a ball of pain. Aaliyah wasn't aware of what happened first, Vik's strong arms holding her, or the sound of cut glass stopping. She buried her face against his chest and held on tight as she quaked with nerves.

Vik held her and gently rocked her for a few minutes. It wasn't until after she stopped shaking did he ask if she was all right.

"Yeah, I'm okay. I think. Shit, Vik, you're covered in blood."

His face was streaked with smears of red and black ooze. It made his blue eyes stand out in startling contrast. His beard was matted with it, as was his hair.

"It's not mine."

Aaliyah eased away from his body so she could look around. She held her arms loosely around him, as his hands rested more on her hips. They both looked at the people and the field surrounding them.

There was an upended truck in the middle of the battle-field. People wandered and stumbled around looking dazed and confused.

The only orcs around were humans in cosplay. No creepy little goblin things crawled around like humanoid spiders. Vik was a Viking again, and not a grizzly bear.

"What the fuck just happened?"

"We need to go," Vik said.

"I've got your axes," Scottie yelled as he jogged past them.

Vik's hand was firm on her upper arm as he guided her out of the area at a run.

"Meet you at your place!" Vik yelled at Scottie and Wolf

as he pulled up next to a hybrid SUV. "Get in," he told Aaliyah.

Scottie lifted a fist with a punch to the air and kept running.

"Vikings drive hybrids?" Aaliyah teased, unable to articulate what she needed to be asking.

"Hey, Swedes are leading the way with all-electric vehicles. What did you expect me to drive? Some oil belching, gas guzzler?"

The car started and was one of the first vehicles on the road as more and more people abandoned the event en masse. Sirens of emergency vehicles filled the air as cop cars, EMT trucks, and then ambulances sped past.

"Can you tell me what the hell happened back there?" Aaliyah finally asked.

"Yes, but it is not going to seem real."

"Look, I have pictures of orcs and what I assume are goblins on my phone. And I know that wasn't some really good cosplay. Neither was Björn the bear. What exactly happened?"

"It's happened before," Vik said as he weaved through traffic.

Somehow his fast driving didn't make Aaliyah queasy, maybe because she was in the front seat, maybe because there was the entirety of 'what the fuck was that?' still occupying her brain.

"How? Wouldn't something like that make it on the news?"

"Big weird news stories happen all the time. Unless it's a slow news day they don't typically get picked up by the big newsagents. You've seen stories circulating on social media of events gone sideways all the time. I mean you've heard of the Fyre Festival right?"

"Sure, that big music festival that ended up being a sham more than anything else."

"Right. You didn't hear about that on the news, you picked that up from social media. Besides, most of those people will not remember what happened. The ones that do, they'll chalk it up to getting carried away in the LARP, or a mass drug episode. Someone will start the rumor of mushroom spores since it was outside."

"And if it was inside, would someone claim a gas leak?" Aaliyah asked.

"Exactly," Vik said.

"Then why did we run away?"

"It's not exactly running away. First of all, I don't want to be detained, and anyone left on that field when the cops get there, trust me, they are stuck there for a few more hours. Secondly, if you figured out the bear was me, well, I don't need anyone else identifying me like that. Neither do the guys. And lastly, well, Wolf needs to get to a robust system so he can start running down code."

"Code? What the hell does coding video games have to do with what just happened?"

Vik pulled his car into a subdivision of McMansions. Aaliyah was glad he knew where he was going, all the houses looked the same to her.

He parked in the drive behind Scottie's familiar sedan. The cooler Scottie mentioned during lunch was still on the driveway. Aaliyah followed Vik in through the front door.

There was no living room, it looked like a light studio, and the area where the dining room should be looked like the command deck of a spaceship. A bank of monitors curved around a chair that looked more like a race car with striping and panels of color. Wolf looked out of place in his grimy Viking furs. But his actions were deft and confident.

He knew how to drive the ship. Or in this case video games.

One monitor ran lines of code, white text on a black screen. Two other monitors looked like gameplay.

"Oh, hey, that one orc looked almost exactly like this guy," Aaliyah pointed to one of the monitors.

"Yeah, those orcs were all out of Realms of Strife, specifically The Codex Wars. The giveaway was the way the goblins moved like spiders. That's all part of the updated release," Scottie talked as he hovered over Wolf's shoulder, the game control in his hands.

Aaliyah pressed her hands to her face. "I'm so confused. What does a video game have to do with what the hell just happened?"

"To the best of our knowledge, it's that someone has figured out how to hack the code," Vik said.

Aaliyah watched Wolf as his eyes darted from one monitor to the other. He didn't talk as his fingers flew over the keyboard.

"Got it!" Wolf announced. He banged something out on the keyboard and then fell back into the chair with a sigh.

"Someone has figured out how to codify magic. They've started hacking into games, and opening portals."

Aaliyah gasped. "Could it have been someone there? I mean there were a few people with their laptops."

Wolf shook his head. "I checked them out before the battle began. None of them were hacking code, or even playing Codex Wars. It was a meet-up group for Edgeland. I was almost too late to get onto the field."

"If what you're saying is true, then some computer wiz out there is really a computer wizard?" Aaliyah asked.

Wolf laughed. "I hadn't thought of it that way, but yes, definitely."

"So are games real? Like there is an alternate dimension that has orcs and shit?"

Scottie shrugged.

Wolf shook his head.

"We just don't know," Vik said.

"How does that explain..." She turned to Vik and closed her mouth. He could turn into a bear. Did that mean his friends did too? Did they even know about his ability?

"Magic," she finally said. "How does that explain magic?"

"We don't know. Isn't science just magic explained?" Vik raised his brows. It was more than a bit disconcerting to see these three grime-covered men in the middle of clean, and mostly empty new construction surrounded by high-tech equipment.

"I'm still confused," Aaliyah admitted. "If someone manages to hack the code of the game on their computer—"

"It's not on their computer. These are social games that run on a remote network. Someone has hacked the main code of what thousands of people are accessing at once," Scottie cut her off.

"We think that somehow the fact that there are thousands of people accessing this section of code through gameplay, it somehow powers the magic. Giving it the spark to manifest," Wolf continued.

"If they hacked the system to put the code in..."

"We hack in to pull the code out."

CHAPTER
FOUR

Aaliyah stood poleaxed in the middle of the practically empty room.

Everything today seemed positively surreal, all the way down to the fact that the hot blonde guy was completely into her, and she could tell. In typical Aaliyah fashion, if a guy liked her, she usually did something to alienate him completely. Case in point, right now she shouldn't be here and Vik shouldn't be smiling at her because earlier she accused him of something rather heinous. Well, Vik was not a normal guy. Normal guys didn't know about magic hacking plots that let fantasy monsters into the real world, and they sure as hell didn't turn into bears.

She looked around. The walls were bare, and still the original contractor's beige. A blue bean bag was piled in a lump with some lighting equipment on it on the other side of the space. A pyramid of empty Mountain Dew cans lined one wall. It looked like Wolf was in the only chair.

"Do you have any place I can sit down?" she asked.

Wolf started laughing. "I told you we needed a couch."

"I'll grab you a chair from the kitchen," Scottie said.

He returned a moment later carrying a plastic lawn chair. She hated those chairs. Her aunt had them, they were cheap, stackable, and not friendly to Aaliyah's wider hips.

"Do you have any furniture?" she asked.

Scottie shrugged.

"Do you at least have a proper bed? Or are you sleeping on a mattress on the floor?"

"She called you out," Vik said as he slapped Scottie on the shoulder.

Aaliyah sat, and looked from man to man to man. "Don't you guys ever want to just sit?"

Wolf chuckled, his focus still on the code in front of him.

"I'm never here long enough to worry about it." Scottie shrugged.

"You shoot your videos here right?"

"Yeah, so?"

"People want to be able to sit. And not in plastic chairs," Aaliyah added as Scottie looked like he was going to say something. She didn't know what bothered her more, the lack of furniture or all the empty wall space. What she would give to have so much hanging space.

Vik placed a hand on her shoulder and squeezed. "I'm going to head upstairs and grab a quick shower, and then I can give you a ride home. If that's okay?"

"Sure. You live here too?"

"No," Vik shook his head. "But I'm gross, and this orc blood is starting to feel itchy. I have a change in the car."

Aaliyah nodded as Vik strode from the room.

"So you live in this big house, all by yourself with no furniture?"

"Not all by himself," Wolf answered. "I live here too."

"And you're okay with not having any furniture?"

Wolf shrugged. "I spend most of my time at the office, or out. I have the only chair I need." He patted the armrest of the very serious-looking chair he sat in.

"You don't have girlfriends, do you? Either of you?" She crossed her arms and sat back, laughing.

"Hey, I feel profiled," Scottie complained.

"At least I didn't say you were living in your mom's basement," Aaliyah said.

Scottie guffawed and pushed on Wolf's chair jostling him.

"Shut up man," Wolf demanded.

"No, I was joking," Aaliyah said.

"Why do you think he lives here?" Scottie asked.

Aaliyah shook her head. "I guess you are moving up in the world, out of the basement and into a really nice house from the look of it. Did you really get the money for this from MinVids?"

"Bought and paid for. MinVids and GameWatch."

"Damn. What's GameWatch?"

"GameWatch is a specific platform where he plays video games and makes a running commentary as he goes, and other gamers watch."

"And that makes money?"

Scottie shrugged and then opened his arms wide, indicating the house they were in.

"It doesn't make money for everyone. It involves a lot of time, a fairly decent personality, and a dose of luck," Wolf said.

"Ah, you think I have a personality," Scottie said, in a mocking little-girl high pitched voice.

"Shut up, dude," Wolf grumbled.

It wasn't long before Vik came practically skipping

down the stairs. He looked like a different man. The missing blood and gore aside, he no longer had dark smears of black and ochre makeup across his eyes. His hair was slicked back into a wet ponytail, and he wore normal clothes. Without the furs, he looked practically civilized.

Somehow the mundane clothing emphasized the width of his shoulders. The slate hue of his Henley certainly did a good job of making his eyes pop, and the slim-fit cargo pants made his legs look even longer than before.

Aaliyah swallowed a hard lump that formed in her throat. Vik was stunning. There was no way she was reading him right. He couldn't be into her. Men who looked like him— and then she shut herself down. Men who looked like Vik were not automatically misogynistic assholes simply because they had shoulders and a six-pack. The man drove a hybrid and fought like a bear. Literally. He wasn't hung up on some alpha or beta-male label.

"You ready?" he asked.

"Yeah," Aaliyah managed to finally say. She wasn't sure how long she had just been staring at him, but his face split with a dazzling smile, and she felt her knees go weak.

He held his hand out to her. She let him help her from the plastic chair that wanted to stick to her backside. The chair lifted from the ground as she stood, the armrests hooked over her hips.

"You need real furniture man," Vik said.

"So embarrassing," she muttered as she shoved the chair off her ass.

"No, what's embarrassing is pulling down six figures from videos and not having any furniture."

"At least I don't have that old shit from my grandmother," Scottie retorted.

Aaliyah placed her hand on Vik's arm, this wasn't worth

bickering over. "It was nice to meet you guys. Hopefully, I'll see you again sometime."

"Totally, you're coming to a con. It will be fun," Scottie said.

Wolf waved, distracted by whatever was on the computer monitors. At some point, Aaliyah thought he had switched over to gaming, but she couldn't be certain.

"So you have hand-me-down furniture?" she asked as she followed Vik out to his vehicle.

"Yeah, when my grandmother died, my mother insisted that I take the furniture. I wasn't living much differently than Scottie. Plastic lawn furniture, a folding table, mattress on the floor. I think the mentality of rent, lights, and food as priorities is a hard cycle to break. You get used to living with a certain level of comfort, or lack of. Furniture becomes an afterthought."

"If he ever wants to get a girlfriend, he's going to need to get furniture," Aaliyah said.

"The kind of women Scottie hooks up with don't care about that. They are more interested in having him as a checkbox than a boyfriend. It's not something that's been an issue for him."

Aaliyah sighed. Money was wasted on some people. What she wouldn't give to be able to buy a house and have it completely paid for before she was thirty.

She gave Vik directions as he drove.

"You're taking everything very well," Vik pointed out.

"No, I'm not. I'm just really good at hiding my anxiety," Aaliyah chuckled. She was a complete mess inside, and she didn't even begin to know where she should focus her energy. On one hand, the hot guy was driving her home, on the other, he turned into a fucking bear. And of course, she would never forget facing down an actual orc, only to learn that video games could be conduits for magic.

"I should be babbling and drooling. But honestly, I'm not sure if any of that was real. Maybe I hit my head and this is all a delusion."

"Do you honestly believe that?" Vik asked.

"No, but how else do you explain everything, and don't say magic."

Vik shrugged and smirked. "Maybe we all live in a video game and someone is messing with our programming."

"That's as good as any explanation. I didn't want to say anything back at Scottie's because I wasn't sure and all, but... Do the guys know about you being able to shift? Is that why you chose to be a Viking berserker?" Aaliyah asked.

"You don't choose the berserker life, it chooses you," Vik chuckled.

"Seriously?" Aaliyah shook her head and suppressed a laugh. "No, but, really, what came first, the shifting or the association?"

Before she knew it his car was sitting in front of her apartment building. It was an older building that at first glance looked more like a large house, than an apartment building with seventeen units. Technically there had only been sixteen, but at some point, the superintendent's workshop was converted into a basement apartment, and that's what Aaliyah rented.

"You wouldn't be interested in coming in, would you?" Her heart pounded in her throat. Had she just invited Vik inside? "I'd love to hear your story."

She braced for rejection.

"Sure," he said as he put the car in park and turned it off.

Butterflies rioted in Aaliyah's stomach as she led Vik in through the main entry, and down the back stairs.

"All comments about living in my mother's basement are valid. However, I would like to point out that technically it's my aunt's basement and I do have furniture."

"Your aunt owns the building?"

"Her husband, same difference. How else do you think I can afford to live in a building like this?"

She opened the door and flipped on the lights.

The ceilings weren't nearly as high as they were in the original units, and her windows were at ground level, which meant up by the ceiling. But the space was tidy if not eclectically decorated with a combination of hand-me-downs and refurbished roadside finds.

She stood, holding her breath, as Vik looked around. He seemed to be drawn to a painting on the wall.

"This is really nice. Did you do it?"

"Why do you assume it's mine?" she asked tartly.

He shook his head and shrugged. "You seem very artsy. It's not a print, and"— he leaned in close, and pointed at the lower corner of the artwork— "that looks like your name. And that"— he turned and pointed at the art table covered in cups of brushes next to a shelf unit of nothing but paints and jars of pigments— "is clearly where you work."

"Busted," Aaliyah chuckled.

"I bet you did that too," Vik said pointing to the multi-hued crochet slipcover on the side chair.

Aaliyah nodded.

"You want a drink or a snack? Some water or something?"

Vik followed her the few steps into her galley kitchen and caught her wrist. He tugged her toward him, and before Aaliyah knew how, she was standing pressed against him with his fingers tracing down the side of her face.

"Or something sounds about right. I've been wanting to do this all day." He lowered his head towards hers, his gaze on her lips.

She closed her eyes and softened her mouth in anticipation.

He paused.

Aaliyah opened her eyes. His face was so close she could barely focus on the way his lashes grazed his cheeks.

"May I kiss you?"

She melted, officially, and pressed into him, making the contact of their lips happen. She couldn't wait the time it would take for her to say yes. His kiss was as potent and incredible as everything about him, packed with a double whammy of consent.

"Hmmm," he hummed. "You are better than I had imagined."

Aaliyah gulped. "And just how much have you imagined today?"

"I have not been a good boy, if that's what you're asking."

Aaliyah stared at him. The words coming from him didn't seem real.

He stepped back and cleared his throat. "I'll take a glass of water, I guess."

Aaliyah smiled. She pulled a glass from the cupboard and filled it from the built-in filter on the fridge.

"Would you like to have dinner with me?" she asked as she handed Vik the glass.

His fingers grazed hers, and she felt it like an electric jolt through her entire body.

"Sure, where would you like to go?" Vik asked.

Aaliyah braced herself, "I was thinking delivery?"

"Whatever shall we do while we wait for our dinner to be delivered?" The smile he gave her was wicked and made her toes curl. He knew exactly what she meant.

Spending time with Vik was the best thing Aaliyah had ever done. He kissed like he meant it. And he touched her like he was worshipping her. And they were still dressed, mostly.

As soon as he started kissing her, neither of them wanted to stop. Vik insisted that they pause long enough to put in a pizza order. "If we don't order now, by the time we remember it will be too late."

Aaliyah had deferred to his better thinking.

But as soon as the order button on the phone app was hit, their lips were back together, like magnets.

They bypassed her couch, more of a settee not meant for heavy making out, and went straight for the bedroom. The front of her sweater was open, Vik's shirt was gone. Neither of them had shoes on.

She would have been all for the frenzied tearing of clothes, but Vik was a freaking romantic. He went slow, he took his time. He asked permission. He was so good, and all they had done so far was some heavy petting.

Aaliyah was startled when the intercom buzzer sounded.

"That must be the pizza guy," Vik said as he rolled from the bed. He leaned in and gave Aaliyah one more quick kiss. "I'll be right back." He adjusted the front of his pants and grabbed his shirt as he walked through her small apartment, leaving the front door ajar.

It seemed like Vik was gone for a long time. Hers was

the only unit in the basement next to the building's laundry facilities. He had to walk the length of the building twice to reach the front security door. She rolled onto her front and pivoted so she was upside down on the bed. With her elbows on the mattress and her head resting on her fists, she was positioned perfectly to see him come back in. She knew he would be back, after all, his boots were on her bedroom floor.

When he came back in through her front door, she couldn't help but smile. He made her feel like a giddy princess. He treated her like his queen.

Vik set the pizza and the other boxes down in the kitchen and stalked back to her in the bedroom.

"Hungry?"

Aaliyah rolled onto her back and looked up at him. "Not for pizza."

Vik quirked his eyebrows at her. They were ridiculously pale, yet very expressive. The downfalls of being blond. Something Aaliyah would never know.

Aaliyah sucked her lower lip into her mouth and bit down on the slightly swollen flesh. "I've always wondered what bear meat was like."

Vik kept his eyes locked with hers. "Are you playing with me, or are you serious, Aaliyah? I don't want you to feel like you have to do anything more than where we're at right now."

Aaliyah rolled and shifted so that she was sitting up on the bed. She pulled her cardigan off, and reaching behind, unclasped her bra. Her nerves thrummed and she shook as her pulse raced through her body. Her bra came off next. Proportionally her breasts were on the smaller side compared to her hips. She still had a copious rack, but instead of an extreme hourglass shape, she was a pear.

Vik didn't seem to care. He licked his lips and stared at her body. His chest lifted as his breathing grew harder. "You don't have to tell me twice."

His hands were already working his belt, and the button and fly of his pants. He shoved his pants down and climbed into the bed in only his boxer briefs. He crawled toward Aaliyah, pressing her back to the mattress with his mouth on hers, and his hands caressing and kneading her breasts. With one hand occupied on her breast, he reached down and hiked her skirt up around her middle. He snagged her panties and dragged them down her hips. With the hindrance of underwear out of the way, he slid his fingers between her thighs and to her core.

Aaliyah gasped as Vik's hand cupped her. She rocked her hips against his hand. She ran her nails over the prickly growth along his scalp until she reached the longer hair of his mohawk. She threaded her fingers through his hair, amused at how much curl and texture he had. Her amusement was soon forgotten as he did something with his fingers against her clit, and Aaliyah lost all reason.

"You are so wet," Vik crooned.

"What do you think all that kissing earlier was doing to me? Oh, damn you feel good."

"Condom?" Vik asked.

"Yes, please and thank you," Aaliyah said. She pointed to the dresser across the room. "In the top drawer, small peacock box."

Vik was out of the bed, and rummaging through her drawer. "First date and I get to look through your panties drawer. This is turning out to be a great day." He held up a collection of red lace and strings. "Please do me the honor of wearing this at some point, and letting me remove it with my teeth."

"Would you stop looking at my undies?"

While he rummaged through her drawer, she shimmied out of her skirt. She giggled as she wiggled her toes still wrapped in knee socks. The socks were going to stay on.

"Ah-ha," Vik made a noise like a pirate before turning and launching himself at the bed.

In what felt like an epoch of waiting, his shorts were pushed off, and the condom ripped open. Aaliyah stared at him, all of him. He was sculpted of marble, and in contrast to her darker tones, almost as pale. She welcomed him to her with open arms. Wrapping her legs around his hips, holding him to her.

He felt as good as he looked, maybe better.

His touch was a contrast of firm and demanding and soft and giving. His skin slid over her in deceitful decadence, promising softness, but hiding a body that was all hard muscle, and driving force. But he was a giver, he didn't take, he coaxed, he teased.

Aaliyah was lost to his touch. She wanted to reciprocate, she wanted to give back as much pleasure as he was giving her. Maybe next time. She was putty under his touch. All she could manage was to react, to rock her hips, to grab him tighter.

As Vik took her body to the edge of ecstasy, Aaliyah could hardly contain her cries. She saw stars behind her eyes. When her muscles clenched and began throbbing and pulsing in a frenzied climax, all she could do was hold on and enjoy the ride. Her muscles had an agenda of their own. As she regained her ability to focus, she began thrusting her hips again in a counter rhythm to Vik's thrusts.

Vik pressed up, holding himself above her. He leveraged against her, stroking harder and with more force. She raked her short nails over the bulging muscles in his arms, reveling in how his body looked and felt.

His face was beautiful as his expression changed from smiles to determination, back to smiling at her, and then, he hit what he was working toward. His jaw dropped, and his eyes rolled back as he closed them. His roar was as fierce as when he was on the battlefield.

Aaliyah welcomed him back into her embrace when he practically fell back into her arms, replete from his efforts.

"You know," Aaliyah said around her panting. "I don't normally do that on a first date."

"Yeah, well I don't typically let my dates know I shift into a bear. So, a lot of firsts for us. It's not a bad thing."

"It's not, is it?"

The pizza and the chicken wings were cold when they finally roused themselves from Aaliyah's bed to eat.

They snuggled together to watch a movie, but roaming hands and kisses distracted them from what was on the television. Vik wrapped himself around Aaliyah after rocking her world again. His face snuggled in against her neck, and he pulled her back against his chest.

"Can you stay?" Aaliyah asked.

"I can't think of a more important place to be right now," Vik sounded as tired as she felt.

AALIYAH WOKE. SHE COULDN'T GET THE VISION OF THAT ORC OUT of her head. It wasn't exactly a nightmare. It was the haunting of a bad memory. She rolled out of bed, careful to not disturb Vik. She stood and watched him sleep for a long moment. Even in sleep, he still had the harsh angles of a

WARRIOR. The bruise along his jaw had bloomed from a red mark to something dark and purple.

She shrugged into a sweatshirt, found her pajama shorts, and pulled them on. Shoving her feet into fleece-lined slippers, she padded out into her living room. It was stupid early. The sun was already up and doing as much streaming in through her windows as she would get all day.

When a thought moved into her head, and she couldn't get it out, she learned that she could force it out through her fingers. She propped up her phone and thumbed through until she found the photos she wanted. She still could barely believe those images were not expertly rendered digital art, but real.

She began sketching shapes and forms on a cheap newsprint sketch pad. She drew and flipped the page to draw more. Her shapes were loosely formed, and probably only made sense to her if anyone else tried to figure out what she was doing. After some time, she knew exactly what she wanted.

Pulling out the good paper, she traded out the traditional wood pencil for a mechanical one with a hard lead. Her marks were faint on the paper, as intended. The orc and the bear caught mid-action in battle was clear enough for her purposes. Once she had the major forms blocked in and refined, she reached for a brush and pulled over a small watercolor palette. Spinning in her chair, she grabbed a plastic cup, covered in layers of paint, and filled it with water from the kitchen sink.

"Morning," Vik mumbled. He stood at her art table looking down at what she had been working on.

"This is fucking amazing. I mean I get a sense of really being there."

Aaliyah laughed. "You were."

He picked up a small painting and stared at it. "I mean, Aaliyah, I feel like I'm here." He held up the painting in his hand. "I can feel the rush as their robes fly past me. I can see the movements."

"I get that a lot. I don't put in that much detail, but people seem to feel like I've taken them someplace."

Vik shook his head. "No, not that. I mean these images are moving, making sounds, putting the memory of scent in my head."

He looked her in the eyes. "Aaliyah, you have magic."

She shook her head frantically. "No, I have a talent that needs to pay better. It's not magic."

"I know magic. I'm part of a small group of men who hunt magic where it doesn't belong. Aaliyah, this is magic."

"Is that bad?" The dancing nerves that Vik's praise had given her suddenly felt heavy, weighted down with dread.

"Not at all. But I can see why Maisie thinks you need to vend in an artist alley. You completely bring these characters to life."

"Yeah," Aaliyah sighed. "I don't do the kinds of characters that people go to those cons for. I don't do superheroes."

"You don't need to. These fantasy martial arts shows have plenty of followers. Hell, anything that's high fantasy has a following, it doesn't have to be fan art. Let me show you one before you decide it's not for you."

Aaliyah placed the cup of water down, and leaned against Vik, pressing her entire length against him. He smiled at her and returned his gaze to the art in his hands.

"I've never been to one. Are you sure?"

"You are amazingly talented. The magic wouldn't be here if your work wasn't any good."

Aaliyah pressed her face into his arm. He was still here,

still saying wonderful things to her. He leaned over and kissed her.

"Do I get to take you to your first con?" he teased. "I get to take your con virginity, now that's a notable first."

"Don't be such a pig." Aaliyah playfully shoved his shoulder.

"That's Scottie. I'm a bear, remember?"

"I think you might need to remind me." She took Vik's hand and led him back to the bedroom. "You still haven't told me how all of that happened."

"Magic."

WOLF

Control the game before it controls you.

Yeardley hasn't been to a con in years. Not only is she looking forward to hanging out with her friends, but she is hoping the hotty Viking cosplayer, Wolf, will finally sit up and take notice.

Unbeknownst to her she's about to walk into battle, figuratively and literally. In an epic maneuver sure to go down in con history, Yeardley offers up a programmer smack down. While still riding that adrenaline high her skills are put to the test as she is thrown into another smack down, this time of fantasy proportions.

You don't choose the berserker life.
The berserker life chooses you.

CHAPTER
ONE

"What are you wearing?" Aaliyah's voice sounded scratchy through the speaker phone.

"Clothes, why?" Yeardley asked.

"Aren't you and Maisie doing cosplay?"

"I am," Yeardley chuckled. "Maisie said she was, but she hadn't decided what yet. Why aren't you dressing up?"

Yeardley leaned in closer to the mirror and swiped the mascara wand through her lashes, blending them into the false lashes.

"I modified my Halloween costume from last year. Red and black Harley Quinn, with long pants, no booty shorts."

"Arg! I don't know what to wear," Aaliyah confessed.

"What, Vik's not helping you?"

"Vik said I don't need to. He's not dressing up. He said his geek cred is secure, and that I should be fine, since I will be with him."

"You don't need to dress up if you don't want to." She pulled back and checked out her reflection. She tugged on her hair, adjusting the high ponytails. Her pale blonde hair fell to just below her chin level.

"Won't I stick out?"

"Not at all, there are going to be plenty of people in just t-shirts and jeans. You'll be fine."

Yeardley's phone started clicking.

"Hey Aaliyah, I'm getting another call. I'll see you there. And if you're worried about it just put on a superhero t-shirt and you'll be fine."

"Bye, I'll see you later."

Yeardley hit the buttons on her phone switching calls.

Maisie's face appeared on the screen.

"Yeardley what are you wearing?" she sounded panicked.

"Why is everyone asking me this? What are you wearing?"

"I found an old Wonder Woman costume in the back of my closet, and it still fits," Maisie said.

"That sounds fun."

"Are you sure?" Maisie asked.

"Maisie, have you put it on?"

"Yeah."

"Send me a pic."

"Okay, you'll be honest with me. You'll tell me if I look too fat?"

Yeardley sighed. "Maisie, I will tell you if you look stupid."

Yeardley picked up her phone and leaned back against the bathroom counter. She didn't have to wait long before Maisie's picture flashed on her notifications. She swiped the screen so that she could see the whole picture.

Maisie looked adorable. Her costume was a more historical twist of the comic book heroine's outfit. Instead of a body suit, she had a short pleated skirt and a chiton style neckline. But all the colors and all the stars, and the large gold bracers were there.

"You look adorable."

"But am I too fat for this?"

"Maisie, I love you..."

"But you are going to tell me that I am fat, but that doesn't mean I'm not also cute."

"Then why are you asking me, if you know that's what I'm gonna say?" Yeardley asked.

"But am I cute enough?"

"Cute enough for what?" Yeardley asked. She knew exactly what Maisie was asking, was Maisie cute enough for Scottie. She didn't have that answer. Scottie didn't seem interested in Maisie. But Yeardley had no idea what Scottie was looking for in a woman.

Scottie was Maisie's big crush. He had been her MinVid crush until she met him in real life, and ever since she had been obsessed with whether he would like everything she did or wore, or... It didn't help that he was a flirt.

Yeardley was busy dealing with her own crush, she didn't have time to also manage Maisie's crush.

"Can I send you what I'm wearing?" Yeardley asked.

"Oh yeah, send me pictures," Maisie squealed.

Yeardley posed in the mirror and took a few pictures.

"Oh, Harley Quinn! It's perfect. Are you sure I look okay?" Maisie asked again.

"Maisie, you look adorbs, you really do. Look, I need to finish getting ready so I can be there in time."

"You look great, I'll see you there."

Yeardley ended the call and tossed the phone back on the counter. Lipstick and jewelry were the finishing touches and she would be ready. Maisie's anxiety over if Scottie would think she was cute, Yeardley keenly felt, but in regards to Wolf.

Wolf was Scottie's roommate. He was also a super gamer, so much so he was a game programmer for the wildly popular Edgeland. Maisie, Aaliyah and Yeardley had met the three men by chance a few weeks ago. The guys, Wolf, Vik, and Scottie, were all dressed as Vikings for a Live Action Role Play event. Even though they had a misunderstanding over Norse Heathen symbols, Aaliyah and Vik hit it off immediately.

After Aaliyah and Vik went from nothing to being a couple in the blink of an eye she had met the other guys a few more times. It made Yeardley nuts because she couldn't get any more information about Wolf out of her friend. It was almost as if Aaliyah wasn't paying any attention to any man other than Vik.

At least Yeardley wasn't as obviously obsessive as Maisie was over Scottie. Well, she hoped she wasn't being as obvious.

She and Maisie had gotten to see their crushes again a few days earlier, when Scottie had arranged a group outing to the movies. The next installment in everyone's favorite super hero saga was being released. It had sounded like a great idea, and Yeardley had really hoped she would get a chance to do a bit more than awkwardly talk with Wolf.

When she and Maisie arrived at the theater, Aaliyah having gone with Vik, Yeardley was disappointed to find it was a large group event that Scottie hadn't organized so much as announced he was going and invited everyone who followed him on MinVid and GameWatch. Yeardley wasn't nearly as crushed as Maisie had been. She spent most of the movie silently crying into her popcorn.

Yeardley had only gotten to say a few words to Wolf, and cast her gaze at him throughout the evening. She caught him looking at her, so she had hope.

An hour in real time and an eternity in traffic later, Yeardley stood in the concourse of the hotel in front of the ticketing room. She was under the mid-century mobile style chandelier where she, Maisie, and Aaliyah had agreed to meet.

Yeardley!" Maisie's exuberant voice cut through the general noise of hundreds of bodies milling about having conversations of their own.

It didn't take her long to find her friend. A curvy, short Princess Diana aka Wonder Woman, not British royalty, hurried toward her. Her costume was a perfect blend of comic book and historical accuracy.

"You look fabulous," Yeardley said.

Maisie put her hands out and danced in a little spin showing off her outfit. When she finished she kicked back her foot for effect.

"As do you Miss Quinn," she offered.

Yeardley struck a dramatic pose with the back of her hand against her forehead.

"This old thing, I found it in the back of my closet." She shifted and began brushing down the sides of her vest. "No, really, I had to dig this out of the back of my closet. I can't believe these jeans still fit."

The jeans in question had one leg in white and black vertical stripes with the other leg solid black. And they were insanely tight. The red diamonds on the black leg were newly added decorations, but the holes in the knees were original. The black vest was from her current wardrobe rotation so the decorations were all safety-pinned on, including the drawing of a certain green haired clown with a giant red X over his face pinned to her back. A red push up bra and a fishnet top finished the look.

"Is Aaliyah here yet?" Yeardley asked. She waved a program around, that she had already rolled in her nervous state. Aaliyah meant Vik, and hopefully Vik meant Wolf would be nearby.

"They're here. Scottie got a new car, so they are out in the parking lot somewhere ooh-ing and aah-ing over it," she sounded a little annoyed.

Maisie sighed. With her breasts and her cosplay, that was a potentially dangerous combination.

"If you want Scottie's attention, make sure you do that around him," Yeardley said as she made a wiggly gesture with her finger.

"Do what?"

"Your boobs, Maise, your boobs." Yeardley did an exaggerated lift and drop of her own chest.

"Look who's talking. You'll put an eye out with those."

"That, my friend, is the plan. Speaking of"—Yeardley unrolled her program and opened it—"I can't find Wolf in here anywhere. I thought he was supposed to be doing some of the gamer panels."

"What do you mean?" Maisie leaned over and looked at the program and Yeardley flipped through the pages. "Maybe Wolf isn't his real name."

"I always assumed it was his last name, or something."

"There you are," Aaliyah said, walking up to them.

"Ladies!" Scottie announced his presence. "You didn't come and check out my sweet new ride."

He already had two scantily clad women clinging to him, one under each arm.

"I just got here," Yeardley said.

Next to her Maisie began vibrating. "I saw your MinVid when you bought it."

"That is not the same. You need to come sit in it. Tell you what after lunch, I'll take you for a ride."

"I want to go for a ride," one of the women clinging to him said. Her innuendo was as clear as glass.

"Of course you do babe, it's an awesome vehicle." Either Scottie was dense and missing the woman's hint, or he was ignoring her.

Yeardley had yet to decide if he was wily smart or a lucky, thick skulled himbo.

"What did you get?" Yeardley asked. She had been thinking about upgrading, maybe he would recommend his dealer.

"Taycan Turbo," he said.

Yeardley gulped. "Porsche?"

Scottie's car capabilities and hers were not on the same playing field.

"Yeah, it is sweet."

"Damn," she let out a resolved breath. "I need to make MinVids."

Scottie gave her a raking glance up and down. "You'd do better with FriendsExclusive."

Yeardley started to growl.

Vik slapped Scottie upside the back of his head. "Don't be a pig."

"Dude?" Scottie rubbed the back of his head and glared at the other man.

Scottie's hand shifted from rubbing his head to rubbing his jaw.

"When did you decide to grow your beard out?" Maisie asked, clearly suckered in by his prompting.

Maisie's hand clamped down on Yeardley's arm. Her friend didn't care if he was a sexist pig, or a dolt. Maisie's crush for Scottie continued to burn bright. Yeardley expected Maisie was holding onto her so that she didn't accidentally reach out and touch the man's face.

"It's about time you noticed. No one has said a damned thing about it."

"Maybe we are hoping if we ignore it, it will go away," Vik grumbled.

Aaliyah pushed on his chest a little. "Play nice."

Neither of them had dressed up. They looked like Aaliyah and Vik always did. Except for the first time they met, Yeardley had no indication that Vik did cosplay, or participated in any of the geekery that Scottie made his living at.

Scottie, on the other hand, was never without some form of cosplay, be it a random helmet on his head or the shield he actually carried to the movie night he organized. Today, of course, he had gone all out, complete with green body paint. He was tall, and with flaming red hair that contrasted intensely with his make-up, he made an impressive orc.

"Can we go already? I don't want to miss the photo ops," one of Scottie's adoring companions whined.

"Duty calls," Scottie said as he let the women by his side steer him away.

"See you later," Maisie said rather mournfully.

"Is Wolf not presenting?" Yeardley turned and asked Vik.

"As far as I know he still is. Why?"

She didn't want to admit that she had gone over the program with a fine-toothed comb looking for his name.

"I'd thought he would be with you guys this morning." She tried to hide her disappointment.

Vik shook his head. "Haven't seen him. He's here somewhere. Shall we?"

"We're going to go check out the artist alley, see you later?" Aaliyah asked.

"Costume contest!" Maisie called out after them. It was important to her that all her friends got together for that. "Costume contest," she said again, a little deflated.

"They'll be there," Yeardley said, bumping her shoulder. "What do you want to do first? The panel I think Wolf is supposed to be on starts soon. Can we go and at least see if he's there?"

"Of course," Maisie gasped and turned, her gaze following an exceptional costume.

Yeardley saw the side of an elaborate blue Elizabethan style dress. It would have been more fitting for a Ren Faire. But a good costume was a good costume, and she understood showing off one's work.

"Hayden?" Maisie asked as she approached the Elizabethan woman.

Yeardley followed, and as they got closer, she realized that the only things the costuming really had in common with a Ren Faire Elizabethan garb was the big skirt and the corseted top. When Hayden turned, Yeardley gasped. Not Elizabethan, dwarf. High fantasy dwarf.

Hayden's dress was embroidered with patterns that looked like magic symbols. The fabric, up close shimmered with different colors— blues, greens and pinks— in the cross weave. She practically dripped with velvet and furs, and obnoxiously large gems. But the crowning glory was Hayden's hair. Piles of curls and braids in a rich dark brown adorned her. Braids traveled across her cheeks, and integrated the dwarf's beard with the elaborate coiffeur on her head.

Her diminutive, yet sturdy stature only added to the overall perfection of the costuming.

"Maisie? I haven't seen you in forever," the regal dwarf woman said.

The friends hugged and Maisie introduced Yeardley.

"May I?" Yeardley asked, reaching for the long draping sleeve of the other woman's dress.

"Of course." Hayden held out her arm.

The fabric was silk, no denying the way it felt to her fingers. "This is simply stunning."

Maisie waved her phone in Yeardley's face. "Take a picture of us. I haven't seen Hayden since— Oh crap, the last time I came to a con."

"Was I seeing things, or were you just talking to Scottie Mann, like it was no big deal?" Hayden asked.

"You follow him on MinVids too?" Maisie practically squeaked.

"Oh, it's a big deal every freaking time," Yeardley chuckled.

"Shut up," Maisie said as she made a face. "Our friend Aaliyah is kind of dating one of his friends."

"So by extension you've gotten to talk to him?" Hayden asked.

"Yeah," Maisie said with a sigh.

"Is he as nice as he seems?"

Yeardley laughed.

"What's so funny?" Wolf's deep voice caught her off guard.

It was her turn to *eep* and get flustered. Every time she met Wolf again she was shocked at his height. She was tall, he was taller. And today his boots gave him extra height, as did the way he had a section of his long locs pulled up and away from his face.

"She was about to pick on Scottie," Maisie said, crossing her arms.

"Well, how can I help?" he asked.

Yeardley swallowed a giggle.

"This is Hayden, one of Maisie's old con friends," Yeardley made a quick introduction.

"Lady Hayden." Wolf took Hayden's hand and bowed low over it.

If Hayden wasn't swooning, Yeardley certainly was.

"Wolf happens to be Scottie's roommate."

"I thought I recognized you," Hayden said with a bit too much awe in her voice. "I had asked if Scottie was as sweet in real life as he seems on MinVid."

"I wouldn't know, I haven't licked him." Somehow Wolf kept a perfect straight disdained expression as the three women around him dissolved into giggles.

"If you are asking if he's a good man, I'd have to say yes. And that's not because he would charge me more rent if I bad-mouthed him. I have a panel in fifteen minutes, I thought I would see if you wanted to accompany me?"

Yeardley's heart bounced around her chest with nerves when he held his elbow out to her.

"Yes, of course. It was lovely to meet you Lady Hayden. Maisie, you coming?" Yeardley asked as she looped her hand over Wolf's arm. She had to fight to focus and not turn into a complete basket case. She was touching Wolf at his invitation.

"I'm gonna catch up with Hayden. If that's okay with you?" Maisie turned to her old con friend for confirmation.

"Lovely, of course. I'm headed to a wing making demonstration and workshop," Hayden said. "I'd love to catch up."

"Oh, that sounds like fun," Maisie said.

Yeardley was not fully certain this was her life as she strode arm in arm with Wolf down the concourse toward the ball room where the panel on programming video games would be held. They looked more like a couple headed out for the club than a couple at a con for all things sci-fi, fantasy.

They looked like a couple, both in black and red. His boots were covered in silver spikes, his knees peeked out from beneath the black kilt he wore. His red shirt had several buttons opened, and he was all wrapped in several straps of a belted harness.

"I know my cosplay is feeble at best, but it's recognizable," Yeardley started.

"You look rather stunning," his voice was low and gravely.

It was doing something to Yeardley.

"Thanks." She blushed. "You look rather stunning yourself. But I don't know the reference," she confessed.

"I'm cosplaying a badass games developer. Sometimes it's hard to be taken seriously in too much costuming. I'll dress up tomorrow when I'm not on a panel, and can play more."

They entered the long hall, and walked toward the front.

"I have to go up and check in," Wolf said.

"I'll grab a seat. Have fun."

Yeardley walked down the empty row and found a seat close to the middle.

Wolf took his place on the stage, greeting the other panelists, and sitting behind a placard that identified him as Simon, Programmer Edgeland. Well, that explained why she couldn't find him in the program. Simon though? Wolf suited him so much better.

CHAPTER
TWO

Yeardley wasn't exactly sure what she was expecting. But the discussion went off the rails quickly and the moderator had difficulty keeping it on track.

One of the programmers, and total douche-bro named Collin spent the majority of his time whining about sexist ideals in games, specifically having to remove certain misogynistic elements from game design. He wanted them in there. He acted like games were for his doughy, white ass alone.

Wolf, and the other non-white, and only non-male, programmer were not letting Collin, or his antiquated ideas slide.

"So you're saying this panel represents gaming segments?" the Asian woman, Amelia, leaned into her mic and spoke. "There are six of us, two persons of color and one woman. We do not represent an accurate spread of the industry."

"That's because more men game," Collin blustered.

"That's bullshit," Wolf started.

"Language, please," the moderator interjected.

Wolf didn't even look at the moderator and continued. "Forty-five percent of online gamers are women, while roughly thirty percent of gamers are non-white."

"Where are you getting your numbers? I think you're just making shit up."

"Oh, like you are with most gamers are men?" Amelia interjected. "A simple internet search will get you this data." She turned back to Wolf.

He continued, "Of programmers, twenty-five percent are women and twenty-five percent are non-white. This panel isn't balanced. With Amelia and I, we represent the non-white programmers, but you need another woman on the panel to better represent female programmers."

"That's because game spaces are predominantly made for men," a small guy, who seemed to be team Collin commented.

Amelia looked at the moderator and closed her mouth. She clearly wanted to say something not allowed. Instead she said, "Game spaces need to be inclusive: men, women, our non-binary friends. Everyone is welcome, should be welcome."

"Oh so you're saying we should provide safe game space for kids in something like Mountains Deep?"

Mountains Deep had been a violent game that included very adult situations, but because it was pretty and had cute fuzzy animals, parents had purchased it without paying attention. It came under a lot of scrutiny when some parents finally paid attention to what they had purchased for their kid, and were mortified that they weren't cute fuzzy animals, but horny furries.

"Games come with a rating for a reason," another panelist said.

"So, are you saying games should come with a designation if they are for men or for women?"

"That sounds useful. I don't want female players in my band of brothers raiding party," Collin said.

"That's some incel shit right there," Amelia scoffed. "Games need to better represent the population of players. And maybe if they were designed with more inclusivity they would attract more diverse players."

"I don't want kids in my type of game," Collin said.

"No one is saying let kids into the more adult oriented games," Wolf responded.

"That's exactly what she's saying."

Amelia mumbled something away from the mic.

Wolf leaned into his mic. "Throwing kids into the mix right now is a red herring. Games do need designations based on age appropriateness, level of violence and sexuality. Gendering game play is not on that list. No one is saying 'be age inclusive,' stop bringing it up."

"This isn't what I signed on for. We're supposed to be talking about programming and game design, not gate keeping who can and can't play, who can and cannot program. I'm out." The guy who had been seated next to Amelia stood and walked off the platform

Collin sat back crossed his arms with a smug look on his face. He would win because he would bully everyone until they were sick of him. He would be the last man standing on his hill of garbage, never realizing it was garbage, and thinking he had won.

Guys like him pissed Yeardley off to the point of sputtering incoherent oaths. She cast her gaze side to side, and then tightened her gut and stood up.

"Excuse me," she said as she stepped over a few other spectators seated in her row and into the aisle. She shook herself and strode onto the platform and sat in the empty chair next to Amelia

"Who the fuck are you?" the little guy next to Collin asked.

"Language!" the moderator yelled.

"I'm Yeardley, I'm a woman, and a programmer. I'm here to represent."

Amelia reached up with a fist. Yeardley bumped it.

"I'm sorry, what are you doing here?" the moderator asked.

"Well, if twenty-five percent of programmers and almost half of players are actually women, I am here to represent."

"And how does that add to the conversation?" Collin asked.

"I'm pretty sure I just told you," Yeardley said.

The audience gasped, and a few clapped.

Amelia rummaged for something behind her, and then reached in front of Yeardley grabbing the name card that had the name of the guy who left. She bit off the cap of a sharpie and wrote "Yardley- Representing"

"I hope I spelled that right," Amelia whispered.

It was close enough for today's purposes.

"You can tell when a game company has brought in too many women," Collin stated.

"How's that?"

"The quality of the game drops. I've had that happen at a few places, and I've had to move on. I can't work in a subpar programming environment," Collin stated.

"I can't say I've ever noticed anything like that," one of the other panelists said.

"I have to agree with Collin."

Of course his minion did. Yeardley wondered if Collin's

proctologist didn't see that guy's photo during rectal exams.

"Females in the workplace really change the dynamic and the work suffers."

Wolf barked out a laugh. "You mean you have to behave like a human, and you can't go around making sexist jokes. You just don't like getting called out on your inappropriate behaviors at work."

"And you work for who?" the minion man asked.

"I work for Sunrise Enterprises. The makers of Edgeland. We have a diverse programmer pool."

"Yeah, I used to work on that one. When it was good," Collin sneered.

"Bringing up that you used to work on Edgeland isn't the flex you think it is," Wolf scoffed.

"Why? Because I was smart enough to leave?" Collin asked.

This was no longer a conversation to inform people interested in becoming programmers, but was some kind of pissing contest for Collin. And he was cranky that no one wanted to pee with him.

"Gentlemen, please. We have already gotten off topic. Let's not air our dirty laundry as well," the moderator cut in.

Yeardley leaned forward, righteous indignation overrode any nerves she may have had. "I think the conversation has touched on an important aspect of programming that those who are interested in it, need to be aware of. There are a lot of old school ideals that simply do not have a place in the industry anymore. In any industry. Women and people of color are underrepresented in these conversations. I had a manager who was told on his first day that his job was to let go of all the women in the department.

Needless to say, not only did he quit, he took all of us with him."

"What company was that? I think I'll apply for a job there." Collin's comment was met with jeers.

"I said I'm here to represent, and that is an important aspect of the conversation that is so often swept under the rug."

"Oh wow, um, typically we would open the panel up to questions from the floor, but we are out of time," the moderator cut in. "I want to thank our panel for a discussion that I am sure will go down in con history. And probably the last one they will let me moderate. Okay folks, next up in this room is Sci-fi writers and world building, and be sure to go into the main hall with the vendor room and the main stage for the costume contest starting at twelve-forty-five."

Yeardley pushed her chair back. Her nerves were jangled, that was intense, and more than a little unexpected.

"That went off the rails," Amelia said.

Wolf loomed behind Yeardley. "I need to see you for a minute."

Yeardley gulped, fully distracted, she didn't get a chance to properly introduce herself to the other woman.

Wolf's voice was deep and menacing.

Yeardley inwardly winced as he wrapped his long nails around her arm and led her from the dais.

She didn't say anything, waiting for him to berate her for having embarrassed him, and for having done something so completely rude.

They turned left instead of right, and he directed her into an empty hallway. Before she could explain, he had her pressed against the wall, and his mouth was on hers. His lips were soft but their pressure was firm and commanding. His entire body crushed against her. His hair fell around their heads, blocking out the rest of the world.

Yeardley whimpered at the unexpected reaction from him. Her body wanted to go limp, but she also wanted to wrap everything around him and pull him in closer. She hiked a leg over his hip. He ran a hand over her thigh.

"That was so fucking hot," he growled.

He didn't give her a chance to answer. She wanted to say... she couldn't remember what she was going to say. He erased her memory with his touch.

"Oh oops," Amelia's voice cut through the lust-filled haze in Yeardley's mind.

Wolf eased back. He kept his grip on Yeardley's thigh, and didn't really ease away from her body.

"Hey, you need something?" he asked.

Amelia shook her head, a smirk on her face. "I was basically coming to do the same thing, but you beat me to it. Yeardley, that was a bad ass, sexy as fuck power move. And if you decide you're done playing with him, give me a call." She shook her head and turned. She lifted her hand and twirled it in the air. "Carry on my man, carry on."

Wolf dropped his head forward with a heavy sigh.

Yeardley started laughing. She covered her mouth and kept giggling.

"That was intense. She's right, you know. You are fucking sexy, and that move was bad ass. You just fucking walked onto the stage and sat down like you owned that room."

"It seemed like the right thing to do. That Collin is such a bully. I bet he doxes people who piss him off in games."

Wolf started to say something and then shook his head. "Can I kiss you some more?"

"I feel like I've been waiting for you to clue in for the longest time." Yeardley lifted her face to his.

His lips were back on hers. He knew how to kiss. He used the perfect combination: press, slide, suck, tongue.

Yeardley moaned into his mouth.

"You can't keep doing that," he said between pants.

"Doing what?" she asked.

"You make noises, and"— he dropped her leg and stepped back— "I only have so much control."

Yeardley bit her lip. "You too huh? Too many clothes and they are getting uncomfortable. Maybe we could continue this conversation later, somewhere more private?"

"What's your definition of later? Like in fifteen minutes, or tonight?"

"Fifteen minutes?" Yeardley asked. She furrowed her brow in confusion. "What's in fifteen minutes?"

"I figure that's about how long it would take to get up to my room."

"You have a room?" Yeardley opened her mouth to say something and then shut it. She should not grab his hand and pull him toward the elevators. She should not go fuck him right this second so that maybe she could spend the rest of the day focusing instead of being distracted by promises of naked wrestling, or at least some more heavy making out with Wolf later. "I promised that I would meet up with Maisie for the costume competition."

"That starts in like forty-five minutes."

"Forty-five, hmm, fifteen to your room, fifteen back, that only gives us fifteen minutes and frankly, that's not going to be enough time to get you out of all of that gear."

"Poor planning on my part."

He stepped another step away from her.

She reached out and pulled him closer. "I didn't say I

wanted to stop kissing you. We just can't do anything else for a few hours."

Wolf leaned in. His breath brushed her cheek.

"That's where you're hiding." Vik's voice killed the mood.

When Yeardley opened her eyes, Vik was right there, almost as close as Wolf. He had one hand on the wall and the other on Wolf's back, blocking them in.

"News of your little adventure is spreading like wildfire. You can't hide back here forever. Besides, someone else is bound to find you and then instead of being the ball buster on the programming panel they'll be talking about Harley having sex in public."

Yeardley groaned.

Wolf's hand crossed between them and he shoved Vik back. "No one is having sex in public."

"There wasn't even groping happening," Yeardley complained.

"We're kind of in public," Wolf countered. "Observation, not complaint."

"Well, it looked like he was trying to push you into that wall," Vik said.

"Oh my god, Vik, leave them alone. We're going to go find a snack, you want something?"

Wolf adjusted his various straps, mentally settling back into his clothes. As if the thought of taking everything off and spending the rest of the day up in his room hadn't been very close to the forefront of his mind as it was for Yeardley.

Yeardley shook her head. "I'm not hungry. I want to hit the vendor floor if that's okay? Go get something if you're hungry."

Wolf shook his head. "Meeting up at the costume competition?"

"You got it." Vik slung an arm possessively over Aaliyah's shoulders and they left.

Wolf held out a hand. "Shall we?"

Yeardley slipped her hand into his, and felt a heightened tingle of nerves as their skin glided together.

Damn only having forty five minutes. They probably could have gotten a quicky out of the way, but something in her gut told her this man did not do quickies.

THREE

Butterflies danced in Yearldey's stomach as she held onto Wolf.

Between the adrenaline rush from his kisses, and the way people were coming up to her to tell her how much they appreciated her standing up and taking to that stage like she owned it, had her buzzing.

"I'm so tired of cis white guys thinking that everything is for them," one new fan complained. "The industry is such a breeding ground for incels. I bet you work with a bunch of nice guys." She did air quotes indicating she didn't believe any of them were actually nice.

"It's like that in a lot of tech industries. But I can't speak to gaming," Yeardley said.

Wolf squeezed her hand and she turned to him.

"I can," he said. "And yes, there is still too much of that in the industry. My advice is to keep at it. There are decent people in the industry."

"But the assholes are so loud," the fan whined before thanking Yeardley one more time and running off to join her friends.

"Wow, is it always like that after being on a panel?" Yeardley asked.

Wolf chuckled. "Hell no. What you did was pretty spectacular."

"Uh," she groaned and put her face against his shoulder. "Me and my big mouth. But that Collin guy pissed me off so much."

"That's what Collin does, he pisses people off. I think he thinks it's being clever."

"Distract me," she said.

"You already turned down running off to my room." He smoldered at her.

"Yeah, ok not my brightest move. But seriously, pretend I'm a total nube to cons. What do we do now?"

Wolf scanned his gaze down her front. "Okay, let's go find as many Harley Quinns as possible and take a picture with them."

Yeardley laughed, "Like a scavenger hunt?"

Another Harley walked past, several yards up the concourse. Yeardley grabbed Wolf and hurried after the woman.

"Harley!" Yeardley called out.

The other Harley Quinn stopped and looked around. She smiled when she saw Yeardley waving at her.

"Can I get a picture?" Yeardley asked. "I'm going to see how many different Harleys I can get pictures with."

They posed and Wolf took pictures with both of the Harley's phones.

"That sounds like fun, can I tag along?"

By the time the alarm on Wolf's phone alerted them to the start of the costume contest, Yeardley had collected three Harleys, and they were scouring the convention together taking pictures. One poor Joker, thinking he was getting a fun picture surrounded by women, ended up being threatened by various costume weapons.

He was a good sport and played along.

"The costume contest starts in ten," Wolf announced.

Yeardley's shoulders slumped. "This is fun, but I did promise Maisie I would be there."

"We can always pick this back up. I think we inadvertently started a small horde. Finding them again shouldn't be a problem."

Yeardley waved at her compatriots in cosplay and let Wolf lead her to the ballroom. The door they entered through was right between the split between the show stage, where the costume contest would be, and the vendor floor. The contest stage was set up like a T with a runway cutting into the rows of seats.

"Oh we could have gone shopping," Yeardley said.

When Wolf looked at her, she smiled. "But the Harley hunt was way more fun. Thank you for suggesting it. Come on, let's find Maisie."

The seats were filling up fast with con-goers. Yeardley spotted Maisie surrounded with empty chairs. She had bags spread around her saving seats.

"Let me guess, you're the tall ballsy woman who barged up onto the stage during the panel and began yelling?" Maisie said as soon as she saw Yeardley.

"She wasn't yelling. And there was a vacancy," Wolf defended her.

"Let me guess," Yeardley sat next to her friend. "Some guy told you about what happened."

"How did you guess it was a guy?"

"Simple, because if one of the programming women had told you they would have said—"

"The words epic, badass, and awesome display of

woman power would have been used," Wolf cut her off. "Only the gamer dude-bros are upset by what happened."

"Aren't you a gamer dude?" Maisie asked.

"I am, but more importantly I am a gamer of color, and that changes things dramatically. Just as being a female gamer does. I value a diverse playing field, and having diverse avatars available. CIS-het white guys, for the most part, think the world needs to be CIS-het and white."

"But—"

"Don't you dare say not all men," Yeardley glared at Maisie.

"I wasn't, I was going to say but what about Scottie and Vik. And before you scold me again, I realize how stupid that is. They wouldn't be your friends if they were like that."

"Your own brother is like that," Yeardley pointed out.

Maisie sighed. "Yep, and he's nothing like you guys. Nothing. Sorry, I have a lot of family based internalized misogyny to unlearn. It's right up there with my value has jack all to do with the number on the scale."

Yeardley leaned over and hugged Maisie. "That's my girl."

Wolf reached around her and patted Maisie's shoulder.

"Okay, stop. Change of subject," Maisie wiped her face as if there might have been tears. "I can't decide if I want to do an orc, or a lady dwarf for my next cosplay."

Yeardley gasped. "You're going to make a new costume? That's fantastic."

"Lady Hayden's garb was quite impressive," Wolf said.

"I know, right? And the wig work, ah-mazing. But I don't know if my skin can take all that spirit glue. I get contact dermatitis so easily."

"So latex is out for you then? How do you think you would do with all the makeup?"

"I wear makeup almost every day, so I'm thinking that makeup might be better. I need to get some glue and do a test run." She turned to look at the vendor booths behind the rows of chairs where they sat. "Do you think there might be a vendor selling cosplay stuff? Oh look, there they are."

Maisie raised her arm and began waving.

Yeardley turned to see Aaliyah and Vik walking toward them.

"We brought snacks," Aaliyah announced as they took the seats in front of Maisie and Yeardley.

Vik tossed Wolf a crinkly bag of chips, as Aaliyah handed Yeardley and Maisie bags of M&Ms.

"Have we missed anything yet?" Vik asked. He sat and then spun around so that he was facing them instead of the stage.

"It hasn't started yet," Yeardley said.

"What are we looking for? Do we know anyone participating?"

"My friend Hayden is part of a group of lady dwarves."

"Her costume was gorgeous," Yeardley said. "If the rest of her group looks half as good as she did—"

"Welcome to Fanfun Con sponsored by World Art Games, and Fascination Comics. After the cosplay contest go visit their displays in Hall H. I'm Draco and I'm your MC this afternoon..." The announcer cut her off. Aaliyah and Vik turned around and began sharing snacks like they were in a movie theater.

"At least he didn't tell us his house affiliation," Maisie giggled.

Yeardley missed the announcement for what category

they were looking at, but then a line of paladins and knights awkwardly shuffled down the runway and back to the main stage. She guessed it had to have been an armor category.

THE ARMOR CLASS COMPETITION WAS GOOD, NOT THAT HE PAID much attention. Wolf didn't really care about the costumes or the cosplay. Not today. Not after that spectacular display of intelligence followed by the hottest fucking kiss of his adult life.

His attention was all for Yeardley. He didn't want to fuck this up. She was perfection from that smart mouth to those beautiful eyes. And the way she kissed. Maybe a kilt today wasn't the best idea. But he wanted to look good, for her, and in general, but mostly for her.

Her eyes sparkled as she watched the costumes and laughed and giggled with her friend. And every so often, she would turn that dazzling look at him. He found joy in her joy. Warmth spread through his chest as being someone she wanted near her. And blood rushed to his groin when he thought about having her back in his arms. He tucked the edges of the kilt in and shifted in his seat. Erections and kilts, bad combination.

"This is Hayden's group," Yeardley squeezed his arm and gave it a shake. She had just met this person, yet her nervousness for them and their costuming group radiated from her.

Lady Hayden and a cohort of others dressed as high fantasy dwarves took to the runway. The dresses were a multitude of colors, and the hair pieces were elaborate combinations of Renaissance and mid eighteenth century

French wigs. Piles of braids, jewelry woven in and out of the strands, and hair piled high and sculpted to represent small animals like squirrels and forest floor flora such as mushrooms.

"That looks like a lot of work," Wolf said leaning close to Yeardley. "That's what Maisie wants to do?"

Maisie leaned across Yeardley. "Yes, it's incredible isn't it?"

Wolf had to admit, it was fun to look at. He cut a glance at Yeardley's friend, she was the right stature for a lady dwarf.

"That would be fun, but I'm too tall," Yeardley said. She sounded a bit disappointed.

"You are wonderfully tall," Wolf crooned. "You would make a beautiful elf if you wanted to do high fantasy. But I'd love to see you dressed up as a valkyrie or a shield maid to go with my Viking."

"You want to do a couple's cosplay?" She turned to him with wide eyes and a laughing smile. "Seriously?"

He bumped her shoulder with his. "Maybe, it could be fun."

She slid her hand into his. She didn't say anything, but her smile, and the rise of color on her cheeks was promising. The lady dwarves were leaving the stage when he felt it. A pulse of power that he was beginning to associate with a magical event.

Vik turned to him at the same time he leaned forward to put his hand on Vik's shoulder.

"You felt that too?"

"I've got to find a computer," Wolf said as he sprang to his feet. Instead of stepping over knees to get out of the row of chairs, he climbed onto his chair, and leapt empty chair to empty chair over the rows until there were no more chairs. He hit the ground running into the vendor section. His gaze scanning for a laptop he could borrow.

YEARDLEY LOOKED AFTER HIM. "WHAT WAS THAT?"

"Maybe he really has to pee, I know I do. I was holding it long enough to see Hayden's group. I've got to go." Maisie stood and began wiggling her way out of the row.

Vik looked at Aaliyah and then made eye contact with her. "You might want to leave."

"What?" Yeardley asked.

"Oh shit, you mean like last time?" Aaliyah asked. When Vik nodded, she grabbed her bags and began leaving. "Yeardley, we have got to go."

Yeardley was on her feet and following her friends out of the seating area. "I'm going to go find Wolf," she said.

She left while Vik was kissing Aaliyah.

"Get out of here, Yeardley," Vik growled from somewhere behind her.

She ran, and didn't stop until she found Wolf. Some skinny kid was nervously hovering while Wolf focused on the laptop and typed away frantically.

"Get a computer," Wolf growled. "Find her a laptop. Now!"

The kid scrambled and ran.

"What the fuck is going on?" Yeardley asked.

There was a large oh and ah gasp from the costuming contest. She turned to see a drawn chariot roll in through the ballroom doors. At the reigns stood a dwarf, resplendent in battle armor holding up a gleaming double headed battle axe. The costume was elaborate, beautiful even. The work on the chariot was exceptional all the way down to the really large armored goats that pulled it.

Well damn, they had to have won the contest with that much detail and that entrance. Another loud gasp and everyone's attention, including Yeardley's, was drawn to the opposite entrance. Another battle chariot, but this time. Where the hell did they find dogs that big? This chariot was equally elaborate, but not beautiful. It looked slimy, and shit those dogs were huge and looked really grumpy. The goblin at the reins had gray skin and was emaciated. The foot soldiers who followed moved weirdly low and crept like spiders.

"Do you see this, Wolf? Those dogs are fucking huge!"

"Dire wolves," he said. He didn't look up and kept typing away.

"How can you tell? You aren't even looking."

Wolf pulled the laptop from the hands of the kid. "Thanks, now you need to get out of here."

"Dude, you can't just steal my shit, demand another laptop, and—"

Wolf grabbed the kid's head and turned him to face the contest stage. "You play Codex Wars?"

"Oh, fuck me," the kid said.

"Get out, and take people with you." He glanced up at Yeardley. "You code? Time to code."

Wolf side stepped and began typing on the new laptop. He pointed at the one he just left. Yeardley saw a screen full of code. It would take her a minute to figure out what this was telling her. Especially since it wasn't in configurations she recognized. She scanned and began scrolling.

"Game code. What am I looking at and why?"

"I don't have time to explain everything. Look for

anything that starts with this." With a long nail, Wolf pointed to a line of syntax.

Yeardley attempted to read it, but it made no sense. The part she understood involved opening a gate. No, a gateway.

"Find that, delete that." He sounded like he was in pain. She looked at his face, it was contorted. He wrapped one arm around his middle and continued to hack at the keyboard one handed.

She started with a universal find and replace. Only it seemed to take forever to complete the find function.

"You can't do it that way," Wolf said. His voice suddenly sounded lispy. "The line code is too long, too many instances. Just start scrolling and deleting. I'm going to try to reprogram the portals. Look. I'm not going to be able to finish right away. So no matter what happens to me. Take that laptop and run, keep deleting that line."

He fell to the floor.

"Wolf!" She was on her knees next to him as he convulsed. She looked up for Vik, for anyone she could ask for help from.

She scanned the area and didn't believe what she was seeing. There was a full battalion of goblins, some riding the backs of the dire wolves, facing off a battalion of dwarves. Some people took pictures with their phones while others tried to get out of the way, panic clear on their faces.

"What the hell is going on?" She turned her attention back to Wolf, only he was no longer there. Instead she knelt next to a wolf, almost as large as the wolves in the goblin army. He was mostly gray with a line of brown across his back and shoulders.

She fell back on her ass. The wolf, Wolf, looked at her,

nodded, and then darted into the standoff. He stopped next to a bear. Yelling from the dwarves and goblins got louder, they banged on shields, their battle animals screamed or growled with frightening sounds.

Their characters surged together. There was no way this was some kind of staged reenactment. The bear and the wolf. Wolf, that explained a lot, surged into the fray.

After moments of stunned inaction, Yeardley scrambled back to her feet and began deleting the code that Wolf had identified. He said he was working on portals. She put down the laptop she had been working on and began scanning the code he had been pounding away on. There it was. She watched as a line of code appeared. Someone else was inputting a new source.

She scanned it. There was a rhyming quality to the code. It was different, and it had a unique identifier at the beginning, a bit of non-functional text that served almost like a signature. Whoever was putting in the code Wolf wanted gone was essentially saying 'I did this.' She highlighted the code and deleted it.

She scrolled and found another block of code. All she needed to do was look for that signature. This time instead of deleting the code, she reconfigured it. She knew secure delivery. She secured the portal, basically locking it from one direction. She didn't know if that would help, but she continued locking down the portal.

There was a panicked cry, and she noticed the goblin army was no longer pouring in through the doors to the ballroom. Dwarves armed for battle continued to run in.

With a deep breath, she returned the code. She needed to wrap the portal code in a secure packet, and stop them from functioning. Her fingers flew over the keyboard. There was a battle of programming going on in front of her, and she was pretty sure it was directly related to the battle behind her.

She glanced over her shoulder. Shit, was that a battle boar? Costumed humans had entered the fight, thinking it was something other than what it was, and they were getting hurt. Really hurt.

Every time she encountered the syntax Wolf wanted her to delete, she deleted it. Every time she found mention of a portal she locked it. A new piece of code popped up. She stared at it, evaluating it.

"What if I did..." she began altering the code as it appeared. She turned the laptop around so that she didn't have to keep looking up behind her. Now she could just look up. She typed in what she wanted, and, yes, it altered something in the battle.

Dwarves retreated through their doors, but goblins could not get through that portal. She entered another block of code. Nothing happened. She needed water. A lot of it. She looked up at the ceiling. She needed the sprinklers to activate.

WOLF LEFT THE CODING IN YEARDLEY'S CAPABLE FINGERS AND bounded into the battle. He stopped with Vik at his side. The giant bear was waiting for something. Scottie hadn't arrived yet, but wherever he had been he had to have felt the magic surge. The shift would hit, and he would be here soon.

Anticipation hung heavy in the air. The eerie calm before battle covered his skin, prickling his nerves, making his fur stand on end.

The tension broke and the armies yelled out their battle

cries and rushed together. The fighting armies had entered the ballroom through magical portals. Wolf ran around the boundaries of the battle. As long as the humans stayed clear everything should be fine. His goal was to keep the humans safe when the video games became real.

At first his task was easy. Scare the bystanders away, but then, some asshole thinking he was a genuine badass, in cosplay armor came screaming into the mix. Wolf was too far from him to help, but Vik was there. The bear got between a rampaging dire wolf and the puny human in costume. Soon too many others were doing the same. This wasn't some free for all melee.

Wolf circled round, wanting to make sure Yeardley was safe. Doing his best to keep the edges of the battle from spilling over into the vending booths. When he could spare a glance, Yeardley was gone. Maybe she had run, hopefully she was safe. He didn't have time to be distracted. Didn't have time to wonder what it was about Codex Wars specifically that was letting magic in via code.

He heard the scream of "fire," before he smelled the smoke. Just great, a fire was not going to be helpful right now. Within seconds the sprinkler system spit to life and stale moldy water sprayed down on everyone and everything in the ballroom.

That's when he paused. The goblins and dwarves, and all the things they brought in with them from the Codex Wars realm began melting. They dissolved like the Wicked Witch of the West in the Wizard of Oz.

He leapt back to where he had left Yeardley, hadn't seen her there the last time he looked. Within moments of sniffing for her, he located her, soaking wet, hunched up under a table, computer in her lap.

"It worked!" she yelled triumphantly. "Oh shit!" She

yelled as the change washed over Wolf, and he was back to human form and kneeling in front of her. All of his clothes, a little worse for wear, were still on.

He reached for her, and pulled her out from under the table and kissed her. He pressed his mouth to hers and she returned his kiss with passion.

"We have got to get out of here!" He took her hand and pulled her to the nearest door.

Out on the hotel's concourse people were scrambling, looking for friends, and trying to get out the doors.

Yeardley yelled, and tugged Wolf back.

"Maisie!" she yelled.

"I'll find her, you get out of here."

Yeardley stopped, looked out the glass doors, and then pulled him in close for another kiss. "I'll be under that tree." She pointed out into the parking lot. There were a lot of trees. He'd find her.

She ran, and he began fighting his way back into the crowd. He wasn't too worried about Aaliyah, she would have Vik looking out for her, but... he had no idea where that idiot Scottie would be, and someone had to look after Maisie.

He jumped up, trying to see over the mass of people. She was not a tall woman, and he didn't know where she had gone. He saw Scottie. The tall redheaded man waved at him.

"That was fucking lit!" Scottie laughed as he approached Wolf.

Wolf cut him off. "We need to find Maisie."

"Shit. Where's Yeardley? Vik? Aaliyah?" Scottie asked, his expression changing instantly from exuberance to concern.

Wolf shook his head. "Yeardley is in the parking lot. She's safe. I have to assume Vik is taking care of Aaliyah."

"Scottie!"

Both men turned toward the sound of Scottie's name. Wolf only saw people, too many of them. The entire convention was flooding out these doors, and it looked like other guests staying at the hotel as well.

"Maisie!" he and Scottie yelled.

"I'm here!" Hands shot up in the thick of the crowd and began waving.

Scottie began making his way toward her. Wolf followed in his wake. When they reached her, she was flushed and panting. Her makeup streamed down her cheeks as if she had been crying. She hugged Scottie first, and then Wolf.

"Come on, let's get you out of here, and catch up with everyone."

By the time they fought through the crowd to get outside, emergency crews were already running into the crowd. Wolf led Scottie and Maisie toward the tree he thought Yeardley had indicated.

He sighed with relief when he saw her standing there with Vik and Aaliyah. They were all waving at him. He lifted his hand, his arm suddenly tired and heavy. Maisie ran and crashed into a hug with Yeardley and Aaliyah. By the time Wolf reached the group, Yeardley had disengaged herself from her friends and was wrapping her arms around him.

"I cannot wait for you to tell me how you did that," he said against her hair. "You are a fucking badass."

"What the hell just happened?" Maisie asked. "I went to the bathroom, and then I couldn't get back into the ballroom, the doors were locked, and I could hear screaming. And then chaos, and people were going batshit crazy."

"Gas leak," they all seemed to say at the same time.

"Well Fanfun Con is officially over," Scottie said.

"They haven't had time to make any decisions like that," Maisie said. She sounded more sad than disappointed.

"After this, it's gonna shut down."

Wolf's phone buzzed in his pocket. He fished it out and looked at the message. "Definitely closed. The entire hotel is. I just got a text saying they will relocate me for the night, but I won't be able to return to my room to get my things until tomorrow."

"That sucks," Scottie said.

"What now?" Maisie asked. "I don't want to go home. Can we go get some food?"

"You know what, that sounds like a good idea." Scottie draped an arm over her shoulder and began walking off toward his car.

None of them said much as they followed, but Yeardley kept looking at Wolf expecting him to say something.

"Hamburgers or burritos?"

"I could use some fries, so hamburgers."

The conversation ping-ponged around as they narrowed in on the family owned burger place a little farther away, but they knew would not be overrun by other con goers.

"Okay," Scottie bounced away from Maisie and slid into the driver's seat of his new car. "This is me, race you there."

He pulled forward through the space in front of him and left before anyone could really respond.

"I can't fucking race a Porsche," Yeardley muttered. "Not even going to try. I'm parked over this way." She pointed and began walking.

Vik and Aaliyah continued on to his car.

Maisie didn't move. She stared at the empty parking space. She looked like she wanted to cry.

Wolf wrapped an arm over her shoulder. "He's a fucking idiot," he said.

"Earlier, he said he would take me for a ride, to show off his new toy. He didn't even ask," she sounded numb, past disappointment.

"Scottie is clueless. Come with us, and tell us all about this lady dwarf cosplay you're thinking about. I didn't hear everything you said back there."

CHAPTER

FOUR

As soon as they made it to the restaurant, Yeardley, Aaliyah, and Maisie went into the ladies' room to wash up.

Maisie had a hard time holding back her sniffles. Wolf had done a great job keeping her distracted on the car ride, but as soon as she saw Scottie it was impossible for her to hide her disappointment.

Yeardley ran a paper towel under warm water and began wiping Maisie's face.

"He's a himbo Maisie. He is not worth your tears," Aaliyah said.

"Right," she sniffed. "Boys aren't worth crying over, and the ones who are will do their best to never make you cry."

"Exactly," Yeardley agreed.

"He's clueless. He probably doesn't even realize he did anything wrong. You don't need to waste your time on clueless."

"Cute and clueless," she pouted.

Yeardley sighed and leaned against the sink. She

couldn't think of anything to say that didn't sound hypocritical. After all, it was clear she was connecting with Wolf, and Aaliyah and Vik were stuck together like superglue. Of course, Maisie would want to make that same connection with someone, and how perfect would it be if that person could be Scottie. Not only was he already her crush, but he was friends with her girl friends' guys.

"I don't know what to tell you sweetie. I don't know him that well, and he just seems so self-absorbed. But don't listen to me. I don't know him that well. Listen to Aaliyah, she's been around him more."

"But I like himbos, they don't walk around calling themselves alphas, and just being dicks. They are genuinely kind, do the right thing because it's right. They listen when it's time to listen, and they aren't afraid to show emotions."

"Are you thinking about George of the Jungle again?"

"Listen, that movie and Brendan Fraser single handedly ruined me for men for the rest of my life. Everyone else is walking around blaming animated characters, and I have to deal with the single most himbo of himbo movies." Maisie sighed. "I'll be okay. I can friend-zone myself, and get over him. I just need a harder shell. Look, if anyone asks, I was scared and upset by the gas leak at the hotel. I mean that. It's not a lie, exactly. But I don't want the guys to know that."

"I won't say anything," Yeardley said.

Aaliyah didn't say anything. When her friends looked at her, she shrugged. "I won't mention that he made you cry, but I might say something to Vik. I'm not joking when I say Scottie can be clueless. Vik could be the clue-by-four he needs upside the back of his head. I mean I would tell him that he's a dumb fuck, and he needs to be more mindful of what he says."

Maisie blinked at Aaliyah, the sad expression on her face didn't change.

"Okay, okay, I won't say anything. I promise," Aaliyah said.

Yeardley made an effort to sit between Maisie and Scottie in the booth, so that it didn't emphasize the fact that she and Wolf were clearly leveling up their relationship status.

Many baskets of cheese fries later, Scottie leaned back and admitted defeat. "I think today has won. And I still need to edit some of the video I took today and get it posted. Plus I have got to get out of this body paint. It's itchy."

Maisie grinned at him but turned to Yeardley. "Can I get a ride home?"

"Of course, you don't have to ask."

"You know, Maisie, I did promise I'd show you my new car, you want to ride with me?"

Yeardley felt Maisie start to vibrate, where their legs touched in the booth.

"Are you sure? I live clear over in Inglewood, and you're in the opposite direction."

"How do you know where I live? Have you been stalking me?"

"Aaliyah told us," Maisie answered.

"I suppose she also told you that I need furniture?" he asked. When he stood, he yawned, stretching up, showing off his height.

Yeardley suppressed a laugh at the awed expression on Maisie's face. The last thing she wanted was for Maisie to get hurt, but if this was the beginning of something between the two of them, she was going to cheerlead for it.

Maisie deserved someone who made her happy and treated her well.

"I totally told them you need furniture. I can't believe you bought a car before you bought a couch," Aaliyah said as she shook her head.

"Priorities," Scottie proclaimed.

"Exactly, you have none." Everyone laughed.

"You coming?" When he held out his hand to Maisie, she pushed on Yeardley to get up so she could squirm out of the booth and follow him.

"Text me when you get home," Yeardley called out after them.

"Me too," Aaliyah added.

Vik shook his head as he watched them leave. "I guess that's our cue. What are you up to tonight?"

Aaliyah punched him in the chest.

"What?"

She opened her eyes wide and looked from Vik to Yeardley and back.

"Oh, right. I guess we're off. Have fun kids." He got out of the booth, waiting for Aaliyah.

"Remember condoms," Vik said with a smirk before following Aaliyah out of the restaurant.

Yeardley fell into the booth and leaned forward, hitting her head on the table.

"That wasn't embarrassing or anything," she said.

"Stop, you'll hurt your face," Wolf said as he slid into the booth next to her.

His hand was warm on the back of her neck. She sat up and leaned against him.

"You don't have a hotel room, and I live with my sister."

Wolf let out a heavy breath. "Unless we want any

sounds we make broadcast in MinVid, I suggest we go back to the hotel and let them get me a room elsewhere. Scottie is going to be editing all night."

Yeardley sat up and looked up at Wolf. "Did you say something to him?"

"Oh, like how he was a rude fuck head to Maisie? Yeah, we both did. He said he was so amped from the fight that he jumped in his car and went, and by the time he realized what he had done, it was too late to circle back and ask if she wanted to go with him. I know she likes him. But I don't know if he's mature enough for a relationship. Maisie would be good for him, but would he be good for her?"

"That's what I'm worried about."

"Hey, we'll both keep an eye on him. And I know you and Aaliyah watch out for Maisie."

Yeardley nodded. "Back to the hotel then?"

"But first we need a drug store."

Yeardley raised her eyebrows in question.

"We're going to need condoms, right?" Wolf asked, his own brows lifting.

"Oh, hell yeah," Yeardley laughed.

YEARDLEY LEANED ON THE CHECK-IN COUNTER PLAYING ON HER phone as Wolf made arrangements with the hotel to be relocated. He still wasn't going to be allowed into his room until the Fire Marshall was able to conduct a thorough inspection.

A text from Maisie came in. "Made it home."

"Good," Yeardley typed.

"Did he say anything?" Aaliyah asked.

"Yeah, he apologized, said he felt awful about ditching me like that. I have his phone number now and can text him!!!" There were three exclamation points.

"I know y'all think he's dumb, but he had some really insightful ideas when it came to my cosplay ideas."

"I'm glad he's behaving better," Yeardley typed.

"I never said he was dumb. I said he was an idiot. There is a difference." Aaliyah's message made Yeardley chuckle.

"What's so funny?" Wolf asked.

"Oh, all set?" Yeardley held up her phone. "My friends are hilarious."

"Yeah, I have a room at Ralston Suites. It's about a mile that way," he pointed away from the freeway. "Shall we? I also have a gift card to get some fresh clothes. This is costing the hotel thousands."

"Well, you won't need that gift card tonight, will you?"

"I hope not," his voice dropped and the growl sent shivers up Yeardley's spine.

"Wolf," Yeardley finally got the nerve to ask. They were headed back to her car, in the same lot they had evacuated to after the, was it a situation? A battle? The official excuse from the hotel was a gas leak. But really what had happened? "You will tell me what exactly happened this afternoon won't you?"

He stopped and tugged her hand so she spun to face him. "I will tell you everything. Thank you for keeping it quiet when Maisie was around. The fewer people who know, the better it is. I think. But, I have to ask you, knowing what you saw me do, is that going to change anything between us?"

"We stopped and bought condoms. It's not going to change anything. Now maybe this thing about your name,

Simon, might." She wrapped her arms around his middle and began dragging him toward her car.

WOLF LAY SPREAD OUT ON THE SECOND BED IN THE ROOM. HE WAS forlorn and distracted. Yeardley had expected him to be all over her, or at least animated as he told her what had happened back there at the convention.

They had arrived at the new hotel, gotten the key, and as soon as they walked in the door, Wolf fell back on the bed and groaned.

Not knowing what to do, after grabbing the remote she climbed onto the second bed and pulled her shoes off. After throwing them across the room with a double thud, she sat cross legged, and began flicking through channels. She split her time watching to see if the show was interesting or not—mostly not—and checking her phone.

Maisie had arrived home safely, but was now providing a text recap of her ride home with Scottie in his new car. This was a second by second replay. Yeardley didn't need to reply other than hitting the heart emoji every so often.

She gave Wolf some time. This afternoon had been, for lack of a better word, intense.

She climbed off the bed and began rummaging in the bag from the drug store. In addition to buying condoms, they had gotten drinks and candy, and other snacks. She grabbed the pack of red licorice and returned to her spot in the middle of what she now considered her bed.

She chewed on the candy, watched random bits of random shows, and read Maisie's texts. Other than the fact she was in costume in a hotel room with Wolf, this could have been any other lazy Saturday afternoon. She pulled another licorice stick from the package and looked over at the man sprawled out.

She stood, and taking a giant step, stepped across the gap onto the other bed. It rocked, and she wobbled a bit before finding her balance. She stepped next to Wolf's head and looked down at him. His eyes were closed.

"Whoa," he said as he cracked his eyes open. "You look crazy tall from here."

He closed his eyes again, and she crouched down to be closer.

"You ever just need time to process everything?" he asked. "It's like for a minute, I just need everything to stop moving so I can think straight again."

He reached up and traced his fingers down the side of her face. "You are so beautiful."

"I was thinking something similar," Yeardley said as she gazed down on him. "We need to address the elephant in the room before proceeding."

Wolf rolled and sat up, facing her. "Which elephant is that? There is an entire fucking herd in here."

Yeardley fell back onto her ass. Wolf climbed toward her.

"Simon?" she asked.

He rolled so he was laying back on the bed, but this time his head was in her lap. He reached up and stole the stick of licorice sticking out of her mouth. He took a bite before returning it to her mouth.

"Blame my parents for that," he said.

"And Wolf?"

"That's a bit more complicated. Come here," he wrapped a hand around the back of her neck and tugged her down to kiss him.

She laughed as he raked his nails through her hair as it fell into his face.

"Uncomplicate it."

"I guess it started when I started choosing Viking skins in games."

"So games came first?"

"I'm a half blind nerd boy named Simon who programs video games for fun. Yes, games came first."

"Okay, Simon, so you started playing Vikings."

"And that led to cosplay, and then really getting into it. Like really, really. I follow Odin and Thor, I know that Valhalla is out there for when I die with honor and glory. And that for some reason Odin chose me and my brethren, Vik and Scottie, for some glorious battle."

Yeardley rested back on her hands. "Yeah, but," she looked up, thinking.

"Did your affinity with and name come before or after?"

Wolf twisted so he could see her. "After?"

"I saw you shape shift today. And that might be from the gas leak, but I don't have the headache that usually follows exposure to natural gas. So, either I got a whiff of someone's LSD, or I saw what I saw. And, well, the LSD might be a more acceptable answer."

"Sorry no LSD. My personality of the berserker Wolf was probably the second thing I established after the first time I chose a Viking skin."

"Okay, that's two big elephants out of the way," Yeardley said. "I need a bath, you going to join me?"

"Excuse me?

"If I've been exposed to gas, or LSD, or whatever, I would like to wash it off. I know I at least need to get that sprinkler system water off of me. There is a giant bathtub in there"— she pointed in the direction of the bathroom—

"and there are at least two more elephants we need to address."

Wolf was on his feet and striding into the bathroom. "How hot do you like your bath? Lava or sauna?"

"Not quite sauna," she said.

"I thought all women liked their baths scalding hot."

"I don't want to be boiled. I want to be clean."

"Bubbles?"

Yeardley scrambled off the bed and stopped in the bathroom door. "They have bubbles? Yes bubbles."

She began picking through the towels.

"They never give enough towels. Maybe we should have stopped and used that gift card to get some clean t-shirts and shorts."

"Why don't you call the front desk and order some towels while the tub is filling."

Yeardley left the bathroom and did just that.

Once the towels were delivered, she stripped and wrapped a towel around her. She appeared in the bathroom door again, Wolf's attention was on the tub. "This should be ready for you."

"Good, I'm ready for it." She waited for him to look up before she dropped the towel.

His jaw dropped open, and he seemed to be struggling with words.

Yeardley blamed the steam in the room for the burning flush she felt on her cheeks before she stepped into the tub and sank down into the water, pulling bubbles around her.

"Grab a wash cloth before you get in, so you can scrub my back," She said as she scooted to the front half of the tub, leaving an obvious place for Wolf to climb in behind her.

"Um, wow, ah, yeah," he seemed to stumble over his words. "I guess I'll go change too."

"Yeah, you don't want to leave your clothes in here, they'll probably get all wet."

When he stepped from the bathroom, she let out a big breath as quietly as she could, not quite believing she had just done what she had. But someone had to get Wolf back on track for the evening's entertainment.

CHAPTER
FIVE

Wolf stepped back into the bathroom, a towel low around his hips.

Yeardley, who only moments before dropped her towel, exposing her body to him, now sat in the tub and blushed furiously. Her eyes widened as she looked at him, and when their gazes met, she looked away, and kept her head averted.

"You're cute when you blush," he said.

She didn't say anything, just pulled more bubbles around her.

He stepped farther into the bathroom, so that he was practically behind her, before he dropped his towel and stepped into the tub. He let out a hiss and a sigh as the warm water welcomed him into its depths.

"Better?" he asked.

He reached around her shoulders and pulled her back against his chest, as he relaxed against the back of the tub. Yeardley was stiff for a long moment, and then she relaxed.

"This is nice," she said.

It was. And it was the right speed for them. She still had

questions, still saw elephants, before she was willing to go further with him, and that was okay. Her comfort was his priority.

"You wanted to talk about elephants?"

"Well, yeah. This conversation is about to get really weird, so I thought, maybe I should distract us a little bit," she said. "So you wear contacts?"

"That I do. And I even have glasses. But this is not what you wanted to talk about is it?" Wolf asked.

"Will you be able to sleep in them?"

"Are you sure you want to talk about this weird thing?" He let out a derisive laugh. "You are awfully distracted by my eyes. These are the daily disposable kind. So once they are out, I don't use them again. I have more at the hotel, and of course at home."

"Do you need to go home tonight and pick some up?" she asked.

"To be honest, I was hoping to not have to leave this room once we got here," he said.

"There's no rule that says once you check into your room you can't come and go as you please."

"Well," he lowered his head so that his lips brushed the tip of her ear. "Your pleasure was what I was thinking about.

Yeardley shuddered in his arms. The bath was entirely too warm for her to be cold.

"Um yeah, I think I'd like that." She slid her back against his chest, gliding smoothly side to side, and then she tipped her head back, giving him better access to that ear, and her neck.

Not missing the opening, he placed a kiss, and then scraped his teeth along the skin under her ear.

The noise she made was somewhere between a

contented sigh, and a moan. His hands, that he had been very aware of so that he didn't touch or grab body parts that were not yet offered as available for his caress, ran up along her thigh, her delicious long, strong thigh. He let his nails drag gently over her skin.

"Oh gods, yes, that feels good," she moaned.

Yeardley reached up over her head to grab a handful of his locks. She twisted and his mouth captured hers. She pulled on his hair as if to draw him closer.

Even with her lips against his, Wolf did not forget the way she had reacted to the scrape of his nails across her skin. As he reached up to grab one of her breasts, he dragged his sharp nails up her torso after his fingertips grazed her flesh.

He moved the hand on her leg higher, wrapping around to grab her inner thigh, and to skim over that slit between her legs he had been wanting to touch all fucking day long. He cupped her, and her hips bucked against his palm.

She fell back against him as she pressed her hips into his hand. No longer kissing her, he had a modicum of focus back. He lifted his knees, giving Yeardley more room in the tub to get closer to him, getting his hips closer to her ass.

His cock throbbed with want. It pulsed against her. There was no way she did not know what that was. She pressed back against him with a bit of a hip wiggle. Yeah, she knew exactly what that was.

He ran his fingers over her sex, and then, carefully since his nails were show-off long and stiletto sharp, he pressed the pad of his finger between her folds. She was slick with desire.

He laughed, delighted that they were both on the same page, elephants be damned.

With one hand cupping her supple breast, and the

other stroking her clit, Wolf moved his lips to her shoulder. He licked at her skin as if he could taste the freckles that dotted her skin.

Yeardley continued to whimper and rock her hips against his hand. He couldn't do much more from their current position because of his nails. Letting go of her breast, he reached up and pulled down a washcloth. Slowly, tantalizingly, he dragged his fingers from between her legs.

He grabbed the soap and began lathering up the cloth.

"But I want to be dirty," Yeardley moaned.

"Don't worry about that. This is going to be the hottest, filthiest bath you've ever taken. Turn around and face me."

With water splashing over the edges of the tub, Yeardley managed to turn until she faced Wolf. Her ass was far away, but now he could see her. Her skin ranged from pale to a deep rosy flush. The freckles on her shoulders lighten as they scatter down her arms and across her chest. They were joined by a delicate smattering of them across her nose.

He lifted her leg and began washing her feet, sliding the washcloth suggestively in and out between her toes. To his delight he discovered more freckles at the tops of her knees.

"We have got to get you properly clean," Wolf purred.

"I thought you were going to make me properly filthy," Yeardley teased.

"Everything in proper order"—he held out his hand to her—"give me your arm."

He ran the wash cloth over her limbs before he grabbed her legs and pulled them around his waist, practically putting Yeardley in his lap.

She looked down between them. His cock was on full alert between them, and fully visible like a buoy in a harbor.

"Just checking," she said as she leaned her shoulders closer and claimed a kiss.

He tapped her on her nose, and lightly ran the cloth around her face, wiping away some, but not all of the makeup she had on for her cosplay.

She arched back, lifting her breasts to him. "I think you missed a few spots."

Wolf soaped the hand towel up and began running it in circles over her chest, paying particular attention to squeezing and massaging her breasts. He longed to put his mouth on her, soap be damned. He lowered his mouth to her and sucked in a nipple.

Yeardley wrapped her arms around his head, and held him to her. She wiggled her hips, and he knew she was trying to get closer. The tub was big, but not that big.

She reached between them and wrapped her hand around his cock. He couldn't breathe. He didn't want to. He had her breast in his mouth and her hand on his cock, and fuck if this wasn't the best bath he had ever taken in his life.

She stroked, and tugged on his cock. She could pull it off for all he cared, as long as she held it in her hand. Their position was awkward, and she was the first one to cry defeat. She let go of him, and pulled her boob from his mouth. He wanted to pout.

"I need you to fuck me properly, and it's not going to happen in this tub. Hold on, I'm going to turn on the shower and rinse off."

She stood and, leaning over him, turned the shower on.

Did she not realize that she had put her sex right in his face when she stood? He was staring down a triangle of dark fuzz. It practically taunted him. He looked up, he had to blink against the falling water. Her eyes were closed as the water ran over her. She worked her hands into her hair.

He wrapped his hands over her hips and leaned in. His tongue flicked out and licked between her folds. He laved her clit, and sucked on the soft flesh.

She gasped, wobbled, and then her hands were knotting into his hair and gripping his shoulder. Her knees buckled slightly and then she seemed to find the right placement, better placement, because he now had better access to properly kiss and suck and drink her in.

His tongue dipped in deep, and Yeardley cried out. Oh, she liked that, so he repeated it, loving the sounds she made in response. She was breathing hard, braced against him. He lowered his torso, and twisted his neck, giving himself a different vantage point to access her delights.

"Please," the word was barely a whisper. "I can't hold myself up."

He pulled away from her and looked up.

Her face was anguish and passion, and desperation. She continued to pant for a moment.

"I want to come all over your face, but I can't from here. I'm going to fall over."

"Then let's fix that."

Carefully supporting her, Wolf stood and stepped from the tub. He helped Yeardley out. If the floor and their bodies weren't so wet and slippery he would have swung her into his arms. But his knees felt as wobbly as hers apparently were.

He threw more towels onto the floor to soak up everything that had splashed out during their bath.

He ripped the blanket from the first bed, and wrapped it around Yeardley as he lowered her into the bed. He rummaged through their shopping bags, ignoring all the candy, looking for the condoms.

With his quarry in hand he stepped back to the bed.

Yeardley tossed open the blanket, and he climbed in next to her. Her body was lush and warm. She welcomed him into her arms, and wrapped a leg over his hip.

He kissed her, and never wanted to stop. Their tongues danced, and her skin against his was perfection. He touched all of her, and not for the first time, cursed the vanity that had him get his nails done this long for the con. He broke off the kiss to address the condom issue, it took focus to not drive a nail through it. He returned to her mouth and her kisses.

He slid a hand down her back, and pressed her hips up as he tipped his back finding the proper position. They both sighed as they came together. She was already so close, her inner walls clamped tight around him and began pulsing in time to his thrusts.

Who said chivalry was dead? It was his pleasure to make sure the lady went first. When she went off, she bucked and moaned, and became a wild ride before practically collapsing around him. She was fireworks in human skin. And her spasms elicited the same from him.

He roared out his release as he crashed into a singularity, tipped past her event horizon, and splashed out into a field of stars. His arms wobbled and gave up supporting him. He lay panting against her chest. Her legs twisted around him, her fingers playing with the strands of his locs, her breasts the perfect pillows.

He was safe, he had done his job, he passed out.

Yeardley let Wolf sleep. After about twenty minutes she realized he was down for the long term. Poor guy had to have been exhausted. She, on the other hand, was antsy.

His bedroom skills had amped her up, left her with adrenalin to spare.

Realizing it was only about four, she got dressed, grabbed the room key and left. But not until after she left a quick note, and placed it on his phone, just out of reach of his hand, hoping he would find it.

She didn't know about him, but, she hated the idea of not having clean clothes for later, hated that she was back in the cosplay clothes that had been coated in sprinkler water and panic sweat. Neither the hotel that hosted Fanfun Con nor this one were too far from where she lived.

She ran home and quickly changed into clean clothes. She tossed together a quick overnight bag. She thought about texting Aaliyah or Maisie to help her get in touch with Scottie so he could put something together for Wolf. At the very least he would need...

"He lives where?" she texted Aaliyah back once she asked for help.

Yeardley stared at her phone. That wasn't simply across town, it was across town and then some. No wonder Wolf decided on staying in a hotel. And if Scottie had a new car he liked to drive, he didn't seem the kind to mind the distance. She knew if she had a Porsche Taycan, she would want to drive it everywhere.

"Yikes. I'll hit Wallyworld and grab stuff. Easier, faster."

And the store was between where she was, and where she wanted to be, hanging out with Wolf in his hotel room.

When she walked back into the hotel room, more shopping bags in hand, Wolf was already awake. He sat up in the bed they had already messed up, a towel around his head, and another at his hips.

"You had a shower? Did you find my note?" she asked.

"I did, thank you. You missed my disoriented panic,

waking up, naked in a hotel room with none of my things. I totally freaked out until I found your note in my hand."

"I ran home and got a few things."

"I see that. You've changed clothes."

She nodded. "And I got you a change too. These are probably not your style, but I didn't really think you'd be going out of the room in them. Besides, I have had fantasies about you in gray sweats." She pulled the sweats from the bag and tossed them on the still made bed. And then unloaded a t-shirt and a pack of fresh socks.

"Gray sweats?" he laughed.

"Also," she paused, held up a finger, and pulled more from a different bag. "I got some saline and a contacts case. My sister wears contacts, and I know what a complete pain they can be. This stuff can also double as eye drops, it's just saline."

"You did all of that for me?"

He got out of the bed and held the t-shirt up. It had a cartoon alien making a peace sign with the words 'I want to believe.' He pulled the tags from the sweats, and then removed the towel from his hips.

Yeardley made a low sound in her throat. His ass was a work of art.

He twisted and looked at her, and laughed as he stepped into the sweats. He pulled the shirt on, fighting the neck over the towel covering his hair.

"Watching you get dressed is like reverse psychology or something. Cause that was super-hot," she confessed.

"You're super-hot," he said as he crossed the small space to her.

He put his hands on her hips and stared at her. His eyes kept drifting from hers to her lips. And then they were kissing again, and it was glorious.

"Maybe I didn't need to pick up a change of clothes after all," Yeardley said. She was naked, well satiated, and wrapped around Wolf in bed again.

"No, it was worth it just to hear that you've fantasized about me in gray sweats, and to see that look on your face when I put them on."

"I shouldn't feed your ego and tell you that you are a beautiful man," she laughed.

"Feed me my beauty, feed me. Let me sip from your words and partake of your pleasure." He leaned over and kissed her bare shoulder.

"You can talk pretty too," she purred.

"You are inspiring, and beautiful, and—"

"Oh, tell me more." She wiggled into his arms and ran her face over the skin of his chest.

"Wait, now I'm feeding your ego," he teased.

"Yeah, but I don't reply in poetry. I reply in code." She began tapping on his chest.

Wolf closed his eyes as she continued to tap. "Not Morse code. That's binary. Shit. Do it again."

She tapped and paused and continued the pattern.

Wolf translated, "I want. That's too many for you. Though I do want you."

He opened his eyes at her, and her toes curled. "Try again. The first part is right."

She tapped.

He shook his head. "I'm getting distracted. Stop moving your leg over me like that."

She ran her leg over his again. "You mean that?"

"That's it, uncle. I give up. What do you want?"

She sighed and rolled away from him. She placed the back of her hand on her brow. "I can't believe I slept with a man who doesn't know binary. I've made a drastic mistake. I take it all back."

"You are so dramatic." He said as he swung his leg out of the bed and pulled on the sweats she loved seeing on him.

She sat up. "You have no idea."

"What do you want on your pizza?" He picked up his phone.

Yeardley gasped and threw a pillow across the room at him. "You said you couldn't figure it out."

Wolf ducked, and laughed. "It took me a second. Once I sat up I could think it through."

"My preference is everything: no anchovies, no sliced tomato, extra cheese. But I'm pretty good with anything. And I'm hungry, so we will need a large, or I might have to fight you for the last piece."

Wolf put his phone down on the table. "Done, we have twenty minutes, and you are naked."

Twenty five minutes later, she was still naked, and so was Wolf when there was a pounding knock on their door. She dove under the blanket while Wolf pulled on the sweats and then opened the door to accept the pizza delivery.

"You can come out now," Wolf said as he put the pizzas on the table, and began rummaging through the bags for the drinks. They really should just unpack all of this and line it up on the low dresser.

"If you're looking for the Coke, I put it in the mini fridge."

He opened the mini fridge, and just as Yeardley said, there were the cans of Coke all lined up and chilling. He pulled two out and then set them next to the pizza boxes. He found his new t-shirt on the floor and pulled it on.

"Are we dressing for dinner?" Yeardley asked in a very fake, very posh British accent.

"I am"— Wolf rubbed at his chest— "too many hot cheese accidents in my time. Always practice safe eating. You may live as frivolously and dangerously as you wish. But I would hate to see any of that skin of yours marred by malevolent cheese."

"You convinced me, no rogue cheese accidents."

She crawled out of the bed and got dressed in the clothes she had been wearing when she came back after his nap. He was sad to watch her put clothes on, she was glorious naked. All that skin, those legs.

He started coughing as a piece of pizza went down the wrong way.

"Don't choke on the pizza, that will not be a victorious way into Valhalla."

He wiped his mouth with the back of his hand. "It would be after I told them why I choked. Watching a living Valkyrie getting dressed, most victorious."

"Valkyrie, huh? Can I get a winged helmet to go with that?"

"You know, that would be a pretty spectacular cosplay for you to do," he said before taking a drink of his Coke. The cold bubbles felt good on his throat after his failed attempt at choking.

"You said something like that earlier. I'm not the costume maker, that's Maisie."

A brilliant— no, a perfect idea came to Wolf in a flash. He put his pizza down, and waited while Yeardley finished chewing.

"What?" Her eyes darted about as if she was looking out for something suspicious.

"I have a devious, and ingenious plan."

He let her in on his thoughts. And she lit up with happiness.

"You are brilliant," she said.

"I think you're the brilliant one. No, seriously, this afternoon, how did you know about the portals and the code? I mean deleting that line of syntax in the code was what I thought was needed. But you effectively locked the other guy out."

"Okay, so what was all of that? I wasn't delusional." Yeardley stated.

Wolf looked up, he never had to explain this to anyone before. Vik and Scottie had been there, they were part of the discovery process. And as far as he knew, they were the only ones who knew. Well, and now Aaliyah and Yeardley.

"In a nutshell, someone has figured out how to codify magic. They have hacked into a few of the multiplayer online games and inserted code, which works like magic."

"Shit. So some hacker is opening portals between the real world and the fantasy game world?" Yeardley sat up on the bed and crossed her legs, her pizza and drink abandoned.

"That's it precisely. The Codex Wars seems to be the game that gets hit the most. At least that's the one we keep encountering."

"How do you know it's Codex Wars and not Edgeland, or something else?"

"I work on Edgeland. And this guy"— he took one look at Yeardley's face and changed his words— "person has tried. They use a line of dead code, it's like a signature."

"Yeah, I saw that. It really helped me figure out what didn't belong there."

"I used to clean that up all the time. So they stopped hitting Edgeland. Plus I'm working on a subroutine that will automatically scrub that shit out of the program. That's how I know Edgeland is as clean as it can be. But I don't know about other games. Codex Wars has unique goblin hoards. They swarm like spiders, and they are this funky purple-gray color. Really distinct. They have shown up every time one of these portals gets open. Last time they came in with orcs.

"They respond to real time programming. That's how you were able to lock out the portals. Now that dissolving in water, that was nifty."

"I saw some legs in striped tights sticking out from under a table, like in the Wizard of Oz, so I Wicked Witch of the Wested them. At least that's what I hoped I was doing. I'm shocked it worked."

"Fucking brilliant. The programmers for Codex Wars are going to wonder what all that garbage is in their game when they open it back up."

"So you hacked into the servers for Codex Wars like you were walking into a Seven Eleven. How exactly did you do that?"

Wolf looked down at his hands and shrugged. "I may or may not have built in a back door for easy access. Once we learned what was happening, Vik and I spent a good solid two days remoting into their system, and then creating an easy in and out."

"Couldn't your magical hacker be using the same access?"

"I keep it monitored. I don't want to get shut out, and I'm not out to destroy the game. But when you're dressing up for shits and giggles with your friends, you don't expect to have to battle real fucking orcs. Those things are big."

"How often is this happening?"

"A hell of a lot more than it used to. Vik even took on a contract gig with Chin-tech, the people who bought out Codex Wars to see if there was a way he could get someone on the inside to keep an eye on the code."

"Why not install your subroutine on the Codex Wars servers?" she asked.

"Every time I install it on their servers, it gets scrubbed. That's one of the things Vik tried to do, have the subroutine officially installed. But," Wolf lifted one shoulder. "It's been a weird uphill battle."

"Then why not let someone else handle it?"

He locked eyes with hers, and she shuddered.

"Because that's what the fucking good guys do," she answered. "You're somehow tied up in it and it has nothing to do with the coding, right?"

He nodded. "I'm a wolf. Vik is a bear. Scottie is a boar—"

Yeardley let out a cackle. "How fitting, Scottie a boar. He's such a pig, oh my god, that's why he's always saying that." She waved at her face as she continued to laugh. "I'm sorry it's not funny, but it is."

"Oh it's fucking hilarious. He both loves it and hates it. And yes, we are somehow tied into it. I haven't found out if there is a command sequence that triggers the shift or what. But when we are where the magic happens, we shift. Each of us started off our Viking personas in Codex Wars. We each chose our berserker totem animal there. Well, not Scottie. He wanted to be Loki, the red hair and all. I think the boar was Loki's way of messing with him."

"This whole thing is a lot bigger than I thought it was."

When she got quiet, Wolf's stomach knotted. He should have waited to have explained everything before seducing her in the tub. But how was he supposed to resist her while she was naked in his arms and she had put herself there?

"I get this is a lot. And I get if you—"

"Oh no you don't." She stood up on the bed, jumped down in front of him, and then did her best to crawl into his lap, which was a challenge because he was already a big man in a small chair.

"This is not going to scare me off. I've already climbed a booth and set fire to curtains in a crowded hotel just to trip the sprinkler system. At this point, I'm all in. Besides, I know what you can do in bed. Do you think I'm just going to walk away from that?"

She was still laughing when he claimed her lips in a kiss. She continued to laugh even after he ended the kiss.

"Maisie is gonna freak when she finds out Scottie can shape shift."

"That's got to be something he tells her. You can't say anything," Wolf admonished.

"We just have to get Scottie to want, or need to tell her."

"That's the plan."

"You are going to be such a fun boyfriend."

He kissed her again, and this time, she stopped laughing and kissed him back.

BOAR

It's no longer cosplay when the game gets real.

Maisie is feeling glum about her cosplay and her prospects with a certain cosplaying MinVid celebrity when she is kidnapped. Thinking it's a gym-bro gone too far, she realizes the game is very real when he steps through a portal and transports her to another realm.

Scottie isn't about to let a very real orc take off with Maisie. Shifting into his berserker form, he runs after her, only to get trapped.

They have to work together to stay alive, and hope their friends can rescue them. Only Maisie doesn't want to return to the real world if it means losing Scottie's affection.

You don't choose the berserker life.
The berserker life chooses you.

"What the hell is this?" Wolf walked into the kitchen holding up a plastic soda bottle filled halfway with a yellow liquid.

Scottie was in the middle of setting up his light booth so that he could film a few of his latest cosplay creations that looked like food. The kitchen seemed like the logical place to film.

He smirked. "That ain't Mountain Dew."

Wolf rolled and then closed his eyes and held the bottle farther away from his body.

"I swear you get more disgusting every day."

Scottie took the offending bottle. "Well, I am a pig."

"That excuse is getting old. I'm a wolf. You don't see me peeing on every tree, do you? And Vik isn't heading out into the woods for his daily shit. Find a new schtick. Preferably one that isn't nasty."

"What the fuck has crawled up your ass? Yeardley not putting out?"

Wolf stopped moving.

Scottie shrugged off his friend's mood and returned to adjusting the lampstands aimed at the booth.

"Take her name out of your mouth." Wolf's words were low and clipped. The threat was as blatant as if Wolf had slapped him.

Scottie sighed, he had crossed the line again. He was always fucking up friendships, pushing too far. He was pretty sure the only reason Vik and Wolf had stayed by his side was their mutual trauma. Scottie had plenty of friends, after all, he was a MinVid and GameWatch star. All he had to do was say, "Hey let's all go to the movies," and thirty to forty of his "friends" would show up. But those friends never stuck around too long. They usually wanted him to put them in his videos, or do a collaboration that would get them more followers. It sometimes felt as if there was a revolving door on the front of his house for those friends. They came in, took what they wanted, and left.

His longest relationships were with people he had met online, and never face-to-face. Those friends he met up with regularly to quest together. They didn't get to see him being an idiot at the level Wolf and Vik did. If they had, they probably would have walked as well.

Wolf was one of his two best friends. He didn't want to be a fuck up like this. He liked Yeardley, he liked that Wolf had a great girlfriend.

"Sorry, man. I didn't think."

"You never think Scottie, and when you do, it's like you're some twelve-year-old trying to be a badass. When it comes out of your mouth, you're just a fucking ass."

Scottie leaned against the kitchen counter. The entire kitchen was pristine. Not that he cleaned, but he didn't use the kitchen either. And when Wolf did, he cleaned up after himself. He didn't do stupid shit the way Scottie did.

"What were you doing over by my computer?"

"Cleaning up," Wolf said as if it were the most obvious thing in existence.

"Why are you cleaning?" Scottie asked.

"Did you forget? Yeardley is coming over. You're making her armor and helmet. Today's the fitting."

"Shit, is that today? Crap, crap, crap." He began fumbling with his lights and tripped over a cord trying to get out of the photo setup he had created.

"You forgot?"

"I forgot the same way something just slips your mind. I didn't like forget-forget. I ordered all the supplies I didn't already have. I'm ready, not prepared."

"Story of your life."

"Shut up," Scottie said as he skipped down the stairs from the kitchen into the mudroom that led to the garage that was his workshop.

Wolf followed. He was glad that whatever it was he had done to piss Wolf off was already behind them.

Wolf had put up with his shit for years. So had Vik. Others had come and gone, but those two had stuck with him. At first, he knew it was because they had gotten caught in some magical surge while playing a multiplayer role-playing game. They were in the same Viking raiding party, had been for a good six months. When they found out they were local to each other, they agreed to meet up at a live multiplayer role-playing game event. That's when everything had gone sideways.

Scottie began pulling the various supplies from the storage racks, rolls of butcher paper, and craft foam. He may be scattered when it came to being scheduled, but his maker supplies were always well organized.

"I don't get how you can keep your studio pristine and leave piss bottles in the living room," Wolf commented.

"Priorities. Oh shit, the chairs are in the living room. We aren't going to be in there very long, since I'll need her back here for measurements and all that. Might as well go get them and bring them back now."

"You need furniture, man."

"Furniture only encourages the wrong people to stay."

Wolf snickered, "You mean like Jessica? Whatever happened with her anyway? I thought she wanted to collab with you."

"She wanted to collab with my audience, not my dick."

Jessica, beautiful, sexy, cruel. She had given him all the attention he thought he wanted from a woman like her. She was the type to run her hands over his newly acquired physique and purr seductive words about his muscles and ginger beard. And then when her numbers didn't go viral, she blamed him, called him weird, and not in a fun way.

"You know other people like to sit on couches too, not just people trying to leverage your success for their own."

Scottie stopped organizing the tools he was going to need to begin work on Yeardley's Valkyrie and stared at Wolf. "Name one."

"Me, you, Vik. Scottie, this place is huge, and you have been fighting the furniture issue for a while. You know Vik and Aaliyah would come over more if we had more than plastic lawn chairs to sit in."

"You are more than welcome to buy furniture," Scottie offered.

"Yeah, but it's your house, and when you kick me out, you won't have any furniture again. You could hire a decorator."

"That costs money."

"Says the man who paid cash for his house because it made great content. Turn the whole thing into a series. Your viewers will eat it up."

"That's not a bad idea," Scottie said. He leaned against his workbench and began plotting out how he could leverage buying furniture into content. After all, content was king. If he did it right, he could probably even get some sponsorships and walk away without having to pay for everything. Not that cash flow was a problem.

"Scottie, where'd you go, man?"

Scottie blinked and Wolf was next to him with a hand on his shoulder.

"You know what, that's a brilliant idea."

"Glad you liked it." Wolf turned and looked at his phone. "Yeardley wants to know if she needs to stop and get snacks before they head over?"

"They? Who is they? I thought it was just Yeardley."

Wolf shrugged. "Probably her and Maisie."

"Not Maisie," Scottie sighed.

"What's wrong with Maisie?"

"She'll judge me for not having furniture just like Yeardley did the first time she came over, just like Aaliyah did."

"Maisie, judge you? Are we talking about the same woman? She is probably the one person you know who doesn't judge you, no matter how stupid you are. You know she has a huge crush on you?"

Scottie let out a heavy sigh, "Yeah. Okay, maybe not judge me, but she'll be disappointed, and I don't want to disappoint her."

"Dude, you need to get a couch for Maisie."

"You think she'd want to go couch shopping with me?"

"Oh shit, you like her, don't you?"

"So I finally get to see this place," Maisie buzzed with excitement. She couldn't believe it, all because she recognized her MinVid crush out at a random restaurant a few months ago, that she was now headed to his house. Of course, it bothered her that her best friends Aaliyah and Yeardley had been there before she ever had. But they had gone there because their now boyfriends were friends with Scottie.

As much as Maisie would love to be happily coupled up with Scottie— after all, how perfect would that be, three friends and three friends all happily dating— she was well aware that she was firmly in the acquaintance zone. They knew each other. They had even had a conversation or two, never about anything deep or important. But they weren't friends. And there wasn't any potential romantic spark, at least not from Scottie. Maisie was a freaking lit Roman candle when it came to sparking over Scottie.

"Does he really not have any furniture?"

"He's got a big TV and a gaming chair, and I think a bean bag. There's stuff in the kitchen. But the house is really big and very empty." Yeardley watched the road in front of her as she turned into the gated entry to the subdivision. The gates weren't closed or attached to a guardhouse. They were strictly for show.

"Holy crap, these houses are bigger in person," Maisie said as she looked out the car window.

Scottie had filmed his house more than once. She had an idea of what it looked like, and that it was big. The scale and proportion had been lost on her when watching a short minute-long video clip.

"Yeah, and I'm not gonna say, 'oh you get used to it,' because I haven't yet. These houses are fucking huge."

Yeardley pulled into the drive and shut off her car. "Okay, this is it. Now I suggest you get your fangirl squealing out of the way now. This isn't Disneyland."

"No, it's Scottieland," Maisie was awe-struck.

"Oh, my god, you did not. Please don't tell him that. He'll name the fucking house. He'll get large white letters and mount them on the side of the house, and Wolf will never forgive me, and the homeowners association will kick them out..."

Maisie twisted up her expression and looked at Yeardley. "And you say I have an overactive imagination. I will be as cool as I ever can be around him, which we all know doesn't happen."

"Okay, but try not to start crying if he says something stupid." Yeardley handed Maisie a grocery bag from their stop to pick up snack food.

"Don't worry," Maisie said as she followed Yeardley up the walk to the front door. "He will say something stupid, and I will bite the inside of my cheek until I can get to a bathroom. I'm pretty sure a place like this has at least two of them."

"Four. It has four bathrooms," Yeardley said as she rang the doorbell.

Maisie cocked her head to the side as the unexpected tones of a popular monster family television show sounded instead of a doorbell.

They didn't have to wait long before the door was yanked open by a slightly breathless Scottie.

"You're here!"

His flaming red hair was a riot of different directions and his eyes were wide as if they caught him off guard.

"Hi," Maisie managed to squeak out.

When she had first developed her crush on Scottie, he had been a funny and cute face on popular videos on the MinVid social media platform. He was tall and on the skinny side, with sharp cheekbones and a pointed jaw. Now, he was still tall, but the skinny had been replaced with more defined muscles, and the beard he had started growing had fullness and some length to it.

He was no longer some skinny cute guy. He was incredibly hot. Yet, somehow he still acted as if he was just some derpy guy who made costumes and played video games, but who also worked out.

"Are you going to let us in, or are you going to block the door all day?" Yeardley pushed in past him.

Yeardley had been here enough visiting Wolf that she felt comfortable walking in, but Maisie didn't. This wasn't her house, she didn't have the excuse that on the other side of the door there would be a person welcoming her in with embraces and kisses.

Scottie had stepped back so that Yeardley wouldn't run him over, he stood next to the door, still holding it open. She could simply step inside. It was no big deal, they were expected. She felt a blush burn her cheeks. This was stupid, she didn't need to be flustered walking into Scottie's house.

She didn't need to be flustered around Scottie, yet there she was nervous and jittery.

Scottie took a low bow as he made a giant sweep of his arm. "Enter, m'lady."

Maisie sniffed a small laugh and stepped inside. "Thank you."

She was immediately hit by the scale of the house once under the roof. The living room ceiling was several stories high, making the large room seem even larger. She turned as she looked up and around.

"Holy crap. No wonder you got this place," she said.

"Huh?"

"It reminds me of a Hollywood sound studio. So big and open."

Scottie chuckled.

"What? It's got great lighting," Maisie said with a smile. She mostly said everything with a smile when she was around Scottie. It was a habit that she hadn't managed to break herself of, even if he didn't smile back.

"Most people just complain about there not being any furniture," he said with a shrug.

"Yeah, well, you need some in the places you live. But this is where you film and work, right? Too bad the front door cuts through your studio."

"I think you're the first person to get that. I want to put some rigging up there. The ceiling is high enough it would work."

"Maybe you need a little sign or something telling people this is a filming studio. Right next to a jar for your couch fund. Every time someone says you need a couch, they have to give you a buck. Oh..."— she paused and looked into her bag. There was always loose money floating around in the bottom of her purse. Seeing what she wanted, she snagged a dollar bill and handed it out to Scottie. "You need a couch."

Maisie tried hard to ignore the way her pulse quickened when Scottie smiled at her and began laughing. She dropped her gaze and tried looking at him again. It didn't help.

If there was a Venn diagram for Scottie and the women he liked versus the women who liked him, Maisie knew she would be on the furthest edge of the friend-acquaintance overlap, but she couldn't help it.

"Hey, Wolf said you have something to show me?" Yeardley came back in from the depths of the house.

"Yeah, did he tell you what we were doing?" All of his attention snapped to Yeardley, and Maisie was back in the desert regions of the distant borders of the friend zone.

She followed before she was left all alone, and lost without knowing where at least the nearest bathroom was.

CHAPTER

THREE

"What are you doing sitting here all by your lonesome? You okay?"

Maisie looked up to see Hayden standing in front of her. Today Hayden was in another lady dwarf costume with an elaborate wig and facial hair extensions. Her dress was a mashup of cottage core meets eighteenth-century punk. Instead of the deep rich jewel tones of her last costume, this one featured pastels, copious amounts of lace, and wide hip panniers. And it was all covered in flowers and ribbons. Her wig was a thing of beauty that practically defied gravity. Curls mounted up and up into a pastoral diorama scene of unicorns and sheep in a magical meadow. The wig had to have been two feet tall at the very least.

Maisie felt like an abject failure looking at Hayden's beautiful costume. She wanted to be a lady dwarf so badly, but her skin betrayed her. Even though Scottie had been a wonderful help in finding different glues, her skin would not, could not tolerate the adhesive needed to keep the facial hair in place.

The most recent reaction was so bad that she finally went to the Dermatologist, where she was promptly ordered to stop trying to glue things to her face. She tucked her face to the side, hiding the rough patch of skin. She couldn't cover it. She wasn't allowed to put anything more than water and the prescription steroid cream on it.

The makeup she used around the damaged skin camouflaged the discoloration to appear like special effects makeup. It was visible, and up close, it was obviously not makeup. It worked with her orc girl get-up, but she was still self-conscious about it.

Hayden navigated into the space next to Maisie and with much adjusting and harrumphing. She managed to sit on the retaining wall next to Maisie. Her dress folded up between them and she draped an arm over Maisie's shoulder.

"Why so glum chum?"

Maisie's emotions surged and receded. There were too many reasons why she wasn't particularly happy at the moment. "This list is long and sordid. Starting with"—she trailed a finger down the side of her face—"I can't do the cosplay I want because I reacted badly to some adhesive."

"But orc you is adorable."

Maisie groaned. "That's another thing on my list. Some of the other orcs haven't been receptive, giving me a hard time for being cute instead of going for intimidating or overly sexualized." She didn't mention that those particular orcs were the ones hanging off of Scottie's arms when she saw him earlier. He called her cute, and then somehow the women fawning over him managed to turn it into an insult because she wasn't wearing a chainmail bikini.

"And my friends have abandoned me," she sighed dejectedly. She didn't want to be hurt that Yeardley and

Wolf were off looking epic, and Aaliyah was working the artist alley. With Vik hanging around her, there wasn't room for Maisie to just sit and hang out in the booth too.

"I'm your friend, and I'm right here."

Now Maisie felt like an idiot. She had insulted Hayden. "I meant the ones I came with. I'm sorry, that came out all wrong."

"Pfft," Hayden scolded. She wiggled and produced her phone. "I know what you mean. Hey, I don't have your number, and you don't have mine. I'm glad you're back on the con scene, but we need to connect at least on the socials. I don't want to lose track of you again."

Maisie pulled her sack around to her front and pulled out her phone. "You're absolutely right. What's your number?"

After typing in Hayden's number, she sent a text.

"Good, now we are in each other's phones. We can fangirl over stuff together."

Maisie let out a derisive laugh. "It's not like I don't fangirl over everything."

"Hey, it's a good thing. I need someone who appreciates all the fun stuff, and geeks out over wigs with me."

"Speaking of wigs, this is a thing of beauty," Maisie said looking up at Hayden's hair.

"It's heavy as fuck. I'm going to need a serious massage, and a neck brace after this weekend."

"Yeah, but it's worth it. I wish I could..."

"What's stopping you?"

Maisie pointed at her face. "I got a chemical burn on my skin from trying out spirit gum."

"You know there are some sensitive skin adhesives you can try?"

"Yeah," Maisie sighed. "Scottie started me off with the

most gentle one he had. And it wasn't my friend. He even ordered this special stuff for me. My doc said my mistake was not letting my skin heal completely before pissing it off again. Now I can't have any kind of adhesive for a really long time."

"Wait," Hayden put her hands up. "Wait, wait, back that ass up here a minute. Did you say, Scottie? As in tall, ginger, cosplay Scottie? The same one I saw you talking to at FanFun? You're working with Scottie on a cosplay?"

Maisie shook her head. She would love to have been working with Scottie on anything. Being around him made her so happy. Of course, it also made her profoundly sad. Scottie might work with her in private, but he didn't seem to want to talk to her in public.

"It's a long story," Maisie sighed.

"I've got time," Hayden said.

Maisie began the saga. Scottie had been intrigued when Yeardley announced in the middle of his workshop, "You know, Maisie wants to do a dwarf thing. How are you with wigs?"

He had left Yeardley standing with her hands on her hips, a half-formed section of armor plating wrapped around her leg, to go pull out a hairpiece and some spirit gum. Maisie's heart had been in her throat when he grabbed her arm to do a patch test of the glue.

On their return visit for Yeardley's costume, Scottie had presented an elaborately braided beard that almost perfectly matched Maisie's hair color.

"I took it as a personal challenge. I haven't done a hairpiece to this extent before. I hope you don't mind?"

Mind? Maisie had been beside herself. He had done a beautiful job. It was the kind of hairpiece she had been enviously eyeing at the last con.

"I promised I would finish Yeardley's armor first. But if you have time this evening, we could film it, and do a test run."

"But the adhesive?" Maisie lifted her arm and rubbed at the spot that had turned an angry pink when they patch tested the spirit gum.

"I ordered you some sensitive skin adhesive. We can spot test you now, and see if anything happens while I'm working on the armor."

A few moments later, she was not holding still for him very well.

"Stop wiggling."

"It tickles," she giggled as he painted a section of adhesive on her inner elbow.

While Scottie and Yeardley worked on the armor, Maisie and Wolf ordered pizza for later, and generally hung out and made comments.

After a break for dinner, Scottie explained everything as he set up the camera. Maisie couldn't help but stare at him and his mouth as he worked. He was almost a different person, so focused and knowledgeable. He was in his element, and it made him even more attractive if that was even possible.

"All right? Here we go." He stroked her hair back from her face, and his arms surrounded her as he reached for something on the table behind her. He wrapped her hair in a loose ponytail.

"This is cold," he announced as he swiped cold rubbing alcohol down her cheek.

She gasped and flushed when he looked at her and gave her what she could only describe as a wicked smile. What she wouldn't give for him to look at her like that for real.

His touch tickled and excited her even though he was

not inappropriate, not even once. His fingers were gentle. She closed her eyes since it felt weird to have him so close to her face working. She was aware of every breath, and had to not lean into him when he brushed against her reaching for supplies.

She twitched her nose. The adhesive felt weird and pulled at her skin.

"Hold still Maisie, or your beard will be crooked."

"Sorry, it feels weird."

"Yeah, facial hair pieces feel a little odd at first. You'll get used to it."

"It's getting itchy. Is that normal?" She twitched her face around, trying to get the hairpiece to settle down. "It's getting worse."

"I think I should remove it. Your skin is turning red."

He pressed something to her cheek and she shouted out in pain.

"Ow it stings, it stings. Oh, god, it's melting my face," Maisie could hardly breathe around the sudden stinging pain on her cheek. Her eyes started watering. She grabbed onto the nearest person for support, wrapping her hands around Scottie's wrists to both hold on, and to get him to stop whatever it was he was doing to her.

"What's wrong?"

"It feels like acid. Shit get it off, get it off," she cried.

"I need some water." Scottie reached for something. Maisie saw his camera tip over.

"Your camera! I'm sorry I'm messing everything up, but it hurts."

"Fuck the shot, Maisie. We need to get this off your skin immediately." He smeared a glob of cold cream over her skin and the section of beard that was still glued to her cheek.

"You're ruining the hairpiece," Maisie complained. Tears welled from her eyes as the pain on her face stopped with the sudden application of cold cream.

"Woman, your priorities are worse than mine. Come on, I need to get you under running water. That cream is only going to hold you for a minute. Wolf, I need you to find the olive oil and meet us in the bathroom!"

"Olive oil? On it," it sounded like Wolf, but Maisie couldn't tell.

"You're right, this cold cream is already starting to make everything sting more."

Scottie held her hand and dragged her upstairs. They passed through hallways and rooms she knew she wouldn't remember her way back through. Suddenly they were in a bathroom.

"Take your pants off."

"Excuse me, what?"

Scottie ripped his shirt off over his head. Maisie was in pain, and with the tears, she wasn't seeing things clearly, but she could see enough to tell that Scottie's gym time had been paying off in more than bulging biceps. His chest was thick with muscle, and there was a faint ripple of ab definition.

"Pants off, or everything you own will be soaking wet."

Maisie kicked off her jeans, and suddenly she was standing in a freezing shower with Scottie. He leaned into her, or was she leaning into him?

"Relax, I've got you. The water will help keep things cool as I work on removing this. It's not going to feel good."

And it hadn't, it was sharp and pulled. And at times it felt as if he were peeling the very flesh from her bones. She balled her fists and clenched her eyes shut.

"Oil," Wolf announced at some point.

"Grab me some of those swabs, thanks. You're doing great Maise, we'll have you all cleaned up in a minute."

He had called her Maise, and her face hurt entirely too much to appreciate it. She started crying again, letting her tears mix with the spray from the shower and the oil and adhesive remover.

"Oh god, I'm so sorry," Scottie repeated over and over again.

"Didn't you do a patch test?" Yeardley asked.

Was everyone in the bathroom with them?

"Yeah," Maisie held out her arm. "I didn't react."

"Oh, there's nothing on your arm."

"You aren't allergic to latex are you?"

"No," Maisie whimpered.

"You might be now. Reactions like this can trip sensitivities. It's why you should never use cheap black hair dye," Scottie said.

"I don't dye my hair," Maisie said.

"You don't need to. Your hair is a nice color. What I'm saying is that the cheaper dyes can set you up for sensitivities to all kinds of things. So you need to be careful after this. Bandages might fuck with your skin after this. Make sure you only get the sensitive skin kind without any latex."

"How sensitive are you talking? Ow," she clenched her teeth against the tugging.

"Sorry. Be careful around bananas. You might not want to blow up any balloons. Condoms could be a problem."

"Bananas? Condoms? What the fuck?" Scottie wasn't making any sense. She wanted him to be done torturing her. And she sure as hell didn't want him saying things like condom while she leaned against him.

"Latex, it's related to bananas, it's used in bandage

adhesive. If you are allergic to it, your lips could blister just from blowing up a balloon. And I'd hate to think what a condom would do to your va—"

"Scottie!" Wolf cut him off.

"Right, not helpful."

"It's okay. I know what you're saying. If blowing up a balloon can do that kind of damage to your mouth, a condom is going to shred a vagina," Maisie said.

"You didn't," Wolf groaned.

"What?" Yeardley asked. "Vagina isn't a bad word. It's not worse than penis."

"Penis isn't so awkward," Wolf complained.

"I wouldn't know about that," Maisie said. "Have you looked at one? They are kind of weird."

"Penis is a weird word too. Vagina, though," Scottie said.

"You can stop." By the tone in Wolf's voice, he was uncomfortable. Maisie couldn't look at him, but she pictured him shuddering in distaste.

"Does me saying vagina bother you?" Yeardley asked.

Wolf made a cringing sound.

Scottie started chanting, "Penis, vagina, penis, vagina."

"Vah-gin-ah, vah-gin-a," Maisie counter chanted, the silliness a welcome distraction to the pain in her face.

"You deserve each other," Wolf called out. It sounded as if he were leaving the room.

"Ow, fuck. It hurts." She clapped her hand over the area Scottie was peeling away. She opened her eyes and looked up at him. He looked miserable. "Can we take a break?"

"Sure," Scottie said as he leaned against the shower wall and held Maisie to him.

She found it difficult to breathe as she rested against his

chest, his hand on the back of her neck, holding her to him. She couldn't relax and appreciate her position, every nerve was on fire. Between the pain in her face, and her amped-up nerves from being close to Scottie, she couldn't take it.

"Okay, let's do this," she said, pushing against his chest.

Scottie righted himself so they were both standing under the spray. He had one hand braced around Maisie's back.

"I'm sorry this is taking so long. I don't want to tear your skin, and I'm trying to clean it off as I go."

"How much is left?"

"I've got about an inch off, so maybe another inch?"

"You mean I only had about two inches of hair glued to my face?"

"Yep. And your skin is really pissed."

"Just yank it off. Do the bandaid method and let her rip."

"Not going to happen."

"It hurts, Scottie."

"I know, I know. But it will tear your skin. You're already swollen and blistering. I'm going as fast as I can."

Maisie wanted out of the shower. The water felt good on her face, but the rest of her was cold. And she hated that Scottie was seeing her this way. She wanted him to think she was cute, and now, well, he got swollen and blistered skin combined with tears and she was certain her drowned rat impersonation was going strong.

It felt like forever before Scottie declared he was done. "I want to give that a good cleaning with the oil, hold on, almost done."

When he finished he booped her on the tip of her nose. "All done."

Maisie started to put her hand over the affected skin, but the heat from her hand made the pain in her cheek flair back to life. "It still hurts."

"Maybe an ice pack will help? How about some aloe vera?"

"Aloe vera? You mean like burn gel?"

"Exactly."

Maisie stood dripping inside the shower as Scottie left. He returned from another room a moment later with a bottle of green gel.

"I get enough sunburns that I've learned to keep this on hand." The gel made a squelching noise as he filled his palm with it.

Maisie closed her eyes and let him put it on her face. He was excessively gentle with her. It was a complete contrast to the way he bowled through other situations without paying any attention. It was nice. It was going to be torture.

She had been practicing not thinking about Scottie in any way that could be even romantically adjacent. Now she had to twist every thought, steering them back into a platonic framework. She closed her eyes. He's a friend with a capital F. It was an emergency, and he was trying to not make the situation worse. He wasn't holding her to hold her, he was holding her because she was injured.

As she dripped, she was grateful he had at least thought enough about making sure she would have dry pants. But the rest of her was soaked.

"'Can I get a towel?' I asked, standing there dripping in my panties and wet shirt in the middle of his bathroom. He had vanished somewhere. I hadn't realized at that point that I was in the bathroom in his bedroom." Maisie finished her story.

"He left you soaking wet in his bathroom? Oh, Maisie, that's horrible. But kind of funny. I mean being soaking wet with ADHD boy," Hayden chuckled.

"Oh my god, you're right. I don't know why I never thought about that. Scottie totally has ADHD. That explains so much, like how he can focus so intently on video games and is kind of scattered."

"So, what does his bedroom look like?" Hayden asked conspiratorially.

"Like you would expect. It was huge, and he had gaming posters up, and the bed wasn't made. All he has is a mattress on the floor. Oh, and he doesn't have a dresser, he uses laundry baskets. It's like a teenager's room when their parents don't have furniture. And as you pointed out, that's so very ADHD of him."

"So you really like him, don't you?"

"I think everyone except for him has figured it out. And to be honest, that's why I'm sitting here pouting. I mean, Yeardley and Aaliyah are off doing their things with their guys, and I'm happy for them."

"But..."

"But Scottie is out there with some orc babes, mean orc babes. I just hate it that I'm not what he wants."

Hayden wiggled off the wall they were sitting on. She grabbed Maisie's hands and shook them until Maisie looked up at her.

"That's his loss, not yours."

Hayden's skirts started sounding like speakers at a K-pop concert. She wiggled her arm into one of the pannier frames and pulled out her phone.

"I love this skirt, *so* many pockets. I have to go. I'm modeling in Hall C for a wig presentation. You want to come?"

"That sounds cool. I'll be there in a bit. I think I need to hit up a food vendor first."

"Do that, come find me. And if I see Scottie, instead of fangirling over him, I'll kick him in the shins."

Maisie laughed. "You don't have to do that, but I appreciate the sentiment."

"Oh my gawd, you're so hot."

Maisie looked up to find the source of the loud squeals and giggles. A small horde of women clamored to get the attention of a barbarian-sized cosplayer. His orc game was strong. He was built for it, tall with massive shoulders and thighs like boulders. He seemed to be ignoring all the women that vied for his attention.

She shook her head and continued to pack her things up. Hayden was right, just because the friends Maisie thought she was going to be playing with at the con were off doing something else didn't mean she didn't have friends that were interested, and willing for her to participate in their activities with them. She had friends at the con. She was going to go watch Hayden show off that fabulous wig.

And then she would start to design a lady dwarf costume that didn't involve facial hair. Because, dammit, she wanted a wig like that. It was entirely too much fun.

And she knew if she asked Scottie and gave him free rein that would give her an excuse to hang out with him.

Maybe what she needed to do was tell Scottie that she liked him. He seemed to be scattered-brained around a lot of things. And she knew, no, she thought she knew she wasn't his type. But he had been so sweet and so kind when she had had that nasty reaction to the adhesive. Maybe he didn't know he liked her. Maybe he needed to be told she liked him. She would do it. That's what she was going to do.

She scooted off the retaining wall and jumped back onto her feet. She looked up and the large orc cosplay man was coming straight at her. He was impressive and actually kind of good-looking, but he wasn't Scottie. There was no way he would ever be good-looking enough. Scottie was more than looks. Scottie was fun, all personality and goofy. And if anybody ever matched the definition of adorkable, it was him. And Maisie loved adorkable.

This orc guy looked like a typical gym bro who thought that working out was a personality. The way he was coming straight at her felt like he was going to try to sell her a gym membership or his physical training services. Or talk to her about her weight out of some concern for her health, not that it was any of his business.

Scottie never once mentioned anything like that. He never once said, you know, this costume would work better if, or maybe we could shave this and hide your chin or... no, no. Scottie is your friend and he acts like a friend.

But Maisie wanted to be more than friends. She needed to ask someone for a little perspective. Yeardley and Aaliyah kept trying to warn her off him because they knew he didn't see her in that light, and they didn't want her to get hurt. She shouldn't ask them, they were too far involved. And she wasn't going to ask Hayden because Hayden wanted to fangirl over Scottie. Maisie wanted to do more than fangirl.

The smell hit her first, and then the breath was knocked out of her. The next thing she knew she was upside down and being carried like a sack of potatoes over the shoulder of cosplayer orc man.

Something was off, he didn't smell like a sweaty gym boy. He didn't even smell like a cosplayer who forgot how to clean his clothes. He smelled like an entire herd of cattle, like no one ever taught him how to use deodorant. He smelled like he hadn't bathed in months.

Had no one ever taught him to ask permission before picking somebody up?

"Hey." Maisie thumped him hard on the back. "Put me down."

The man grunted.

"I said put me down. I'm not playing this game." She tried to wiggle out of his grip, but he only held on harder. "Do you need me to tell you how big and strong you are? Look, just because I'm dressed like an orc doesn't mean I want to play with you, or am willing to put up with the misogynistic habits built into the character design of an orc."

He grunted again, and then said something completely incomprehensible in some language she did not understand.

"Dude, put me down or I have to start screaming. Security will come, it will cause a scene, and not in a good way. You'll get blasted all over the internet."

She was annoyed and starting to become a bit more than just concerned.

"Hey, why don't you pick me up? I'm right here." One of

the women surrounding him said. "She's not interested. Her loss."

With a lumbering move, he swept his arm and knocked her over.

"Dude, not cool. Put me down."

And then he was running. Maisie tried to catch anybody's attention, waving her arms and kicking her feet. She screamed for help and begged people to call security. People pulled out their phones, not to make calls but to film and take pictures.

She started hurling curses at them, alternating with pleas for assistance. This was not going at all how she thought today was going to go. Never in a million years did she think that there would be somebody strong enough to sling her over their shoulder and walk away with her.

She managed to shove her hands against his back and push up so that she could raise her head for a better view and look around to see if she couldn't see anybody she knew.

She finally caught sight across the concourse, a tall man with a shock of bright red hair.

"Scottie!" she called out his name.

He didn't look up.

She called his name again hoping he would look up, hoping he would see her. This wasn't fun. And she needed his help. Finally, he looked up. She called out his name one more time and they made eye contact.

Scottie felt the rush of magic run over his skin like an electrical charge. He looked up to see if he could tell where it was coming from. What he saw made his stomach clench

IN HORROR. MAISIE WAS ON THE BACK OF AN ORC— NOT AN ORC cosplay but an actual orc— and she did not look happy. When her eyes met his, he knew she was in trouble.

She yelled something, he couldn't hear her but he could see her mouth and it looked like she was calling his name. He hit the ground running. The shift would be on him soon. And he had to get to her before he couldn't say anything to her or he wouldn't be able to let her know of the danger she was in.

He followed the orc through the con. He got more and more pissed off as nobody offered Maisie assistance and she was clearly a damsel in distress. Fuck, he folded in on himself as a spasm took over

He was going to change right there in the middle of everything and everyone was going to see it. This was not cool. This was so not cool. But the orc was headed straight toward a portal. Hanging in the air was a swirling opening of purple flashes and lightning.

Scottie collapsed to the floor as the shift took over. In another instant, he was back on his feet, all four of them and he was running, running as fast as he could towards the portal. If it closed, with Maisie inside, he didn't know what he was going to do, or how they would get her out.

People were standing around taking pictures of the portal. They had to be thinking it was some kind of live special effect and getting in closer to it instead of getting away from it like they should have been. Fortunately, more people seem to be paying attention to the portal than were paying attention to him.

Maisie could no longer see him. He could tell she was looking for him by the way she cast her eyes from side to side. She didn't know he was coming to get her. She looked lost and ready to give up. With effort, Scottie forced his muscles to push harder, and run faster. He wasn't fast enough. The orc walked through the dazzling lights of the portal, and once he was on the other side, it started to collapse.

Scottie couldn't let that happen, with another push of effort at the last minute he jumped, soaring through the portal as it closed behind him. It made an audible pop sound as it collapsed. He landed in the midst of a jungle. He didn't have time to look to see if he knew where exactly he was. He knew the important things. Maisie was in front of him being carried away by an orc and they were in Austratica, the land of Codex Wars. This was not going to be good.

The combination sound of breaking branches and Maisie's continued efforts to free herself gave him a direction to run. He was not going to let that orc get away from him. Not here, even though he didn't know how he would get them back through the unopened portal.

THEY WERE NO LONGER ANYWHERE THAT SHE RECOGNIZED. NOT that she had a clear view of much more than hard-packed dirt and jungle growth. It was hard to hold herself up in a way that let her see what was going on around her. The air in this new place was heavy with heat and humidity. Maisie could feel her makeup melting off of her face.

The orc continued his run. The bouncing and his shoulder in her gut had gone past uncomfortable, and Maisie hurt. Her hands hurt from beating against the wall of muscles in his back. She was beyond terrified, but crying wouldn't do her any good, and who would hear her if she screamed?

A loud feral sound, some monstrous combination of a

squealing pig and a roaring motorcycle engine, deep and throaty, was coming toward her and the orc. Maisie saw the boar as soon as it broke through the foliage. Her view rapidly changed as the orc spun around to face the attacking beast.

She kicked and beat with renewed vigor demanding to be put down. With a jolt, she was dumped on her butt in the dirt.

"So that's how you treat a person?" she snarked at the orc's broad back. She quickly sucked in a breath and scrambled away, pushing with her feet and crawling backward as she realized what was going on.

The orc's muscles bunched and rippled as he flexed, making himself wider. He lowered into a fighting stance and pulled weapons from his belt. He roared.

Equally as loud, the boar screamed in return. It now stood its ground and shook its massive head. Heavy, deadly tusks protruded from its face.

She got to her feet and began running. She didn't know where she was going. She just needed to get away. She didn't get very far before the sounds of the fight piqued her curiosity more than her sense of self-preservation. Creeping back through the branches and leaves, she found a spot at a distance to watch.

At first, she thought the boar was done for. Red ran along its back where the orc had gotten at least one hit in. It didn't look stable, like one more blow and it would be down. The orc swung a large knife but the boar was more agile than she even knew a pig could be. In a quick succession of side-steps, the boar stepped under the orc's arm and got his tusks lodged firmly in the orc's midsection. With a mighty grunt and thrashing of its head, the tusks ripped through the orc. The sound was indescribable, unfortunately, it wasn't one that Maisie would soon forget. The orc screamed as blood and gore spilled from him.

With a gasp, he collapsed on his side and didn't move. The boar stepped back from its kill and made a rumbling grunting roar and then it looked at her. She screamed and turned and ran.

"Maisie! Maisie!"

She stopped and listened. She had heard her name, right?

"Maisie!"

"Scottie, oh god, Scottie? Is that you? I'm over here. Damn it, I don't know where here is."

Suddenly Scottie was there and bundling her into his arms. Or she launched herself at him, she wasn't quite sure the order of things, but it didn't matter. Scottie was there and she was safe.

"We have to get out of here," she said in a rush. "There's a dead orc cosplayer over that way, and a wild boar out there that looks like it's ready to kill again."

"He's not a cosplayer. You know that boars are wild, you don't have to say wild boar. It's implied in the name."

She gripped his arms and stared at him. She fought her thoughts around her panicked breathing. "Now is not the time for mansplaining pigs. The point is we have to be careful, there is a killer swine out there, it already killed a man."

"That wasn't a man."

"What do you mean that wasn't a man? He was big and strong and stinky and didn't listen. Sounds like a man to me."

A pained expression crossed Scottie's face. That's when she noticed his hair was different.

Maisie eased away from Scottie and began pulling at his

clothes. "What happened to your cosplay? You were a barbarian orc man the last time I saw you."

Scottie had been wearing a combination of fur-wrapped boots up to his knees, tattered leather miniskirt-sized loincloth, and assorted belts. The only armor he had worn covered one shoulder and one arm only, leaving his chest and abs exposed. His skin had been covered in green body paint, and his hair had been left a mess.

His hair was now plaited and pulled back. His beard was groomed into a braid with a silver bead. All vestiges of green makeup were gone. He was sun-worn looking with freckles standing out against a burn across his nose. And he was fully covered, no expanse of half nakedness showing off his new gym gains.

He wore a brown tunic with green embroidered edging over a maille shirt. Tied at his waist were a collection of belts and satchels. Over all of that, he wore a long leather vest, and he wore pants with heavy boots.

Scottie looked down and smoothed his hands over his chest.

"Yeah, about that. This is going to sound really weird."

FIVE

Maisie looked terrified. He couldn't help but smile. She was safe and she was unhurt.

"What is going on Scottie?" she asked.

He held her hands and looked into her eyes. Her beautiful big eyes pleaded with him to make sense of everything happening.

Scottie scrunched up his face, how did he do this? How did he say what he needed to say and still have Maisie trust him?

He stared at her, she was still scared, but putting on a brave face. Her brows twisted, and her pointed little chin quivered. She deserved the truth. He started talking, at some point in time during his story he sat and started picking at rocks and sticks in the dirt.

"So what you're telling me is that we are stuck in some video game? And that wasn't a person in cosplay but an actual orc? What kind of drugs are you on? And why did you give them to me?"

"You're not on drugs and I told you it was gonna be weird. Remember the gas leak at FanFun?"

"Yeah, the ballroom got all locked up. That was the day you showed off your new car."

"Well, it wasn't a gas leak. There has been some weird, what can only be described as magic shit going on, bringing creatures from video games into the real world. And it's almost exclusively with Codex Wars that it's happening. And somehow, I'm linked into it." He plucked at his garb. "In Codex Wars my avatar is a Viking Berserker."

Maisie nodded slowly.

"It's all very intertwined. But this…" he tugged at his clothes again. "These are my avatar clothes. And we are inside of Codex Wars."

"Are you saying we are trapped on a mostly undiscovered island with monsters?"

"You're familiar with Codex Wars? You have to be to know that. Most non-players are only aware of the northern continent with the Ice Mountains if that much at all."

"You've been playing Codex Wars almost exclusively on GameWatch for over a year now. I remember when you came questing over to the island."

"You watch me on GameWatch?"

Maisie sighed. "When my brother started watching GameWatch, that's when I discovered you were there too."

A smile danced across his lips. Maisie watched him. He liked that.

"Okay, we are stuck on a semi-tropical continent populated by raiding parties of orcs, humans, and various monsters. Now, what do we do?"

"I need to get oriented as to where we are. We should head toward the gorge and canyonlands. That area is full of caves and we'll be able to find shelter. If we're in the more southern part, there's pretty much no geographical variation. It's just thousands of square miles of jungle and we'll have to basically play keep away and hope we don't stumble into an orc enclave, goblin nests, or any wyverns."

Maisie buried her face in her hands. "Oh, fuck, I forgot that this place had dragons. Are you sure we're not experiencing another gas leak and that we're having a mass hallucination and that we're really just in one of the party rooms at the con?"

"Wouldn't that be nice? We're inside the game, or at least in some dimension that is exactly like the game. I've never traveled into the game before. I've always just tried to keep the creatures from the game from being able to come into our world. Whenever the magic that allows the game to open to our world happens I'm forced to shapeshift into a boar."

Maisie looked up at the sky, her hands still on her face. Disbelief still in her expression. "You were a boar. So if that was you, and you're forced to shift, how can you be human right now?"

"I don't know what's going on." Scottie ran his hand over his hair, smoothing back the braids that had not been there when he had gotten dressed that morning. "The best I can figure is that in gameplay my character can only shift while I'm in the midst of battle."

"You can't control your shift?"

"I've never been able to. The only time I ever shift is when I am fighting with creatures, orcs, or goblins. Things that have come through the game. I shifted at the con when I felt the magic. That was right about when I saw you being carried off."

"Does that mean if we run into orcs that you'll shift again?"

Everything about Maisie broadcast how afraid she was.

But she was doing a great job of pretending to be rational and calm. Scottie didn't like admitting he was way out of his depth here, but he wasn't going to let Maisie know he was also nervous and uncertain about their situation. She was relying on him to save her, and save her he would.

"I honestly don't know how it works, but there's a connection. That's all I can tell you." He sighed and got to his feet.

"Does this mean that Wolf and Vik also shapeshift?"

"Yeah." Scottie nodded and gave her a sheepish grin.

In a burst of energy, Maisie threw her arms out, and then let them fall as if gravity suddenly made them very heavy. "Which means that Aaliyah and Yardley both know, and nobody bothered to tell me."

She rolled her eyes in obvious frustration.

"Nobody was allowed to tell you, Maise. We thought it would be safest that way."

"Safest for me to not know, but it's okay for them to know? That just doesn't seem fair."

"Well, they were there. They witnessed us shifting. It wasn't so much about keeping you in the dark as it was—"

"Sure it was. Nobody seemed to think that I was going to be discreet enough to be able to tell me. God, do my friends even really like me?" She turned in circles, making herself more and more upset.

Scottie grabbed her arms, stopping her movements. "Hey, stop talking like that. We were trying to protect you."

She shrugged out of his grip. "I don't need your protection, Scottie."

"Yeah, you do. I don't think you're gonna survive very long out here on your own."

She crossed her arms and braced herself. "I've been

watching your GameWatch enough that I should be able to figure this out. So we need to head north and find some caves. And we're going to need fresh water. And oh my god, what can we eat here?" She began rummaging through her hip bag. "I have two granola bars. Do you have any food?"

"I don't have anything," Scottie said with a shake of his head.

"Okay. Well, I'm not hungry right now. So we'll save the food for later. And then I guess... shit. You're right. I don't know the game well enough. What kind of food can we eat? Can we hunt? Oh, this is so fucked up." She pressed her palms against her temples as if she could squeeze her head together.

"How do we get back? Have you opened and closed portals before?"

"We've never opened portals before but we've closed them. It usually involves Wolf doing some serious hacking."

"Scottie?" Maisie turned to him in full panic. "How are they going to know we're gone?"

He bundled her back into his arms, finding comfort in her warmth. Finding strength out of nothing because he had to take care of her, he had to. "I don't know Maisie. I don't know."

She didn't know how long Scottie stood there holding her. She probably could have let go, but she liked the way he leaned his face against her hair and made soothing sounds while running his hand over her hair and down her back.

They couldn't stand there like that all day, no matter

how much she wanted the comfort, wanted Scottie paying attention to her. With a steadying breath, she eased away from his grasp. She liked how he didn't simply drop his arms away from her, but slid his hands along her arms. Maybe he needed the comfort and support as much as she had.

"What are we going to do? Should we hang out here to see if the portal opens back up?"

"I don't like being out in the open. I think we should head north, there are cave systems that should offer shelter and defensive protection."

Maisie looked straight up in the sky. What she saw through the leaves was perfectly blue, and clear. There were no clouds. "Does the sun rise in the east and set in the west here?"

"Yeah, as far as world-building goes, the programmers kept it pretty basic. However, there are two moons."

"How do we tell which way is north? There are no shadows under all this foliage."

Scottie glanced up. "I guess we don't until sunset. Or if we find a way to get above the trees."

He squatted down and ran his hand over the dirt creating a smooth surface. He reached next to him and picked up a stick and began drawing. He created a potato blob shape.

"The whole continent is a jungle like this. Except for the desert region and that's in the north."

He drew a line bisecting the potato at an angle.

"How familiar with Codex Wars are you? You watched my GameWatch feeds right?"

Maisie nodded.

"So you know on Austratica the typical middle ages

quest games with the taverns and the wizards don't apply here."

She nodded more.

Scottie pointed with the stick into the upper right quadrant of the potato shape that he had divided out with his line.

"This is the desert."

He ran the stick over his line. "This is what we call the continental divide in the game. And it is Canyon Country. That's where we want to go. We can't accidentally get lost in the desert without first hitting the canyons and the caves."

"Okay, but what if we're like way down here?" Maisie pointed into the farthest opposite corner of the blob of Scottie's rough map.

"Well if we're here, and we head north, we hit the beach. And we follow it around until we get to the canyons."

"How far is that?"

"In real-time? I don't know. In GameWatch. It would take several sessions. I don't know how time works here because you can encounter several days in a gaming session, or you can just have a single afternoon battle in a gaming session. I don't know if we will run into those inconsistencies or not."

Maisie sighed. "How do we find food here?"

"We'll forage and we can hunt. Now, the problem with foraging is can a human eat what an avatar eats? Are the proteins digestible for us? We have to assume wherever we are, it acts like the game. At least until we learn otherwise."

"Shit, I hadn't thought of that. Well, whatever we do, we're going to need to find water and we're going to need to find something that I can wash in. My face is starting to feel itchy under this makeup and my skin is pulling." She gently touched the side of her face. Not quite putting her hand over the scab-bing rash region where she had reacted badly to the adhesive.

Scottie reached out and dragged his knuckle down her skin just in front of the damaged area. "I am so sorry about that. It is taking its time to heal, isn't it?"

"I will get you water and I will get you shelter." Scottie stood. "We should get going."

"But we don't know which way yet."

"No, but we can look for water in the meantime."

The sun set sooner than Maisie had anticipated. They found their direction.

Maisie pulled out one of the granola bars from her pack. Breaking it in half she handed a portion to Scottie.

"I've got another bar for tomorrow, but then we're out of food."

Scottie grunted. He pulled branches together and used the vines that tangled through it all to lash the branches together.

"Let's try to get some rest. Are you a night owl or an early riser?"

"What does that have to do with anything? I tend toward night owl."

"Me too. It's so that someone can keep an eye on things. You look exhausted, why don't you try to sleep."

"You're going to have to rest sometime Scottie."

"I'll wake you up when it's your turn."

"It's not even all that dark yet."

"I know, but as soon as the sun is completely below the horizon line, it's going to get really dark. I don't want to try to set up shelter when I can't tell if the thing I'm grabbing is a vine or a snake. I'd feel better if we had more than a tree trunk at our backs and some leaves over us."

Maisie crawled under the sheltered space Scottie had managed to pull together from nothing. He sat in front of her as she lay down.

"Yeah, but it's a big tree. And you're here." She reached out for his hand. His fingers were rough against her skin. She held on to his hand as she fell asleep.

CHAPTER
SIX

Maisie bumped into Scottie's back when he stopped suddenly. He turned and gestured for her to get down as he lowered himself to a crouching position.

"What?"

He put a finger to his lips, indicating she should be quiet. She nodded, and then let her gaze follow where he pointed down below. At first, she only saw leaves moving, and then she saw the shoulders of an orc. This time she could tell the difference between an orc and a man in cosplay. They were definitely bigger and she knew from experience that they were definitely smellier.

"We'll circle around and see if we can avoid them," Scottie whispered. "But something tells me that's not going to happen."

"Look no matter what happens, you stay safe. In Codex Wars when a character dies, they typically blip out and disappear. We need weapons, if you can get the swords from the fallen orcs before they vanish, that will be helpful.

I don't know if that's going to happen with us really being here, but I just have to assume it's going to."

"What makes you think the orcs are going to disappear?"

Scottie cringed against a shiver. "Call it a gut feeling."

He handed her the short sword he had been carrying.

"What's going on?" Maisie asked.

"I'm getting that feeling that I would get before a portal opens. Assuming I only shift before I fight, that's what's happening."

"Oh crap."

Scottie wrapped an arm around her back and pulled her tight. He gave her a quick kiss and then cringed away folding in on himself as if he was in a great deal of pain.

Maisie stared, in shock that Scottie's lips had pressed to hers. The shock took on a new form as Scottie shifted in front of her.

The transition was fast and smooth. And one second, he was a human then in several quick contortions he was a boar. Large with bristled fur, and tusks protruding from his snout. The beast grunted, and then turned to face the area of jungle to their side. The leaves just beyond where they crouched began to rustle and suddenly one of the orcs that they had observed stood before them.

Maisie retreated, carefully paying attention to make sure she didn't run into the rest of the orc party. She already witnessed how Scottie fought. She knew he was very capable. But she also knew that the fight would be very gory and bloody, and it wasn't something that she needed to see again. Battles in GameWatch streaming were much less graphic in detail. But that was the difference between being in a game and being in reality.

Listening to the fight was bad enough. She wasn't going

to watch it. She clamped her eyes shut and sent all of her energy and will to support Scottie in his fight. When it sounded like the orc had fallen, she cracked one eye open and saw Scottie, still in boar form, with a bloody snout. With a large gulp swallowing down her bile, she ran over to the orc and took the weapons just as Scottie had instructed.

She watched as the form of the orc began to shimmer and sparks flew in the air. Suddenly, there was no more orc.

Scottie grunted and dove into the underbrush. There were two more orcs out there. Maisie followed and spotted another fallen orc. Trying to avert her eyes from the gore, with a side step, Maisie gathered the weapons.

"It's a video game character," she reminded herself repeatedly as she pulled weapons from the belt of the dead orc.

It moved. She gasped and jumped back before she realized it moved because she was jostling it around. All at once, the body of the fallen orc began to shimmer and dissipate into what looked like dust and sparkles. They died gruesomely but they disappeared with party glitter.

There was a muffled *eep* behind her and she spun around. She came face to face with a very nervous man who was hiding behind a laptop. A moment later Maisie realized he wasn't simply holding a laptop in front of him, but he was bound to it with rough ropes. She pulled the ropes around his mouth down so that he could talk.

"What are you?" he asked.

"Who are you?" she asked.

"You don't look like an NPC."

With an exasperated sigh, Maisie put her hands on her hips and tilted her head to the side. "I am not a non-playing character."

"Okay, I admit you don't look like an NPC. I don't recognize that avatar. Who are you supposed to be?"

"I'm supposed to be Maisie. You haven't told me who you are yet."

"My name's Harold. Did you kill all of these orcs?"

"Do I look like a boar?" she asked as she examined the ropes to see if there was a way to untie the man, and keep the ropes intact.

"Well, it's not polite—"

Maisie yanked the ropes back over his jaw, shutting him up.

Scottie entered the clearing, patting himself down.

"Did you get any weapons? It looks like they already shimmered away."

Maisie stood and pointed at Harold. "Look what else I got."

"Who the fuck is that?"

"Harold."

"Why is he all trussed up still? Wait, how can he... you shoved the gag back in his mouth to shut him up, didn't you? That bad huh?"

Scottie hunkered down in front of the bound man and stared at him.

"Don't piss her off, I'll let her gag you again. Don't piss me off, or I'll abandon you without a thought. Understood?"

Harold nodded.

Scottie lowered the gag.

"Who are you? How many of you are there? Did you come to rescue me?"

"Slow down, man, I can only answer questions if you give me a chance to talk. It's just the two of us. We did not come to rescue you, but the opportunity has presented itself. I have to ask you a very important question, listen carefully. Where are you located, and I don't mean your avatar, I mean the player."

"I'm the player, and I'm right here. Are you not player avatars either?"

"Fuck." Scottie surged to his feet and crossed the small clearing where moments earlier he had battled orcs.

Maisie followed. "What are you thinking? He called me an NPC at first."

Scottie twisted and looked at Harold, who they left bound on the far edge of the clearing. "No wonder you gagged him. I think he's real, stuck in the game realm like we are."

He spun and stalked across the clearing. He pulled a long knife from his belt.

Harold gasped and wiggled as if he were trying to escape.

"Hold still unless you want to get cut. Harold," Scottie said before replacing the knife in his belt. "How did you get here, and can you get us out of here?"

"How... how did you get here?"

"I asked first," Scottie said. He shook his head. "Fine, we came through a magic portal. Some idiot managed to put into the programming."

"If somebody could program a portal, I wouldn't exactly call them an idiot."

"I would because I have to fight the things that come through the portal. Now, how did you get here?"

"What do you mean you have to fight?"

Scottie sat back on his haunches. He made a sweeping gesture with his arm, like he was about to tell a story. "Portals open up. And orcs and goblins and war come through. And they're looking for a fight. Somehow my friends and I are connected to all of this. And we fight them because they hurt people."

"What do you mean they hurt people?"

"What do you think happens when a large raiding party comes into a crowd of hapless cosplayers or a bunch of LARPers beating on each other with fake weapons? But those orcs don't have fake weapons. They have very real weapons. They start smashing, and playing golf with battle axes because they don't realize they are fighting foam swords. It's not pretty. There's a lot of blood involved."

"That's not the work of an idiot. That's the work of a damned good programmer." Harold started laughing. "I've made a VR so good it's real."

"This isn't virtual reality. This is real reality," Maisie said.

"And you fucking programmed it." Scottie shook his head. "You're fucking Harold Whittaker"

"Yes, I am." Harold wiggled in place.

"That explains a lot. I should have left the gag on him."

"What do you mean, who's Harold Whittaker?" Maisie asked.

"I designed this game. And this is a virtual reality model of the game. Unfortunately, my laptop died and I seem to be stuck. So I can't program myself back out. I can't program the VR to end."

Maisie stared at Scottie and then looked at Harold.

"Are you guys just gonna stand there and stare at me, or are you gonna untie me?"

"Oh right." Maisie took a step forward, but Scottie clapped a hand on her shoulder.

She looked back at him. "What? We should untie him. We can't leave them like this."

"Are we so sure?" Scottie's expression made Maisie think he smelled something bad.

She held out her hand, palm up, and blinked at Scottie a few times.

Reluctantly he unsheathed the knife and carefully placed the handle in her hand. She began cutting away at the ropes that bound Harold.

"How did you guys get in here?"

"In here?" Scottie scoffed.

"We traveled through a portal," Maisie explained

"This game doesn't have portals, you must be confused. If there were portals I would know about them and we could use them." Harold sounded excited for a moment.

"Nope, the portal collapsed. We have no way of opening it."

"Then why did you bother stepping through? That's rather irresponsible don't you think?"

"We didn't exactly have a choice. Not like you, who created this whole mess."

"It's not a mess, it's a VR simulation, and I simply need the escape button."

"He doesn't get it does he?"

"You mean that this is reality and not virtual in any form?"

Scottie crossed his arms and glared at Harold.

"Why are you talking like I'm not even standing here?"

"Because you aren't listening like we aren't telling you what's going on."

Harold's pinched face got even more pinched. "Fine. I'm listening."

"One of your stupid orcs walked out of a portal in the middle of Warpcon, picked me up against my will, and carried me back here."

"Why on earth would he do that?"

Scottie made wild gestures at Maisie. "Look at her. She's dressed up like a cute orc. He probably was bringing her back here to…"

Maisie whimpered.

"Hey." Scottie wrapped an arm around her shoulders and pulled her in close. "I'm sorry, I didn't think before I ran my mouth off. That didn't happen, did it?"

She shook her head as she pushed out of his embrace. She knew what he had meant, she just didn't want to think about it. Ever.

"That explains how she got here. But what about you?"

"I'm here to rescue her. And I guess I'm here to rescue you too," Scottie shrugged.

"If you don't know where there's a portal to let us out, how are you going to rescue us?"

Scottie looked from Harold to Maisie. "Not sure yet, but I'm gonna do my best. How long have you been stuck here? We've been here overnight."

"I've been here since yesterday when my computer battery died."

"Why did you let that happen?"

"I didn't exactly let it happen! I was picked up by a raiding party and they wouldn't listen to me that they had to let me go and I couldn't keep playing." Harold shook his head and muttered.

"Where were they taking you?"

Harold shook his head. "I don't know."

"Did it ever occur to you that you were maybe picked up by actual orcs and not a bunch of players putting together a raid?"

Harold opened his mouth to say something but hesitated.

"Actually, I didn't think about that at all. Ever. That wasn't even an idea until you mentioned it. So what are the plans now if we're stuck here?"

"We're heading north," Scottie said.

"How do you know which way is north?"

Maisie stared at him in disbelief and shook her head. "You set up this game with the same cardinal directions as our real world, so north is north." She pointed off to her right somewhere.

"And we're gonna keep going in that direction."

"But without a compass..."

"But without a compass, you pay attention. There are some basic rules of north south east west. You know, like how the sunrise is always in the east and the sunset is always in the west."

"Well, we can't stand around here and wait for another group of orcs to come pick us up. Let's go." Scottie hitched a thumb over his shoulder.

Maisie got to her feet and brushed dirt from her knees before picking up the newly acquired weapons and following Scottie.

"Where are we going?" Harold asked as he clamored after them.

"Not here."

"There are some cave systems in the north by the gorge and we'll be able to find shelter and have natural protection," Maisie explained.

"Why?"

"Because"— Scottie spun to face Harold— "you designed a continent with no towns and no villages. And no one we can rely on but ourselves."

"You seem to know this place pretty well."

"Yeah," was all Scottie said as he continued barreling forth, taking his anger out on the foliage in his way.

"He's been playing your game for a long time. He's also been fighting orcs in the real world. He knows what he's doing. Not that I want to be stuck here, but I'm glad I'm stuck here with him. I don't trust anybody more."

"Now that you've got me, why are you going to listen to him?"

"Are you serious? You don't even know which way is north. Scottie knows more about this place than either of us."

"I designed it," Harold complained.

"If you're the one who designed the game you should know how to get around, but you don't. You can't tell the difference between reality and virtual reality. I bet you can't even tell us where on this continent we are, can you?"

Scottie loomed over the smaller man who retreated behind his laptop.

"We go north, where we are more likely to find some offshoots of the Great River so we can get some freshwater."

He turned from Harold to Maisie, and picked up a sword out of her arms and tucked it into his belt. He held out a second blade to Harold, but he shook his head.

"I've got these," she said.

"I want you to have your hands free, and they are heavy." He hefted a sword that looked like an I-beam and planted it into the ground. "That one can stay here, it's too big even for me."

"If we want to get to the Great River we should veer slightly west," Maisie said.

"Oh yeah? I thought you didn't play?" Scottie glanced at her.

Suddenly she felt a blush burn her cheeks. She rested a hand against her chemical burn.

Scottie gently eased her hand away and narrowed his focus to her skin. "The humidity is keeping it from drying out."

"I have the steroid cream in my bag. I think you're right, I haven't had to use it as much since we got here."

"So how do you know so much about the location of the Great River?"

"I told you, I watch you play. And because I'm not a player, I tend to pay attention to different things." She wasn't going to tell him she mostly focused on his face and the way he smiled when he was having fun.

Scottie examined a smaller blade and looked at her bag. "I think we can modify your bag so you can carry this one. It's a good size for you."

He handed her the sword. It was heavier than expected. Trying to hold it with one hand by the handle was completely different than cradling several blades across both arms.

"That will be a good weapon for you. But use both hands." Scottie turned his attention to the programmer. "Harold, can you pick up that other sword?"

"I can't carry that I still have to carry my laptop."

"Why did you even bring your laptop here?"

"So that I could tweak the code as needed. But instead, I got captured."

"It's dead now. And we can't plug it in anywhere. Why don't you just leave it and help us carry these weapons?"

"I can't leave my laptop. I'm going to need it."

"But you're going to need some kind of protection," Maisie said.

"Do you know how to use that?" Harold tipped his head toward the sword she held.

"Not exactly." She made awkward chopping motions. "I've seen enough movies that I should be able to fake it."

"We can practice as we go. It will be good for you to learn."

"I can practice while I'm walking."

"I don't want you to get too worn out. We have a long trek ahead of us. But you can practice after setting up camp. Okay?" Scottie took the blade from her and helped her strap it to her waist.

There wasn't exactly a path that they were following. Scottie trailblazed through the jungle. After what seemed like hours, he found a clearing near a thicket of trees that formed a natural shelter. He stomped around, kicking rocks.

"This will be good. We can camp here for the night. Harold, you can take the first watch. I'll take the second, Maisie—"

"I know when you wake me up. It's my turn."

"What do you mean it's my turn to watch?" Harold whined.

Scottie was already busy pulling down vines and tying branches together to reinforce the walls of the natural enclave they found.

"Well, since there aren't any places with much protection, we have to keep our eye out for creatures, especially orcs."

CHAPTER
SEVEN

O ver the next several days, they fell into some form of routine. They would hike, they would set up camp, and if they were lucky, they would have food for a meal. In the evenings Maisie would practice with her sword. It was getting easier. She still felt weak as a newborn kitten, but she was getting stronger. She was able to hike for greater distances and hold the sword higher and practice for longer.

"I don't know why you're doing that," Harold complained. Harold complained a lot about everything and anything. And he seemed to complain the most about anything that Maisie did.

"You look ridiculous."

"She looks fine. She's got good form."

She bit her lip against the complement from Scottie.

"It's not like it's gonna do her any good. She's not ready for any kind of battle."

"I don't see you practicing. Are you ready?"

"I don't need to practice, I already know how to fight. I don't need to train. It's a video game."

"Fighting in a video game is not the same," Scottie said

"Oh, yeah? What kind of practice have you done? I don't see you training with a sword."

Scottie crossed his arms. "I don't fight with swords, but she needs to learn, and I think you do too. If something happens to me, you'll need protection against the orcs. We've already had a run in with more than one group of them."

"Oh big tough guy, you fight with your fists?" Harold mocked Scottie.

Maisie was ready to turn the short sword in her hands against Harold and the laptop he was constantly clutching.

"I do battle with nature's weapons."

"What the hell is that supposed to mean?"

"He doesn't know? It's his game and he doesn't know?" Maisie looked at Scottie.

For someone who was smart enough to create and program video games, Harold was incredibly dumb.

"He clearly doesn't know a lot of stuff."

"You're doing that again. You're talking about me as if I'm not sitting right here."

Maisie gestured toward Scottie. "What is his avatar?"

Harold shook his head. She didn't know if he didn't have an answer or if he was going to be stubborn and act superior because he had created this reality somehow.

"What do you mean? Is he not an avatar right now?"

"No, we've gone over this. We are not avatars. But he's actually wearing his avatar clothing. And he is dressed like what?"

"He's a Viking raider. I still haven't figured out what you think you are."

Ignoring his commentary on her clothing, Maisie continued. "Congratulations." She applauded his effort.

"He's a little bit more than that. He's a Berserker. You've seen him fight."

"No, I haven't."

"When we saved you from the orcs who had you tied up."

"No, that orc encountered some kind of wild creature."

"Exactly. I'm a creature. Most people just call me a pig." He gave Maisie a wink.

"When he fights, he shapeshifts into a boar." She clapped her hands over her mouth. "Oh shit."

"It's okay. He should have figured it out by now."

"You're telling me that you're some kind of magic shapeshifter? And in the same breath you're telling me all of this is real?" Harold rolled his eyes.

"I can't explain it. You're the one who designed it and you're the one whose virtual reality code made all of this into reality."

"What do you shift into?" Harold asked Maisie.

"I don't shift. I told you. I don't play this game, therefore, I don't have an avatar in this world. So this is me. Frankly, I want to know how to protect myself. In case..." she paused. "In case I get caught without him."

She continued moving through her forms, which to her resembled swinging a baseball bat as if she was playing the game, right-handed and left-handed. Scottie added a new swing that made her think of playing golf.

As she swung through her forms she repeated 'swing batter batter swing,' in her head. Or if she was doing the low upward swing she would think, 'four.' She hadn't come up a battle cry for swinging the sword straight down, or for stabbing. Saying stabby stabby just didn't seem very badass of her. However, it did help her practice. Swing batter batter swing, swing batter batter swing, four, stabby

stabby, four, stabby stabby. She chuckled and continued practicing.

As she continued through her forms, Scottie drew pictures in the dirt.

"We should be coming up on a river soon. At this point I no longer know if it's the Great River or not. But the creek we've been traveling parallel to is getting bigger and deeper. I expect it will branch into another river soon."

"What do you mean the creek is getting bigger?" Maisie stopped her practice and leaned on the sword with its point in the dirt.

"It's deeper. I've been able to catch more fish. You haven't noticed that?"

"I didn't really think about it. Is it deep enough that I could take a bath?"

Scottie crinkled up his face and made a hissing sound as he sucked air in between his teeth. "I don't want you going off on your own."

"Scottie, I still have makeup on my skin." She held up her hands, there were remnants of green smeared on her arm. "I still have cosplay stuck to me. I would really love an opportunity to get it off."

"Oh right. Of course, of course you need to get that off your skin. I didn't think about that." He let out a low groan.

"I'm still worried about leaving you alone. I'll come with you."

"No, you won't," Maisie said.

"I am. I promise I won't look. I will just need to be nearby to make sure you're safe."

"What about me? You're going to leave me all alone?" Harold asked.

"You'll be fine. You know how to fight," Scottie smirked at the other man.

"Well, here it is." Scottie announced as he swept his arms wide. "It probably only goes up to your knees."

"That's better than nothing," Maisie said as she immediately sat and began pulling off her combat boots. She was glad that she had picked them for her cosplay.

"Are you just gonna stand there while I do this?"

"What else am I supposed to do?"

"Turn around, close your eyes."

"How am I supposed to keep watch if my eyes are closed?"

"Watch the jungle don't watch me," Maisie directed.

"But you're vastly more interesting," Scottie said with a smirk as he turned around.

She watched his back for a minute making sure that he wasn't going to peek.

"Are your eyes closed?"

"My eyes are not closed but I'm not going to turn around."

She waved her hands wildly behind him.

"You can't see me?"

"No I can't see you doing whatever it is you're doing to test me."

"Then how did you know I was doing something behind you?"

"Really, Maise? I have you somewhat figured out by now. I do know you."

You don't know me as well as you think you do. She shrugged out of her tunic. She pushed down the knee length cut off pants that looked and fit more like ratty biker shorts and served a similar purpose of not exposing her ass and to prevent massive chub rub. She unhooked her bra and set it aside with her other clothes. She thought about taking her panties off for a minute. What she wouldn't give to be able to put on a pair of fresh underwear.

She contemplated the benefits of wearing the underwear out into the creek and scrubbing them like some old washer woman by beating them against the rocks. Sure, her pants wouldn't be as comfortable without the panties, but that would give her a chance to let them dry overnight. In the morning she could pretend she was putting on fresh undies.

She stepped into the water and let out a shiver. "It's colder than I expected it to be."

"Are you okay?"

"Don't turn around," she chided. Even though she didn't look at Scottie, she imagined that he would have turned around. She clamped one arm over her breasts and used the other one to help steady herself as she stepped deeper into the water.

"You're right, this only goes up to my knees," she said when she was in the middle of the stream. She dipped down until she was almost sitting in the water splashing the water up and over her arms and under her breasts and into her armpits. She wiped off days of smelly panic sweat and rubbed her arms to get rid of the remaining vestiges of makeup.

She wiggled out of her underwear and began hitting them against rocks and scrubbing them together. She glanced over her shoulder to make sure Scottie wasn't looking. She surreptitiously sniffed her underwear, making sure that it smelled better than before.

She laid her head back in the water and closed her eyes as the water surrounded her head. She didn't want to think about how gross and oily and sweaty her hair was. She scrubbed at her scalp with her fingers and wished she had some form of shampoo or soap. What she wouldn't give for a bubble bath.

She did her best to clean her face. The cool water felt good on the angry skin of her chemical burn. Fortunately, she had carried her steroid cream with her to the con to put on through the day.

"Are you almost done?" Scottie called. "Can I turn around now?"

"I'm naked."

"So I can turn around?"

"Scottie!"

They were in a perilous situation and yet the man proved to be an incessant flirt. She was grateful for it, he was doing his best to keep her motivated and her spirits up.

"Fine, I won't turn around."

Maisie's hand bumped into something and she snatched it back with a startled gasp.

"Are you okay? I heard you gasp."

"I just bumped into a rock," she said as she got her feet back under her.

As she made her way toward the bank, something slithered along the side of her leg. She didn't gasp, this time she screamed and jumped.

Scottie turned.

She froze as he looked at her.

"Oh my god, turn around," she screamed.

"Why are you screaming?" Scottie asked as he obliged and spun putting his back to her.

"There's something in the water."

"Of course, there is. It's full of fish."

"I'm not fish food."

She ran up to the bank and got behind him putting her

hands on his waist so she knew that he could not turn to look at her. "Don't look Oh, my god, close your eyes."

He turned, and she stayed behind him.

"Fine." Scottie's tone was laced with exasperation.

"I need you to turn around and put your hands over your eyes. I don't trust you."

"Seriously Maisie, what are you so afraid of?"

"I don't want you to see me naked." She didn't want him to be repulsed.

"Too late. Is that your underwear?"

"Yes, the fish can have them."

Scottie sighed. "I'll go in and get them for you."

"No, no you don't have to. I don't need them anymore."

"Maisie, you're being ridiculous. You will be miserable without your underwear."

"Then close your eyes."

"I'm not going to wade into a creek with my eyes closed."

"But I don't want you to see my underwear."

Scottie made a series of frustrated sounds as he stepped into the water. He scooped her underwear from the water. He didn't understand what the big deal was, they were cotton, they were pink. They were hers.

CHAPTER

EIGHT

S cottie couldn't help the grin on his face. He smiled a lot around Maisie. She made him happy. When he returned to shore and held the wet underwear out, she snatched it without any thanks. Her face was pinched as if she were angry.

They didn't speak the entire way back to camp.

When she stepped into the clearing Herald announced, "Hey, your hair's wet though. You actually did take a bath."

"Thank you, Captain Obvious," she bit out and then sat next to the pile of branches that were not on fire.

"You didn't start a fire," Scottie said. He kept casting furtive glances at Maisie. She was really pissed at him, and he didn't understand.

"Well, no, that's not my job," Harold quipped.

"It's anybody's job. You still could have done it," Scottie grumbled. He was sick of Harold's attitude. They should have left him tied up with the orcs. But he had the code for the portals in that stupid dead laptop he carried around.

Maisie made an aggravated sound and crossed her

arms. She stared at what should have been their campfire as if she could light it by sheer will of indignation alone.

She kept her distance from Scottie for the next few days, much to his disappointment. He couldn't get the vision out of his head of her jumping out of the water and freezing in place as she stared at him. She looked like Venus emerging from her bath. Yet she had been terrified, and then she had been so angry. Did she not realize how incredibly beautiful she was?

She was all softness and ample curves. And so beautiful. He could hardly think straight. Well, his dick was thinking hard and straight enough for the two of them.

As he had expected, the farther north they hiked, the wider and deeper the stream they were paralleling grew. Soon he could hear the rushing sound of the river.

Harold complained that Scottie was doing everything wrong on their push north. But when pressed to step up into the lead position, he always declined.

Maisie wasn't talking to him. But he could tell she was physically hurting. It was a lot of walking, and they didn't have consistent access to food. But they couldn't slow down, they had to get to shelter.

He continued at a slower, steady pace. It was still too much. Maisie fell farther behind.

"Do you even know where you are going?" Harold asked.

Scottie rounded on the other man. "Do you? You fucking designed the game, and created this death trap of a continent."

Harold literally shook in his boots.

Maisie gave a tired shake of her head. "I am so tired of the two of you constantly bickering. I'm tired from lack of sleep and not having eaten since last night. Scottie may be a little scatter brained, but there is one thing I trust him on, and that is navigating Austratica. Scottie is an expert, not of just the game, but of the location we are trapped in. If anyone knows where we are it's going to be Scottie," she said.

Both men stopped and looked at her.

She averted her eyes and ducked her head, as if she was embarrassed for having spoken up.

Scottie brushed past Harold, and stopped by her side. He reached out to her, but then dropped his hand uncertain if she would let him touch her.

"You're tired," he said.

"Yeah," Maisie managed between labored breaths.

"I'm going too fast for you. You should have said something."

"I can keep up."

"It's not about keeping up, Maise. It's about being able to keep going." He lifted his head and looked around. He paused and tilted his head. Closing his eyes, he continued to move until he stopped. The river was close, and hopefully, that meant so was the gorge, and then Canyon Lands. A slight smile crossed his face and he nodded. "I'd say we're about a mile from the gorge."

"We're nowhere near the gorge," Harold snapped.

"If I'm wrong I catch and gut the fish for dinner. If you're wrong you gut the fish," Scottie smirked.

"Why not make me catch them too?" sneered Harold.

"Because I would like to eat tonight." He turned his attention back to Maisie. "Do you think you can make it? There will be some rocks where you can sit and rest."

Maisie nodded. "Yeah, I can keep going."

Scottie pointed in the direction they had been headed. "That way. Head out."

Maisie waited for Scottie to pass Harold and begin the march again. Breath caught in her throat when he picked up her hand and walked with her, at her pace. She looked down at their intertwined hands and felt like crying.

She never admitted to anyone that she subscribed to GameWatch just for him. To give him more views and more thumbs-ups. And to give her more time watching his face. If anyone ever asked, and the stories she told to anyone who knew, hell the story she told Scottie was that her brother had gotten her into it.

Her little MinVid crush had been so much more than she let on. Only now that they were trapped in Austratica with Harold, she wished she had paid more attention to the game as Scottie played. Of course, he played different games including Edgeland. At some point, he seemed to only be playing Codex Wars, and she didn't think anything of it.

Her brother hyper-fixated on single games at a time. At the time it just seemed like another manifestation-slash-confirmation that Scottie was Mr. ADHD. Only now she knew better. Yes, Scottie had all the earmarks of having the attention span of a kid who needed Ritalin to get through school, but it also just drove home how smart he was. He had been studying his enemy, becoming familiar with their abilities, tactics, resources, and tools. Because all the orcs and goblins he said he fought came from Codex Wars.

It didn't take long before they were next to a raging river.

"Let's find a good site for setting up camp. I think we can stay here for a couple of days, and rest."

"Why here? What makes this place any better than any other for staying?" Harold snapped.

Maisie was really tired of Harold being so aggressive when he didn't understand something. "Have you ever tried just asking nicely when you don't understand something? Or is everything a challenge to you?"

Scottie didn't say anything, he simply pointed to the river. "That's why. It's a source of fish, water, protection. Let's see if we can find an area that's relatively clear."

It didn't take long to find a sparse outcrop of rock.

"Why don't you rest for a while. Those boulders back that way about twenty yards should give you some privacy while I'll still be in ear shot."

"Why does she get to rest?"

"Shut up, Harry."

"I told you not to call me that. My name is Harold."

Maisie closed her eyes for a moment before limping back to the boulders they had passed only minutes earlier.

She sat on the rock with a big sigh. In front of her, the river rushed and flowed over broken rock, creating dangerous rapids. She hated camping. And this was so much worse, everything hurt, and there was no bug spray or s'mores over a campfire.

She had embarrassed herself in front of Scottie. How could she even talk to him again when he had seen her naked? He was being so nice to her. It had to be out of pity. She just knew he was comparing her to those super fit cosplay girls who wore bikinis and had zero body fat.

She hated being trapped here. But she still couldn't think of anybody else she would rather have been trapped with. He knew the land from gaming for hundreds of hours. He clearly knew how to camp, and fish. And he knew that she couldn't take another day of walking.

"Are you still mad at me?" Scottie's deep voice asked from behind her.

She nodded and then she shook her head. "Not mad, Scottie just mortified. That was embarrassing the other day."

"You have nothing to be embarrassed about." He stood next to her and looked out over the rushing water.

"You're sweet to say that but I know better. Can we just forget it happened?"

He sat on the rock next to her and picked up her hand.

"I'd rather not but if you say so, I will forget, and I will forget completely that you are wearing pink cotton panties."

"Oh my god." She shoved on his shoulder.

He laughed.

And something in her melted, as if she could fall in love with him any more than she was. She laughed and leaned against his arm.

"How much longer before we can get to those caves? And then how do we let anybody know we're here?"

"I've been thinking about that. I hate to admit it, but I think the best solution is one Harold came up with. Once we get to the caves, maybe we do need to push through to the coast. If we can find a raiding party of players, maybe we can get them to make contact outside of the game with our friends."

"But if Harold is stuck inside with us and the magic coding is in that laptop, what good is that going to do us?"

"Wolf is pretty fucking smart. From what I saw Yeardley do with code at FanFun, I trust them to do their best."

"So what did happen at FanFun? That wasn't a gas leak was it?"

He shook his head. "Definitely not a gas leek. Harry

over there must have created a personal VR entrance for himself. It opened up two massive portals in the middle of a goblin dwarf battle. I was talking to someone on the concourse about maybe doing a MinVid collab when I felt the surge hit. It's like a magical ripple over my skin." He ran his hand down his arm, waving his fingers up and down, creating a visual of magic ripples to go with his description.

"I got into the vendor room as people were running out. That's when the magic overtook me and next thing I knew there were goblins and dwarves and battle goats. It was a pretty epic battle. Yeardley did a piece of code that made all of the video game characters dissolve when they got wet. And then she shimmied up a set of dividing curtains and held a lighter under the sprinkler system. That's how everybody got all wet."

Maisie laughed as she pictured her friend being a total badass and saving the con. "And the gas leak was just the excuse for explaining a mass hallucination?"

"I'm sure some people are gonna say it was a presentation during the costume contest that went wildly wrong. Others are going to say it had to have been a mass hallucination triggered by the gas leak."

"So this isn't a mass hallucination we're sharing here and now?"

"Unfortunately, I'm gonna have to go with no. Not that I wouldn't have you in my hallucination. But I wouldn't put you through this if I had a choice."

She stared up at him. His forehead and nose were sunburned. His braided hair was unruly. There was dirt smudged across his cheek. She reached up and ran her fingers through his beard. Trying to smooth it down.

"Yeah, everything's a mess right now." Scottie followed

her hand and pulled his beard into some shape. "I must look like some kind of crazy giant leprechaun," he laughed.

She looped her arm through his and leaned her head against the shoulder. "Well, if you are, that would explain why you're so lucky."

Be my lucky charm. She sighed.

"You think we should get back to see how Harold is doing? I can't believe you're making him gut fish. I got the impression he doesn't know how to do anything without game controllers in his hand."

Scottie laughed and the movement bounced her head against his shoulder. This was nice, why couldn't their exile be like this? Why did it have to be full of orcs and scarce food and no plumbing?

"Do you think we're gonna run into any more raiding parties? It's been at least a week."

Scottie shook his head. "We should practice some tomorrow."

"Do you think we need to?"

"I don't know where any of them are. And unlike playing the game, I don't have an eagle eye view option to know where things are. I don't get to make the choices of confronting or avoiding. We could run into danger at any time. I really hate first person shooters, and that's what it's felt like the entire time we've been here. I don't know what's around the corner, or behind that tree."

"Can we just sit here for a minute longer? It's nice to have a moment of peace."

"It is." He pressed his face against her head, and placed a kiss against her hair.

She sighed, it was better to not be mad at him and be talking to him than it was to stew in the miserable embarrassment of her own making.

They didn't get another moment of peace. Harold's screams had them both on their feet and running to their campsite.

"What is it?" Maisie asked as she looked around.

Scottie crossed the area they had cleared and picked up a sword and tossed it to her. He held the other one out for Harold.

"There's something out there." Scottie dropped the sword at the other man's feet when he refused to take it. He ran his hands over his arms. "It's big, and I can feel the magic. My hairs are all standing on end."

"You've got piloerection?"

"Jesus, ew no! Unlike you, I don't get a hard on when I think of fighting."

"Piloerection means your hairs bristle up and stand on end," Harold explained.

"That's what I just fucking said." Scottie continued to keep his focus on the jungle just beyond their camp site.

They stood braced for action staring out into the jungle. Scottie eased his posture and began moving around.

Maisie, not yet convinced the danger had passed, continued to hold her sword in front of her.

"So, this hair erection," she started.

"Don't call it that," Scottie sounded pained.

"Do you normally get that before you change?"

Scottie shrugged. "Yeah, that's part of it. It seems to have gone."

"What was out there?" Harold asked.

"I don't know, you're the one who screamed."

"A bug crawled over my foot. It was big."

Scottie pointed a loaded finger at Harold. He just stood there pointing and glowering for a moment before he stormed off.

Maisie tossed her sword down. "You could have said something earlier. Scared us half to death."

"You're just overreacting."

"And you have been under reacting, and he"— she pointed in the direction Scottie went— "has been keeping us alive. It's time you figured that out. You know for someone so fucking smart, you really are clueless."

CHAPTER
NINE

Maisie worked through her forms. She hefted her sword over her shoulder, ready to swing like a bat.

"In the morning, we should head out," Scottie suggested as he watched her practice. She moved with the grace of a dancer, but the heavy weapon caused her to hit awkward spots in her practice.

"So soon?" Her arms swung in rhythm. She was getting stronger, and that's what mattered most.

"The gorge won't be as easy to trek, and we've had a few days to rest up. To be honest, we could find the perfect spot to set up a permanent camp within a few miles of where we're located, or it could be days."

"That would be fantastic," Maisie dropped her sword arm.

It was hard to avert his eyes from her heaving chest. If he didn't stop staring other things would get hard too. Correct that, harder. Even scraping the insides of fish out didn't put a damper on his growing affection, attraction, and ardor for her.

"This place seems perfectly fine to me," Harold interjected.

Harold was always interjecting. Scottie found it difficult to put up with the man's constant smarter, holier than thou bullshit. He was constantly reminding them that the dead laptop he carried around like a baby held the code that would get them out. Continually professing just how smart he was, how he dropped out of college because he was already making so much money from game sales.

Scottie never once pointed out that when it came to financial windfalls, he had Harold beat. Harold may have sold his first game for a cool one point five, but that's what Scottie made in the first six months of this year. He was a top earner on the MinVid and GameWatch platforms, but none of that mattered here. Just like the dead laptop didn't matter.

Harold's ability to program is what got them into this mess, while Scottie's cosplay creations and gaming antics had zero impact on their survival. It seemed like a weird flex for Harold to constantly be bringing it up.

"It's not ideal," Scottie answered, less than thrilled to be speaking to the man.

"And what exactly is ideal?"

"For starters, I want a roof over my head and a wall at my back. If we could create a barricade, then maybe I could get a decent night's rest."

"Oh, a little cave of our own with a front door?" Maisie clasped her hands under her chin and blinked up at nothing. Completely mocking him.

"Hey, don't knock having a front door," he half grumbled at her. It was hard to be mad, she was in a good mood, and exceptionally cute this afternoon.

"You mean don't knock on a front door?" she teased. "Whose there? Not the door."

"Did you just make a knock-knock joke?" Harold asked.

With a flourish of her hands, Maisie took a bow.

"That's not how they work."

The smile fell from Maisie's face. "I know that. I'm just trying to have a little fun."

"How about instead you try to do something useful, like getting rid of those smelly fish guts, or starting the fire, or—"

"She's allowed to have a little fun. We could all use some levity right now," Scottie cut him off.

"Well, I for one don't need little Miss Mary Sunshine to put on a comedy sketch."

Maisie closed her eyes and took several deep breaths.

"Are you done with that?" she asked Scottie, pointing to the fish guts that he had piled up on a large leaf.

"Yeah."

She held out her hands and made give-me grabbing motions. "I'll be useful and go dump it."

For a split second, Scottie thought she was going to dump it on Harold. Now that would be some well deserved comic relief. He folded the leaf over on itself, making an envelope for the contents, and handed it to her.

Without a glance at Harold, she walked off.

Scottie watched her shoulders drop as she walked away.

"What the fuck was that? Huh? I have half a mind to pick you and that fucking laptop up and throw you into the river."

"Half, that's about all you have. She's always swinging that stupid sword around, and trying to be funny."

"And you don't do anything other than complain and

hug your computer. Put it down and help out around here occasionally."

"That's what NPCs are for."

Scottie got to his feet. "We aren't goddamned NPCs. I'm getting sick of telling you that."

"She might as well be one for all the use she is," Harold pointed in the direction Maisie had gone in.

"She is of more value than you and your dead computer." He stormed out of the campsite and followed Maisie. Something he should have done when she first left.

When he caught up with her, she stood on the bank of the river, staring out at the rushing water as it crashed against rocks.

"Hey."

She turned and glanced at him.

"Sorry about that." She gestured toward their camp.

"Being silly? Having fun? There is no need to apologize. I came to see if you're okay."

She shrugged. "I'm fine, I guess. No, I'm angry and I don't know if I'm mad at myself or Harold."

"Be pissed off at him. I know I am." He stood next to her and brushed her shoulder with his.

"I've been standing here fantasizing about having thrown Harold in instead of a leaf full of fish guts."

Scottie laughed and wrapped an arm over her shoulder and pulled her against him. "That's my girl."

"Assholes like him—" she started.

"I'm gonna stop you right there. There aren't other assholes like him. He is a unique species of super dick."

She giggled.

He relaxed a bit knowing her feelings weren't terribly hurt, maybe just a bit bruised.

"Oh, no, he is from a subspecies of jerk that I have to

deal with all the time. You don't see them because they camouflage themselves around other guys. You might just see some generic dickish behavior but you don't get the full experience."

"Oh, yeah? And how's that?"

"I have boobs and you don't."

She was not wrong, she had amazing boobs.

Scottie flexed. "I have pecs."

"Yes you do, and they are very nice. Thank you for sharing your workout videos."

He smirked. He knew hundreds of thousands of people watched his videos, but it was Maisie admitting that she liked his workout videos that felt like winning an award.

"But you having pecs doesn't automatically make gamer and con goers think you don't deserve to be in their spaces."

"If you game, and you like all things sci-fi and fantasy and comic adjacent you belong in those spaces."

She leaned her head against his shoulder. "Not all men think that way. And the ones who are willing to concede that women can be in those spaces don't want women like me there. And they aren't afraid to tell me." She let out a heavy sigh. "Harold is just another one of those guys."

Scottie stood back from Maisie, put his hand on her shoulder and looked her in the eyes. "What the fuck is that supposed to mean? Don't want women like you there?"

She gave him a weak grin and turned so that she looked out at the river again, and not at him. Wrapping her arms around herself, she rubbed her arms as if she were cold.

Scottie stepped up behind her and put his arms around her, holding her back to his chest. She didn't relax against him. Whatever it was she wasn't saying, was hard for her.

"You know you can tell me anything." He kissed her hair.

She let out a derisive chuckle. "It's part of the reason I stopped going to cons."

"That asshole voice actor who was rude about your cosplay?"

"You remembered? Wow, yeah. But he was rude about my cosplay because I'm fat."

"Maisie," he started.

"No, Scottie, don't try to placate me with other words that mean the same thing. I'm fat, and to some people, that's inexcusable. And to some guys, like Harold, that puts me in open season for hurling insults at, and telling me I don't belong. You know when that fucking orc was coming at me before he dragged me off, I actually thought he was some gym-bro coming over to tell me I needed to work out and go on a diet."

"That doesn't happen."

"Yeah, it does. It happens more than most people realize. And it's not just that. I can and have to do everything perfect, better than perfect, or I'm perceived as being stupid. Do you know how many people, not at the con, but in general, treated me like I was dumb for having a chemical burn on my face?"

"Jesus, Maisie. I'm sorry."

She leaned against him, and he felt her relax.

"Thank you," she said, "for listening."

"You know, I think you belong in those spaces. I think you're smart, and funny."

"That's because you know me. But people like Harold aren't willing to get to know me. All they see is a fat girl."

"I don't see a fat girl."

Maisie started to say something.

"Let me finish. I see a cute girl, and sure you've got a bit more going on than some of the other women there, but it's your smile that makes me want to smile. It's your pain that causes me pain. And it's your pink cotton panties that haunt my dreams."

"Oh my god, Scottie, you didn't—" She spun in his arms.

He cut off her words with a kiss.

Her lips were soft and confused for a second. But Maisie was smart, and she leaned into the kiss, wrapping her arms around his neck. He eased back a bit, and Maisie whimpered. Clearly, he needed to keep kissing her, so he did.

She slid her tongue across his lower lip, and he took that as permission to double down on his efforts. He had Maisie in his arms, and she was kissing him, this was something that he had been thinking of for months.

It was hard to breath around the tightening in his chest when the kiss ended. He traced his fingers along her cheek. "This is healing up nicely. And I'm sorry my poor skills caused you pain, and people are idiots because if anyone was being stupid it was me." It's not what he had intended on saying, but his brain had short circuited out, and all he could really think was how amazing Maisie felt in his arms and against his lips.

She caught his hand. "It's no one's fault. It was a reaction. Are we just going to ignore the elephant between us?"

"Hey, I know my dick is big, but I wouldn't call it an elephant."

"Scottie!"

He leaned back with a laugh, and looked down at her. "You are adorable, and I've wanted to kiss you for the longest time. What's your elephant?"

"I'm trying to forget that you've seen me naked, and you keep bringing up my panties."

He leaned down and put his mouth next to her ear. "I never want to forget that I've seen you look like a goddess emerging from the waves. That will be the memory I take to my deathbed. You are beautiful."

She blazed like the setting sun with a deep pink blush. She bit her lower lip and blinked up at the sky.

"Really? You don't think I'm in the way, or Miss Mary Sunshine?"

With a finger under her chin, he tilted her face so he could look into her eyes. "You are my sunshine. You are what keeps me going."

He kissed her again, now that he had started, he didn't know if he'd be able to stop.

CHAPTER
TEN

The trek into the gorge was nowhere as easy as the long tiring days that hiking through the jungle had been. The jungle floor had been a series of sloping hills, and for the most part, the sky was obliterated from view. But walking into the gorge had them following narrow paths on the side of a cliff face.

"I feel exposed out here," Maisie said. She didn't want to complain, but the sudden ability to see the creatures that flew in the sky had put fear into her that she had gleefully been unaware of previously.

"Wyverns aren't going to come along and pluck us from the trail for an afternoon snack, if that's your concern." Harold said.

"Really? That's good, because I had almost forgotten they were out here." Her gaze tracked the wings of a pair of pink and blue wyverns skittering along the treetops below them.

"We have more to be concerned with the day bats," Scottie said.

"Why?" Maisie, gasped as several of the aforementioned day bats, terracotta colored winged creatures with cream under bellies, erupted from the cliff face into the sky.

"Day bats eat bugs, they are harmless," Harold pointed out.

"Yeah, but their droppings are all over the trail up here, and it's already narrow. Slippery isn't a good addition."

Part of Maisie was welcome for the distraction the continuous conversation provided. She didn't have to think about the drop to oblivion on her right as she followed Scottie. But part of her wished they would just all be quiet so she could focus on not dying.

"Maise." Scottie held out a hand to her. "Let's go slow."

She didn't rush to reach him, but as soon as he had a grip on her hand, she felt safer.

"Watch your step through here. This is where the bats were hanging out."

Her foot slipped. By force of will, and a desire to not die, she found stable footing. Her heart pounded against her ribs as if it were trying to escape.

"Shit."

"Exactly. You okay?"

Letting go of Scottie's hand she hugged a little closer to the cliff face and gripped the wall. She closed her eyes and pressed her face against the rock. She didn't want to do this. Every adventure movie she had ever seen with an epic journey, they all lied. There was no glory in walking across the continent. This was hard, so hard. She was scared and felt defeated. She wanted to take the easy way round, only there was no such thing.

"Why did you stop?" Harold asked.

"Maisie, I need you to look at me, Sunshine." Scottie coaxed her to open her eyes and turn her head.

He smiled at her as if this was nothing more than a walk in the park.

"You are doing amazing. I just need you to come a few feet closer to me. The path gets wider."

"You aren't lying to me?"

"Hey, it's me. What do you think?"

"I think you'd say what you need to manipulate her to get out of the way," Harold piped up from somewhere behind her.

Maisie couldn't help but laugh. Harold was so much a comical stereotype of the gamer guy who did not like girls, and he fit it so well. Almost as if he were trying. Only he was actually being a jerk.

Scottie held out his hand to her again. This time he pulled her toward him.

"That's it, baby steps."

After what felt like forever, but what was probably a dozen yards at most, the path grew wide enough for Scottie to pull her against him, and hold her for a few moments.

"How much more of this?"

They had been following a trail to the bottom of the gorge for two days now. The first night had been miserable, with Maisie constantly dreaming that she would roll off the ledge. Even though she had slept sitting more or less upright while leaning against Scottie's chest as he held her. She didn't know if she had a second or third night in her.

Scottie tilted his head back to look up. "It's hard to tell. It would be easier if there was a staircase, but we have these paths that keep going for miles before they are obviously getting us lower. We're more than halfway there."

"Can we rest for a bit?" She hated that this was getting the best of her. She tried hard to muster through when her feet hurt, and when her legs cramped. She knew she wasn't as fit as Scottie, or, much to her chagrin, Harold. But she did her best. Only right now her best was struggling.

"We'll never get to the bottom if you keep stopping." Harold complained.

Making their already perilous situation even more awkward, he tried to step past her. Scottie grabbed the other man's arm to keep him from over balancing.

"I had it," Harold snapped.

"You gonna keep going?"

"Some of us want to get to the bottom."

"Some of us don't want to take the one-way elevator down. You should rest, it's good to not tax ourselves."

Maisie put her hand on Scottie's arm. "Let him go on. I'm sorry I'm slowing you down."

"Never say that, okay? For someone who is afraid of heights, you are doing a fabulous job."

"Am I that obvious?"

"Pretty much."

"I've been obvious in other things and you never clued in. How come you caught onto this?"

Scottie chuckled. "That's easy, I'm not directly involved. Also, you've been muttering pretty constantly about not looking down, and there are rocks under your feet. And clutching to the cliff face. They're all pretty much little hints. And about the other thing, I've known. But you were doing your best to not let that interfere with us being friends, so I let it be."

Maisie felt as if her stomach took the plunge off the side of the cliff. He'd known. She'd been foolish thinking he had been clueless.

She lowered her gaze, only to bounce it back up, and

stare out into the sky. It was a lot less nerve invoking than looking down on the tops of trees.

"Maise?"

She didn't let him pull her face back to look at him. His fingers dropped away.

"Are you mad that I knew?"

"You could have said something."

"I didn't want to hurt your feelings. But if we are going to talk about missing the obvious, how come you didn't pick up on when I started to crush back on you?"

"Because you've always been nice to me. And I didn't want to get my hopes up."

Scottie leaned back against the cliff. "We're a pair, aren't we?"

"Yeah, look at us being nice to each other, and thinking it's something other than what it is. In case you've changed your mind, I'm good being your platonic friend."

"Seriously? You want to go back to that earlier mess that was us? No thank you. I think being up here is fucking with your head. Let me be perfectly clear. I do not want to be platonic."

"Really? You aren't just saying that to be nice?"

"Let's get off this fucking cliff and I'll show you how much I mean it."

"Well then, what are we hanging around here for?"

The trek wasn't any easier, but with the promise of more kisses from Scottie, Maisie could pretend that she wasn't afraid of heights. It wasn't long before they caught up with Harold.

He stood frozen, back plastered against the cliff face.

"Problems?" Scottie asked.

"I slipped and dropped my laptop."

"I'm surprised you didn't follow it over the edge," Scottie said bitterly.

"Well, I don't know how many lives I have in this version, and—"

"You have one life in this version, Harold. One," Maisie bit out.

"You don't know that."

"You're right, I don't. And I don't want to find out. But without your laptop, you can use your hands to hold on."

"All my code is on that laptop."

"And the battery has been dead for at least two weeks. We can't stand here staring down all day."

"If the code is lost will we ever be able to get out of here?"

"I don't know, Maisie. I don't know."

The path stopped. Boulders created a natural staircase for several yards, before another narrow path hugged the side of the cliff. Eventually, the path smoothed out and took them all the way to the base of the gorge near where the waterfalls from the Great River created a series of pools before continuing along its path to the coast.

"Let's set up camp for the night. We can start looking for caves in the morning."

"We need to go look for my laptop."

"No, Harold, we do not," Scottie countered.

Maisie placed her hand on his arm. "Let him go."

She grabbed his hand and walked toward the falls. They stood on an outcropping of rock about a hundred yards from the base of the first significant drop. The water collected in a still pool, before swirling around the rocks they stood on, and continued in a series of smaller cataracts.

She sighed, and smiled back at him. It was good to see her calm again. Her fear had become his fear when they were traversing the wall of the gorge.

"It's beautiful here," she said in wide eyed amazement.

He figured the elation of having successfully made it to the bottom had given her a renewed sense of appreciation. He looked around. It was pretty enough, but nothing compared to her and her smile.

"You are."

"I meant this place." She blushed when she looked back at him.

He dragged her back against him and wrapped his arms around her. "I meant you. I believe I owe you a dramatization of exactly how non-platonic my intentions are."

He pressed his lips to hers, letting the kiss start sweet, almost chaste.

"I need you to know that for as long as we are here, I will do my very best to protect you and keep you safe. Your concerns are my concerns. I could feel how scared you were up there, and I have never been more proud of anybody in my life."

"Scottie," Maisie said his name in a breath.

"Please don't tell me I'm being sweet. I don't have sweet intentions, not with you. Not anymore."

His mouth claimed hers again, this time he wasn't satisfied with simply pressing his lips to hers. He needed to claim her, to give over his intent. Lips parted, tongues twined.

"Do you want to make love with me? I mean, could we?

When you say not platonic..." She looked up at him, her hands still braced on his shoulders.

Scottie stared at Maisie in disbelief. He swallowed around a lump in his throat. He was going to get to see her naked again.

"I, ah. Fuck. Yes, the answer is yes. It doesn't matter what I was thinking, because I can't think of anything else at the moment. I was all set for a long seduction, whatever pace you're comfortable with."

He looked over his shoulder. "Shit, what about Harry?"

"I'm hoping he gets lost," Maisie giggled. "Oh god, I'm suddenly very, very nervous."

Scottie stepped back and began pacing. "Me too. How do you want to do this? We should just take our clothes off and..."

Maisie covered her face and groaned. "Are we always going to be this awkward?"

"The first time is always awkward," Scottie laughed. "Sorry, if I'm making it worse."

"I wouldn't know," Maisie said with a shrug.

"Oh, fuck." Scottie started shaking his head. "Really? And you want me?"

"Is that bad?"

He reached his hand out to her. When she slipped her fingers against his, he knew with perfect clarity that he was going to spend the rest of his life making her happy. He didn't want to fuck this important step up for her, for them.

"I'm honored. And I think making love to you under a waterfall seems like the most amazing thing ever."

He pulled her back into his arms and this time when he kissed her, he slowly began running his hands over her body. He would have been satisfied with a really good make out session, and maybe he knew there was a reason he was willing to go slow with her. He was going to have all the time in the world to learn her body, and the way she liked things. This new, unexpected, turn had him shaking.

"Are you nervous?" she asked.

"Yeah," he let out a nervous chuckle.

"Why? I'm the virgin here."

"That's exactly why. This matters. You matter."

CHAPTER
ELEVEN

Scottie looked around, and while the setting was beautiful and romantic, there really wasn't any place that would be comfortable.

"You're thinking about it," Maisie said.

"You want me to stop thinking about it?"

"I didn't mean to put extra pressure on you. Oh geez, forget it, forget I said anything."

He reached out and grabbed her hand as she turned from him.

"I don't want to forget it. I want you, but I also want this to be magical for you."

Maisie raised her hands and spun in a slow circle. "Look around, Scottie. There is this gorgeous waterfall, we are surrounded by lush green jungle, and there are fucking dragons in the sky. And I know I might not be—"

His lips stopped her from saying anything more. She pressed into him with a moan that effectively rerouted the blood in his brain straight to his cock.

"Whatever you were about to say, shut up. You are everything amazing and beautiful. Never forget that."

He was kissing her again, and touching her. Her breasts were heavy in his hands, and his brain short circuited. He began easing them back toward a boulder, working on his belt. He dropped it and kept moving. They separated long enough for him to pull his tunic off. He had to lean over and have Maisie pull the heavy chain shirt over his head. It caught in his hair. With a yank, and the loss of a few strands of hair, it was off.

Maisie stood back and stared at him. Not his face, but his body. He dropped some weight the few weeks they had been trapped in Austratica. Those defined abs he developed working out for hours at the gym, now stood out in high relief. His muscles had toned further, and there were other changes she noticed.

When she tentatively reached out to touch him, he grabbed her wrist and pressed her hand to his chest. It tickled as she gained courage and traced over his ribs and stomach.

"I'm not like you," she whispered.

"Thank god," he muttered.

"I'm not toned and firm. You can't see my hip bones."

"I don't want to see your bones. I want your softness."

He sat and pulled her into the space between his knees. He pressed a kiss on the exposed flesh of her breasts, wrapping his hands around them, skimming his thumbs over the fabric of her tunic until he found her nipples, and continued to rub in circles until they peaked hard.

"Are you ready to let me see you? In your pink cotton panties?" he teased.

Maisie's eyes went wide and he followed the gulp in her neck. She bit her lip and nodded.

Scottie reached for the hem of her tunic and lifted it, exposing the pale expanse of skin, and her bra-clad breasts.

He sucked in his breath. She was a siren calling out for his touch. He buried his face between her breasts, and inhaled her. Her scent, her warmth, the sound of her racing heart. He filled his mouth with her soft skin, and grazed his teeth across the fabric of her bra. He reached behind her, and looped his fingers in the band where the hooks held her contained.

"May I?" he asked as he looked up into her eyes.

She nodded.

He closed his eyes, remembering how she had looked coming out of the creek. How her nipples had been a deep rosy pink against her skin. He removed her bra by touch alone, anticipating seeing her again, as if she were a gift for him. And she was. When he opened his eyes, all he managed was a guttural sound deep in his throat before he wrapped his mouth around a nipple. He crushed her against him, losing himself in the feel of her breast against his mouth, her hard nipple teasing his tongue.

Maisie wrapped her arms around him and clutched his head to her.

"Jesus," she gasped.

Scottie slid one hand down her smooth back, continuing to slide it past the waistband of her pants. He kneaded her ass with one hand, and held her breast with the other as he sucked, and licked and teased her nipple.

He let go of her ass as he released her nipple. He didn't relinquish the breast in his hand as he pulled her face down to his to kiss her again. Their tongues twined. Maisie moaned into Scottie's mouth. He moved his hands over her, grabbing her breasts, running over her arms, down her sides.

He hooked his hands into her waist band again, this time pushing her pants down.

Maisie worked her legs, stepping out of her pants.

Her legs were soft under his touch.

She righted herself with a small gasp, ending the kissing. She looked down between them. He followed her gaze.

He chuckled. "You know, I kind of want to shout, release the kraken right now. But I don't think that's the right mood. You sure about this?"

"If there is one thing I'm sure about, it's this."

With a nod, Scottie eased her back so he could stand and push his pants out of the way. Her eyes went wide, and she made an O with her mouth.

Scottie started to laugh. "That ugly, huh? Ready to change your mind?"

"You're a big idiot, you know that? Right?"

He looked down at the erection protruding from his body. "Slightly larger than average, but yeah, I'm an idiot. A fucking lucky idiot."

He took her hand as he sat and leaned back, guiding her closer. With his longer reach, he picked up their discarded tunics. "Here, put these under your knees."

She nodded and straddled his lap.

"Are you ready?" He helped to balance her with one hand, while he held his cock back.

He sighed with a shudder when she pressed her damp heat against him. This was for her, at her pace.

She slid her hips back, gliding her wet folds over him.

She ground against him, her clit bumping against his head as she slid back and forth along his length. Maisie gasped and mewed as she continued to rub. Scottie's eyes wanted to roll up into his head. She was heaven. He dug his fingers into her thick thighs, rocking his hips along with her.

She increased her speed, and her whimpers came on every breath.

"Ready, Sunshine?"

She nodded her head furiously.

Scottie reached between them and aligned his cock. With the next roll of her hips, Maisie took Scottie into her depths. He slid in perfectly. She was tight and hot, and her walls were already clenching in rhythm, ramping up for a frenzied release.

"Oh," she moaned with a hint of a whine.

"Are you okay?"

"Scottie? Oh," she cried. "Oh god, oh fuck, oh."

The orgasm rolled through her body. He felt her grip and release his cock in greedy spasms. Her body sucked and pulled at his cock.

He leaned on one arm, and held her hip hard with his other hand, giving him some leverage. As Maisie was unable to move, he began thrusting hard into her. She continued to whimper with each breath. Her inner walls grabbed at him wanting to hold him in tight.

"Oh, fuck is right, damn you feel so hot."

Maisie leaned forward and braced against his shoulders. Her breasts were right in his face. He captured a nipple in his mouth. He sucked in time with his thrusts and the feel of her body pulling on his cock.

He spilled into her with a roar. His hands clenched and he pressed into her.

Everything tightened and then all of his muscles relaxed at once. Maisie collapsed against his chest.

He brushed her hair back from her face, and kissed the top of her head.

"You okay?"

"Is it always like that?" she asked.

"Depends on what you mean. Did I hurt you? Cause that part will feel better."

"It gets better?"

"I'm not gonna lie, that was fucking phenomenal. For your first time, you know what you're doing."

She giggled, and her entire body jiggled against him, her skin against his. "You can thank romance novels."

"I like what you read." His hands ran up and down her back. She felt so amazing. He wanted to stay on that uncomfortable rock with her plastered to him forever.

"Am I squishing you?"

"Hm mm," Scottie hummed.

"I'm sorry" Maisie said as she started to push away.

Scottie tightened his arm around her to hold her in place. "That didn't mean I wanted you to get up. But we should move. Do you want to take a quick bath? We're both naked, and there is a pool of crystal clear water. Shall we?"

Maisie rolled off Scottie. Her legs felt wobbly.

"Is this normal?"

He looked at her legs and then smirked. "Noodle legs? That means I did my job well."

"Not that I have anything to base it against, but I'd have to agree."

She squirmed a little, the pressure between her legs wasn't uncomfortable exactly. It was just different. He said that would go away with time. For her first time there was no sharp breaking of skin, and no real pain. He had filled her and given her nothing but pressure and friction, and everything had been amazing.

She wobbled as she tried to gather up her clothes. She wished she could wash them and hang them out to dry. She missed clean clothes.

"Come here." Scottie stood knee-deep in the pool created by the waterfall. "It's a bit cool, but it feels good."

She slid her hand into his, and let him help her into the water. She gasped as he pulled her down into a deeper section so that their bodies were submerged. He kept his arms around her.

The slippery glide of their bodies in the water had heat pooling between her legs again. She wanted him to touch all of her, wanted his mouth back on her breast.

"This feels so good," she purred.

"You feel so good." He kissed her again and buried his fingers in her hair.

She reached up and began pulling her hair out of the messed-up braids she had put in days earlier.

"Here." He eased her head back and began massaging her scalp and trailing his fingers comb-like through the long strands as they floated in the water.

They bounced slightly in the water. Maisie had no idea how deep it was, she had wrapped her legs around Scottie and he supported her. She ran her hands over his shoulders and pecs.

"I like you touching me," he said with a husky rumble.

"It's weird, you know. I've thought about this so many times. It doesn't seem real. And you like it, and you want to touch me back."

"I want to do so much more than touch you. Maisie, thank you."

"For what?" She smiled at him, and played with his beard, noticing how the water droplets looked like glitter.

"For this, for having patience with me. For not wanting anything from me but my attention and friendship."

"What else would I want from you?"

He closed his eyes, and she saw raw hurt cross his face.

"You aren't using me to get views, right?"

She squinted at him.

"I'm joking. With you, that's a joke. I know you aren't using me."

"Why would anybody use you like that?" she asked.

"Maisie, I have almost ten million followers on a collection of platforms. I'm seen as easy access to a large audience."

Her mouth dropped open, and she looked horrified.

"I would never."

"I know you wouldn't. The last couple of mistakes, well, they were mistakes for a reason. But you have never pretended to be my friend. You've honestly been my friend, and that makes this so much sweeter."

He held her chin and kissed her mouth, and whatever she had felt for him before dissolved and was replaced with a love she didn't even know could exist. Not wanting him to see her cry, she let go and ducked under water.

"We should get out, and look for a good campsite," she said as she paddled back to the rocky edge of the pool.

"I don't want Harold to find us all naked."

"You know, I had successfully forgotten about him."

Scottie caught up with her in two broad strokes. He was out of the water before she was. She took her time and admired him as he pulled his clothes back on. He had fiery hair, and pink skin. Paler than she was, but with arms and neck darkened with freckles from their endless days in this place.

His muscles rippled and bunched, and he had that fucking amazing Adonis V groove at his hips. She couldn't believe someone who looked like him had wanted to be with someone shaped like her. And he wasn't just anybody, he was Scottie. Her Scottie.

CHAPTER
TWELVE

They encountered caves much sooner than Maisie had anticipated. Not even a few miles from the last pool of the waterfalls, where the river reformed with a gentle pebble beach, they located a suitable cave. Scottie had a checklist that Maisie had to agree with. She would have gleefully gone into the first one she found, not thinking about bats or other creatures that might live in there.

So after an entrance that didn't require more than bending over to get in, knowing how deep was the second requirement. If they couldn't follow the cave all the way to the back, if they just couldn't tell, that was a nope.

The cave they found had an entrance Maisie felt comfortable fitting through. Harold complained about hitting his head. But Scottie, who was so much taller, didn't. The cave itself was fairly shallow, only going back into the canyon wall about fifteen or twenty feet. It was wide and had plenty of space for everyone to lay down and be within the shelter.

"The plants do a fairly good job of hiding the entrance, but I still want a door."

"Oh lordy, you aren't going to do another one of those stupid knock-knock jokes are you?" Harold whined.

Ignoring him, Maisie turned her attention to Scottie. "So we can stay here for a bit? Set up a more permanent camp?" She didn't want to get her hopes up, but she desperately wanted to stop trekking through the wilds every day without a destination.

"I still think we should go to the coast and try to find other gamers," Harold said.

"I agree," Scottie started.

"What? You never agree with me."

"Well this time, you actually have a point. But we need a break. We are all tired, hungry, and stressed to the limits. Here we have easy access to the river." He ticked items off his fingers. "That's fishing, fresh water, bathing, all right there. I saw some citrus looking trees between here and the falls, so another food source. I don't know if this place has a rainy season like the game, but we would stay relatively dry here."

"While you get what you need for a door, I want to see what I can find to maybe make mats to sleep on. So I don't have to put my head in the dirt when I sleep."

Scottie cleared his throat. "You've got me."

Warmth spread throughout Maisie's being. She did have Scottie, and in the few hours they had when they weren't keeping watch, he held her. Letting her rest her head on his chest.

She sighed. "I still woke up with rocks in my hair."

"Sorry about that Sunshine. Sleeping mats sound like a good idea. Tomorrow we can forage for what we need."

"Tomorrow, I'm going back out to look for my laptop," Harold informed them.

"I wouldn't expect anything less." Maisie turned her head so that Harold wouldn't see her smirk. It wasn't to save Harold from her expression but to save herself from his incessant judgmental commentary.

It took several days for Scottie to collect the necessary branches and vines he needed to make a door.

Never wandering far from Scottie's side, she collected palm-like fronds. With another gratitude nod toward all the romance novels she read, she thanked those authors who would put random dumps of historic information into their narratives. If it weren't for instructions on weaving rushes into mats, she never would have thought about weaving palm fronds together to make mattresses she could stuff with other leaves.

As expected Harold complained that it was taking too long to build the door. But he never offered any help. Not with the direct task at hand, or even with fishing and gathering citrus for their dinners. The only thing he provided was negativity. Of course, Maisie wasn't going to get into it with him. Even Scottie left him alone

His absence was a contributing factor to how long everything was taking. And she didn't want to change that for anything.

"Has he left yet?" Scottie asked.

Maisie pretended to weave a mat together. Pretended because she spent more time watching the jungle and listening for Harold than she did working the fronds.

"I think so." She put the weaving down and entered the cave.

Scottie was right behind her. As soon as she turned, she

was in his arms. Their lips pressed together, their tongues fighting for dominance.

Scottie pulled his tunic off. Now that they had set up camp, he didn't walk around in all of his layers of tunics and chain maille. It also made getting undressed quicker. Maisie took his tunic and spread it over the dirt floor with her own.

"I really need to finish one of those mats."

"What I need is this," Scottie practically growled as he leaned over and lifted her breast to his mouth.

She gasped, and clutched him to her.

They weren't getting nearly as much work done as they could be because with everyday came another opportunity to spend hours exploring each other's bodies.

Maisie pulled Scottie down with her, cradling him to her body between her thighs. She loved how he worshiped her body with his hands and his mouth. She was lost to sensation as he discovered what made her cry out with lust and need. And she loved how it felt to have him deep inside of her, his hips pressed to her, his strong arms holding himself above her. In those moments, the way he looked at her, she convinced herself that he was in love with her, and it wasn't a case of being convenient.

By the time Harold returned from an unsuccessful laptop hunting mission Maisie was back to weaving the mat and Scottie was grunting out his frustration over the door not coming together to his satisfaction. It took days of distracted work to complete the door. It took even longer to make several mats.

Scottie wished he could lose track of the days. He wanted to lose time to simply being with Maisie. But his brain clutched onto the oddest things. Why would he forget an appointment or a promise to make his best friend's girl a set of Valkyrie armor, but he could perfectly remember it had been thirty two days since he chased that orc through a magic portal because Maisie was in danger.

He didn't mind clinging to every moment of the past month with Maisie. Especially the last twelve days since he finally took her in his arms and declared his feelings for her. Twelve days of her knowing smiles, and perfect kisses. Twelve days since she practically demanded he shut up and take her virginity.

He knew there was a significance to thirty one days. But he couldn't remember. His house was paid for, same for the car. Wolf would take care of the utilities. Other than Game-Watch, which he streamed live, all other platforms were recorded and scheduled a month ahead of time. It wasn't his bills or his social media presence. Hell, other than those people he saw on a daily basis, Vik and Wolf and the delivery guy, no one would know he was missing yet.

Maisie's family, on the other hand, had to be sick with worry. She would have lost her job by now. Hell, he didn't know if she rented or had roommates, or still lived at home. That was all fucked up now.

Thirty one days, and the beginning of their new life in this place. This was not the life he wanted for Maisie. He wanted a king size bed and a big screen TV with her curled up next to him on that mythical couch he still needed to buy. He wanted her to buy his couch because it was the only way his brain had figured out that he wanted her in his house.

She cuddled against him, warm with sleep. She was his

everything. And he knew he was missing something. He kissed her soft cheek and wiggled out from under her and she used his shoulder for a pillow. He folded up his extra tunic and tucked it under her head. Before stepping outside.

If they were going to push on for the coast, he should start smoking some fish. It would be better if he actually knew how to do that. It was one thing to know what needed to be done, it was fully something else to know how the fuck to do it.

He walked down to the river. He squatted at the water's edge and scooped cool water into his cupped hands and splashed his face. The hairs on his arms pricked up, and he got a shiver of nerves along the back of his neck. He couldn't tell where the danger was. Twisting around, he tried to sense why he felt magic roll over his skin.

He shifted to his boar form as a screech from the sky caught his attention. He rolled just as talons scraped the air above his back, raking through the course bristly fur at his shoulders. He didn't know how to fight an airborne foe in this form. He needed a crossbows and bolts, hell a sword even. Tusks were for up close and personal fighting. For ripping an enemy from navel to neck.

The wyvern that was now taking practice grabs for him was too far out of his reach. His only option was to run.

MAISIE WOKE UP, COLD AND ALONE. WELL, NOT COMPLETELY alone. Harold complained about something from his preferred spot in the cave. But Scottie was gone. She rubbed the sleep from her eyes and tried to stretch through the morning's new set of aches and pains.

Sleeping on the ground, woven mat or not, was still uncomfortable.

If they ever made it back to the real world, she was never going to have delusions of camping again.

"Have you been up long?" she asked.

Harold had taken to completely ignoring her. Something she wasn't particularly upset by. It bothered her more that she disliked him as completely as she did. She used to think of herself as the type of person who could get along with anybody. Harold didn't even want to try.

She wasn't going to waste her time on him, not when she could give all of her attention to Scottie. And Scottie was willing to give all of his attention to her.

She picked up her short sword and opened the door to step outside.

"Scottie?"

He didn't seem to be nearby. She decided to head to the river, it was close, and while Scottie didn't like to let her go alone, he wasn't around. She should be safe enough, she had her sword.

She didn't begin to worry until he wasn't by the river, and she saw the rocks on the beach were all messed up, like there had been a fight.

"Scottie!"

She ran into the jungle, not knowing how to find him, but desperate to do so. After what felt like hours, she returned to the cave. Harold was still inside.

"Have you seen Scottie?"

Harold blankly stared at her and then turned away.

She was done with his bullshit. She crossed the small space and shook him. "Where the fuck is Scottie?"

"How should I know? He left." He got to his feet and walked out the door.

Maisie stared in disbelief. He had simply walked away from her. Scottie was missing and Harold didn't care. Didn't he realize the only reason any of them were still alive was because of Scottie?

She stormed out the door and followed Harold into the jungle.

"Where the hell do you think you're going?"

"Away from you."

"We need to find Scottie," she felt like she was begging for blood from a turnip.

"Why? He'll come back. It's the nature of the game."

She stopped, dumbfounded that Harold, after all this time still thought this was a game. Maybe it was the only way he could accept what was happening? It seemed entirely too far-fetched to be real, but Maisie knew it was.

She continued to follow Harold, uncertain what to say. Arguing with him was a moot point. Maybe she could appeal to his sense of self-preservation.

"We should head back and go fishing."

"Why? Scottie will take care of it. That's what he's programmed for."

"Oh for fuck's sake, Harold." She stopped following him. Her shoulders slumped. Had the poor man had some kind of mental break when the orcs had captured him, and she hadn't realized it? All this time she had thought he was an arrogant self entitled prick. Maybe he was both.

He vanished behind a wall of leaves.

"Shit, Harold, wait up, we shouldn't wander away from camp like this."

She ran into him as he stood still.

A giant serpent of a monster hissed at her. The thing was beautiful in its terrifying way, pink and blue with a long head with frills and large nostrils. Fangs, easily as long as her fingers filled the beast's mouth. Small blue wings rattled along its back.

Harold put his arm out, keeping her from passing him. Not that Maisie felt like charging the beast. She wanted to run in the opposite direction.

"It's a wyvern," Harold said.

"I can see that. Maybe if we back away slowly it won't charge at us."

"It's a juvenile. It won't hurt us. I programmed—"

"Harold," Maisie snapped. "You programmed a game. That is not a game. It's very real, and it's very angry right now."

"I'm trying to tell you, I programmed it so that players can't interact with the juvenile wyverns. Instead they have to deal with the mother. I can't even get close enough to touch it."

He took a step forward.

The wyvern screeched and leaped.

Maisie screamed.

She moved through her forms as she had been taught. Only now she had a very real foe. She needed to drive the monster away from Harold. And hopefully, get them both back to safety. The short sword was barely long enough to keep her out of reach of the monster's claws while hitting it with the sharp point of her sword.

She swung through batter batter, and followed the action with stabby stabby. She felt like a fool yelling "stabby stabby," as she drove the sword point at the beast's face. She was driving it back. She now stood between it and Harold. He was on his knees and holding his gut.

She knew there was a lot of blood, she didn't know how much damage he sustained. She wasn't going to know until the thing turned and ran away, or she killed it. She didn't think she was going to be able to kill it. Especially as it managed to stay just outside her reach.

A squealing roar came from somewhere to her right. She wanted to cry, she didn't have it in her to fight another monster. She was tempted to drop her sword down and chance her luck with running away. Screw Harold, it was self preservation time.

Suddenly a very large boar stood between her and the wyvern. They screamed at each other. The wyvern lunged for Scottie.

"Oh no you don't," Maisie screamed and brought her blade down on the creature just behind its head.

Momentum carried it forward, and its lifeless body crashed into the jungle floor, siding to a stop near where Harold lay collapsed and bloody.

"Scottie, oh my god, Scottie, are you okay?"

Maisie watched in near disbelief as the boar thrashed and with a painful set of convulsions and sounds, shifted back into Scottie.

"Oh fuck, that's starting to really hurt."

She flung her arms around his shoulders and sobbed.

"Hey, my brave girl. You did amazing." He held her as she continued crying.

"You went away."

"Sorry, Sunshine. I had a run-in with a bigger one of these. What are you doing out here?"

"I wanted to look for you, but... oh shit! Harold." She ran back to the other man. He was covered in blood.

"I've got him," Scottie said as he scooped Harold up.

Back at camp, Maisie followed helplessly as Scottie carried Harold to the river.

"We need to see how bad this is. We should wash away

as much of this blood as we can. Go get my tunic, we can cut that into strips and make a bandage."

Maisie ran. When she returned, Harold looked pale. His eyes were closed.

"Is he... is he gonna make it?"

Scottie shrugged. "He's torn up pretty bad. His insides have stayed inside, but I have no way of telling how deep the lacerations are. The best we can do is bind him up and hope for the best."

With a little help from the sharp end of her sword, Maisie was able to cut and tear the tunic into strips that Scottie wrapped around Harold's middle.

"How is that mattress idea of yours coming?"

She shook her head. "It's nowhere near being finished. But let me see what I can do while you finish up here." She retreated to the cave and their campsite. Grabbing an armful of leaves from the pile she was collecting for an attempt at making a padded sleeping surface, she layered leaves and the woven mats into a crude attempt at a mattress.

She may not have liked the man, but she didn't think he deserved this, not even with his delusion that they were in the game.

She didn't leave his side for days. She slept in fits and bursts, and tried to make him comfortable.

CHAPTER
THIRTEEN

Days went by and there was no change. Harold did not seem to be recovering, yet he wasn't getting any worse until he started the fever. Maisie knew at this point that there was no hope, no medicine, no medical intervention for him.

"Any better?" Scottie asked.

Maisie shook her head.

"Why don't you try to get some rest. I'll watch him."

"Are you sure?"

"Yeah, ah..." Scottie clutched his middle. He convulsed and collapsed in on himself. He fell to the ground.

Panic and concern welled up in Maisie. He couldn't get sick, not here. They had nothing here that could take care of him. She would have to leave to find medicine if Scottie got sick too. She wasn't a healer, or a cleric. She didn't have magical potions, and this stupid place didn't have a drugstore on the corner with antibiotics and bandaids.

Scottie was heavy in her arms as she tried to hold on.

He pushed her back. "No, it's magic, it's..." he couldn't finish talking as his body began to change.

She stepped back and wrapped her arms around herself. She winced empathetically as Scottie groaned in pain, tusks ruptured from his gums. The change had once been so fast and effortless was taking a toll on him. It grew more painful each time.

He hadn't shifted since the wyvern attacked. Did this mean there was something coming?

She turned to Harold on the bed of leaves. Sweat beaded on his brow. His skin was sallow, and his breathing was shallow and coming in fast gasps. She didn't know how she would be able to protect him. As far as she knew he was their only way out. If he died, she was afraid they would be trapped forever.

There may have been a point in her life where being trapped with Scottie in a magical tropical near paradise would have been ideal. Now that she'd done it, was in the middle of it, and they spent all of their time struggling just to stay alive, she ditched the fantasy.

"Harold, are you still with us?" At some point she stopped saying she would find help, they simply had no idea where they were, or what help they could find. He needed antibiotics, and unless he had programmed them into existence, there weren't any here.

He slowly opened his eyes and stared blankly at the ceiling.

"No!" She shook the man. There was no response. She pressed her fingers to his neck. No pulse, nothing. "You insufferable, selfish dick."

"Scottie," she cried and sat limply on the cave floor. "He's dead. We're trapped here forever."

The boar gently nudged and snuffled at her until she wrapped her arms around his thick neck. The bristly fur poked at her cheeks, but she didn't care. She held tight, knowing that they didn't have long to mourn. Scottie had shifted into his boar form, which meant they would have to fight soon.

He grunted and she looked up. Harold was dissolving into shimmering dust like all the orcs and other beasts they had encountered and battled.

Scottie moved to the front of the cave. He stood guard at the entrance to their small shelter. Maisie followed, picked up her short sword, and placed her hand on the back of the giant swine. She was comforted by his fierce presence. And knowing it was Scottie ready to fight gave her courage.

The sounds of foliage breaking as something large moved through the jungle alerted Maisie that whatever was coming would be upon them soon. Unexpectedly, a large bear loomed into the small clearing of their campsite. The opening to their cave safely hidden behind the branches of leafy trees.

Muscles in the boar's back bunched, and his legs braced for a lunge.

She didn't know there were bears on this forsaken island. Scottie backed up, forcing her to move deeper into their shelter. Maisie gasped and stepped back. Suddenly Aaliyah was in the clearing hitting the bear.

"That's a door! Maisie? Please be in there!"

"Aaliyah?" Maisie could barely talk. She started crying with relief, and by the time she pushed past Scottie and fell into her friend's arms, she was sobbing.

"Come on, we don't have much time."

"What? How?"

Aaliyah started pulling on Maisie's arm. "I'll explain later, we have to go!"

Maisie pulled back. "Harold's dead."

"Who?"

"Harold Whitaker, he's the original programmer of the game. He's dead. His body just turned to dust like he was a video game character."

"There's nothing we can do for him. We've got to go," Aaliyah said urgently

With the bear in the lead, Aaliyah and Maisie followed. They ran. The boar followed in the very back. For the first time in weeks, Maisie wanted to give up. She was weak and tired.

"Hurry before anything else knows there's a portal."

"But how did you get it open? Harold has been inside with us. We figured that once he got trapped without access to programming an escape portal, we would be forever cut off. His laptop ran out of battery."

"Wolf and Yeardley have been working on this for weeks. We were only able to get through just now."

The jungle growth gave way to a swirling portal surrounded by lightning creating an opening into what looked like Scottie's living room.

As they ran down through the overgrowth, a party of orcs approached the opening into the real world.

"No!" Maisie yelled.

Both the bear and the boar increased their speeds and raced past the running women. They attacked from behind, catching the orcs off guard. Somehow there was a wolf involved in the mini-battle. The swirling opening grew smaller the closer Maisie got.

Aaliyah jumped through first, she turned and reached for Maisie's arms, dragging her through the swirling lightning storm. Maisie sat, stunned, on the carpet in Scottie's house. Aaliyah yelled into the portal.

"Now, get over here now!"

A large gray wolf came sailing through the portal first.

Maisie watched in horror as the portal seemed to be continuously getting smaller. The boar jumped into the room next.

Maisie screamed as the bear was stopped on the other side of the portal by an orc attack. It was a decision the orc would regret, if it lived. The bear fell into the living room, the orc's arm still in its claws

"Now, close it now!"

With a thundering crash of lightning, the portal collapsed.

On the floor around her, panting from the exertion of running and battle were Vik, Wolf, and Scottie. All in human form.

Maisie started giggling with manic stress relief. "You're back in your stupid orc costume."

Scottie looked down at his chest. "I am, it's cold in here. I think I prefer my other clothes." He crawled over to her and pulled her into his arms.

"We made it back. We made it back."

The giggling turned to sobs. Maisie clung to Scottie. They were home, no more orc attacks, no more midnight watches. She cried against his chest.

"We left Harold. He's dead and we just left him."

"Hey." Scottie wiped tears from her cheeks with his thumbs. "It's what he wanted all along. We didn't leave him, we gave him his wish. He wanted to live the rest of his life in the world he created."

"Who are you talking about? Who died?" Yeardley asked.

"Are you talking about Harold Whitaker?" Wolf asked. "He's been missing for weeks. Almost as long as you've been gone."

"Exactly as long as we've been gone," Scottie said. "He

wanted to create a virtual world but instead found a way to move in and out from his game to reality."

"So he knew he was opening portals?" Wolf growled.

"He did, but he never realized they were opening other portals in different places. He thought once he shut the portals down from inside the game, that would end it."

"We were trapped."

"Oh, shit. We can talk about this later. We need to get you two taken care of. What do you need?"

"Food. And a soft bed."

"I can have something delivered in twenty minutes. Why don't you go and get a shower?" Aaliyah said.

"You guys food. Aaliyah and I will grab some clothes for Maisie. Scottie and Maisie can get clean, and we can all be back here in no time." Vik got to his feet and offered a hand out to Wolf.

"You two take your time, we'll be back soon," Yeardley said as she followed Aaliyah out the front door.

Maisie stayed on the floor, Scottie continued to hold her.

"Shower?" Maisie said after all of the commotion ended with everyone running off to their errands.

Scottie pushed up to his feet and offered a hand down to Maisie. "Come on," he said as he pulled her to his feet. He wrapped an arm around her and held her close as they stumbled toward the kitchen.

"I have to have some chips in here somewhere."

"Chips and Mountain Dew?" Maisie snorted.

"I may not have any actual food, but I always have those," Scottie confirmed.

"You have a half barrel of cheese puffs in here," Maisie said as she stared into a tall cupboard.

Scottie moved behind her and reached over and picked the container up one-handed. "These will do."

He tossed the lid onto the counter and reached in for a handful of orange cheese puffs.

Maisie reached in for her own handful. They ate in silence as they climbed the stairs.

Maisie stopped as Scottie walked into his room.

"What? Don't you want to take a shower?"

She pointed awkwardly down the hall. "Shouldn't I use the other bathroom?"

"Why? All my towels are in here."

She didn't have words to say what she was thinking. They were back in the real world, she would accept that what had happened between them would stay in Austratica. As much as she hated being stuck in the game, she had loved her time with Scottie. But she also knew it wasn't exactly real. It was a fantasy, in a literal fantasy land, now they were back... well she didn't know how to tell him she understood if he also went back to how they were before. There was no reason for them to rely on each other anymore.

She hated everything about being back. Everything. She was glad to be home, but not. Surrounded by the empty luxury of Scottie's house, she felt a deepening hollowness in her core. She didn't want what they had to be over.

Tears dripped down her face and she began to sniffle.

Scottie turned and looked at her. "What's wrong, Maise? I thought you wanted a shower?"

She swiped at her nose, and rubbed her palm across her cheek, grinding the tears away. She stared at him. He was so far away. She could already feel the chasm between them. He may have been standing ten feet away, but in this reality that was on the other side of an insurmountable, uncrossable distance.

"Sunshine, what's wrong?"

Her insides did one last dying flutter as he called her that name. How long before he forgot? How long before it came to mean nothing? She would never be the same after their ordeal. But they were back, and wasn't the goal to return to normal as quickly as possible?

Scottie stepped back into the hall, running his hands down her arms. "Hey." He dipped down so that he was at her level.

"I'm so tired," Maisie started, "in my bones tired. And I'm hungry. I'm covered in bug bites. I'm pretty sure I have fleas. And I'm still scared. I still think that around the next corner we'll run into an orc scouting party, or a wyvern nest. I'm afraid." She sniffed.

Scottie didn't say anything, he wiped her tears and kept his eyes on hers. She lay her hand along his face, cupping his cheek, letting the bristles of his beard tickle her palm. He leaned into her hand, holding it in place with his own.

"I'm afraid that everything is going to go back to normal, and I don't want it to go back like before. I don't know how I'm supposed to sleep in my own bed alone after this. I'd stay in Austratica, as horrible as it was, not to have to go back to how things were between us."

Her stomach tensed as she said the words, voiced her fear.

"What are you saying, Maisie? I thought you were falling in love with me. Was I wrong? Was all of that between us because you thought we were trapped?"

She furrowed her brow and looked at him, her confusion reflected in his eyes.

"I've been in love with you for a lot longer than we were trapped in Austratica, you just never realized it."

He slowly began nodding. "Yeah, I can be an idiot. But I totally fell in love with you, and that's not going to change. I don't want us to go back to whatever it was we were doing before. I'm a better man with you, because of you. You make me want to be smarter, stronger, faster."

"Really?"

Scottie stood, and Maisie let her gaze follow him up. He pulled her into his chest and dipped his head to kiss her.

She tasted her own tears.

"When I said I would be there for you, fight for you, do what I needed to keep you safe, that wasn't just because we were stuck. I meant it, forever. I want you here with me, not alone in your own bed."

"You want me to move in?"

Scottie sank back to his knees. He held her hands tight in his, gently kissing her dirty and bruised knuckles. "Maisie, my Sunshine, when I made the promise to always take care of you, I realize now that maybe my intentions were not as clear as I felt. Let me be as clear as possible. In my heart, I was promising myself to you forever. In my heart, I married you that day at the waterfall. I live, and I fight, and I survive for your smile. I don't know how I managed without you. I don't want us to ever go back to how things were before. I don't want to be without you. I love you. I want to marry you. Please. Will you marry me?"

As she stared, he closed his eyes and pressed his lips to her knuckles again.

She sniffed. "I think I married you that day too. But promises our hearts make don't count much here in the land of document everything, do they?"

Scottie opened his eyes and looked up at her. He was

everything she ever wanted, and he was on his knees telling her he was hers, asking her to claim him.

"Come on, let's get cleaned up. We can fly to Vegas tomorrow and get married, or go to the local courthouse here. I don't think I can wait for a long engagement or a big wedding. But if you want a big wedding, we can do that. We can do whatever you want."

"Scottie, I just want you. Vegas sounds too much like an adventure, and I'm kind of done with adventures for a while. The courthouse tomorrow sounds good to me."

EPILOGUE

A year later...

Maisie fought her way upstream through the crowd like some kind of spawning salmon.

Where the hell was he? He said he would be right here. With his height, and his shock of red hair, and the hat he was supposed to be wearing, Scottie should be relatively easy to find.

She needed the concourse to not be so crazy crowded. She caught a flash of the bright flaming hair that she associated with Scottie. She made her way through the crowd to get to him, and, yep, that was one of Hayden's wigs.

There were times she regretted introducing them, like when she wanted to go to bed, and they stayed up all night collaborating on the most amazing wigs ever. But mostly she was happy they hit it off, and were able to work together. After all, she got to try on all the wigs, and model them during the creation process. Hayden had been right, the wigs were incredibly heavy, and these days Maisie's cosplays needed to be a little easier to wear, and get in and out of.

"There you are." Maisie clutched her breasts. "I've been looking for you. It's lunchtime."

Her blue dress had a modified pinafore front that looked like a second piece worn over the dress, but really camouflaged the nursing access sides. Her hair was brushed back and secured with a white headband. Black mary janes and white knee socks completed her look.

"Are we glad to see you!" Scottie turned, a huge grin on his face. He had one large hand wrapped around the kicking foot of the baby he wore in a front infant carrier. His clothing was a mismatch of plaids and polka dots in a variety of colors. Having extra sewing supplies was both part of the costume and practical, since in the past year, he decided to start attending cons as a cosplay cleric, and provide last minute fix-it assistance. His shirt sleeves had been cut off at the seam and frayed.

The shirt showed off his shapely defined muscles, and the large celtic boar design tattoo. Something he, Vik, and Wolf had all gone out and gotten done about six months after he and Maisie had returned from their stay in Austratica. Vik had gotten a bear tattoo, and Wolf's tattoo was a wolf. They chose their berserker aspects after they realized they were no longer being taken over by magic and shifting.

The baby, with a hint of pink fuzz on her bald head, opened her mouth wide in a happy baby grin and squealed with more kicks and arm flails.

"I swear that's the last time I let you wander off with my baby." Maisie reached out and began unstrapping the baby from the back.

"Your baby? Woman, I swear," Scottie chuckled.

"Has she been fussy? My boobs have been screaming at me that we're late."

"Astra has been a perfect angel," Hayden said. "She's only pulled out part of my wig twice."

"Oh, crap is that what you've been up to?"

"Yes, our daughter has destructo hands."

"It's a good thing her daddy has fix-it hands. Have you seen any places to sit down? I hadn't expected Warp to be so busy this year," Maisie said as she lifted Astra from the pack.

"Last year there was some kind of secret special effects show, and now everyone wants to be around in case something exclusive like that happens again. Rumors were crazy about how it was supposed to be an announcement about making a Codex Wars movie. But when that game designer went missing, I guess they canceled it. I don't know. Didn't you see it? I was doing the wig demo. Apparently, there was some super awesome orc cosplay."

Maisie and Scottie exchanged glances. "We must have missed all of that, somehow."

"Well, you came to the wig presentation, you missed it too." Hayden said to Maisie.

Maisie had never made it to the presentation. At least Hayden wasn't aware of that. Maisie hadn't missed any of it, she had been in the middle of it, so had Scottie.

Free of the grabby baby, Scottie finished whatever little fixes he needed to make to the wig while Hayden and Maisie talked.

"All set," Scottie announced.

"Thanks, I'll see you guys later. Bye Astra. She makes the cutest piglet." Hayden turned and entered the throng of con goers.

Maisie had wanted a name reminiscent of the location where she and Scottie finally realized they were in love. Astra, the name seemed nerdy enough to meet expectations, and secret enough for her and Scottie to never forget the waterfall where they conceived her.

"The ballroom right behind us has a small presentation in about forty-five minutes, that should be enough time to feed the munchkin." Scottie ran a hand down her back, guiding her in the right direction.

"Oh look, it's Scottie!" Loud giggles caught Maisie's attention for a moment.

A gaggle of bikini-clad orc girls came in their direction.

Scottie leaned down and kissed Maisie. "Fans, give me a minute." He shrugged into his coat and put the hat back on his head.

"You make the best Mad Hatter!"

"Is your wife dressed up like Alice? That's so cute."

"Why don't you do orcs any more. I miss those cosplays."

"Do you like my orc?"

Astra started fussing, just as Maisie was prepared to wait for Scottie. In the past year, he had developed a real knack for handling the types of fans that Maisie used to be jealous of.

"Thank you. Your costumes look lovely. I don't cosplay the bad guys anymore, it sends the wrong message. You'll have to excuse me but my wife and daughter need my attention. Maybe we can get a selfie later in the day."

He perfected the hello, goodbye, and leave strategy. He opened the door to the ballroom and stood by as Maisie got situated and Astra latched on and began nursing.

"You do make a cute Mad Hatter," Maisie said, smiling up at him.

"You don't miss my orc cosplay?"

"If I ever see an orc again it will be too soon. I most definitely do not miss your orc cosplay."

"You did make a cute orc, but I do like you this way so much better."

"As Alice?"

"As my wife and mother of our girl." He leaned down and kissed her. It was the best kiss of her day so far.

Keep reading for a preview of more shifters from
Lulu M. Sylvian with Cougar Hunt, Shifter Vacation Stories

COUGAR HUNT: SHIFTER VACATION STORIES

Plus sized loved interests, reverse age gaps, and hot shifters...

Saffron's fling was supposed to be meaningless. it was supposed to help her forget about her ex husband.
Stranded with nowhere to stay, Ann ends up in a high end restaurant, covered in seafood... and a selkie's coat!
When a freak thunderstorm traps Quinn in a secluded cabin, Caleb shows up on her doorstep, wounded. But maybe there's more to get freaky than just the storm...
Hot shifters will save the day in this collection of vacations gone awry.

Stories included:
Cougar Hunt
Seal with a Kiss
Loaded for Bear

EXCERPT FROM COUGAR HUNT

Cougars on the loose...

Music thumped heavy in the air. And in Saffron's chest. It was uncomfortable and fought with her heartbeat. It reminded her that she was getting older. Scratch that, she *was* old. Old and discarded. Forgotten, forlorn, and following her friend into the cruise ship's night club.

They were there to celebrate being free of the shackles of marriage— Kelly was five years marriage free and counting like it was recovery. Saffi, three hundred sixty three days, not that she was counting— and to get their groove on with any willing body they could corner for the week. They had ten days and Saffi wasn't sure she would be able to find anybody interested in grooving with her in that short of a time.

Kelly didn't seem to realize, or care that she was closer to fifty than not. But then again, Kelly had always had a level of confidence that Saffi had lacked. Not that Saffi wasn't capable. She was. And she was confident within her area of expertise. Being a raging extrovert, and now landing men, were not in her wheelhouse. Hell, they weren't on the same block as her wheelhouse. Everything about this trip was far and away from anything that resembled a wheelhouse, a comfort zone, or any area of competency Saffi may have ever claimed at any point in her life.

Dragged along in her friend's wake, Saffi felt the sharp gazes of everyone questioning her presence. She needed to get a grip, a firm one on the back of her neck and shake hard. Reality was that no one cared, no one was glaring judgement at her. For some reason that was so much more scary than thinking someone might resent her presence.

Once inside the club, the throb was more music than noise. Saffi bounced with the beat. She didn't know the band, but the music was familiar. Her step daughter listened to this kind of dance music.

"You good?" Kelly yelled over the loud music.

"I'm fine," Saffi lied. She was in fake it 'til you make it mode. In her head, like a bodysuit under her flippy skirt and low cut lace-up blouse, she pictured herself in a confidence suit. Right now it was itchy and ill fitting, but it was there providing the confidence she naturally felt was lacking in her life. It wasn't working very well.

"Want a drink?" Kelly asked nodding toward the bar.

Saffi nodded and they made a bee-line for the bar. With their hands around ridiculously large, and probably prohibitively expensive margaritas—that pay in advance and swipe your ship ID card thing was dangerous—Kelly and Saffi scanned the club for a place to park and drink, before they headed to the dance floor.

"Come on." Kelly grabbed Saffi's wrist. They skirted the dance floor and slid into a shell-shaped half booth.

Saffi's exposed thighs stuck to the sticky pink vinyl.

"I feel like we're sitting in half a vajayjay," she smirked.

Kelly looked over her shoulder and around the curved booth. The back was taller than the sides, and the upholstery was fluted with deep grooves. "I think it's supposed to be a shell."

"Vagina, shell, same diff," Saffi giggled as she took another drink.

The alcohol hit her system as if they were up the side of some mountain in higher altitudes than cruising along at sea level. The invisible fake confidence suit she mentally pictured herself in seemed to fit more comfortably with more reinforcement along the spine. She didn't care if some twenty-something thought her almost fifty-something ass shouldn't be wearing the short skirt she had on. She looked good, and she knew it. Well, at least the margarita knew it. With the help of the drink her inner bad bitch could reign and those other Hugh-sounding voices in her head could shut the fuck up and get locked away for the night.

The beat of the music changed to something Saffi knew well. It was her "stand up, and strap in," she "had this" anthem. She had been listening to this song on heavy repeat for the past year.

"I'm gonna dance, you coming?"

Kelly, straw artfully between puckered lips, blinked and shook her head.

"Watch my drink." Saffi bounced her way out of the booth, leaving behind what felt like patches of skin on the vinyl.

The dance floor wasn't crowded, and from what she could tell, it was mostly couples dry humping instead of dancing. She didn't care. Years earlier, she and Madison took a mommy-and-me dance class. It had been the smartest decision she made, forming the strong bond she still had with her now grown step-daughter. It also had been the start of two decade's worth of dance classes the two of them had taken together. Saffi used those skills now to roll and sway her hips. When she had the space, she incorporated foot work, and when the music ramped up she could shimmy and shake, and even twerk her back side.

At some point she found she was not grooving to the beat alone. An attractive morsel—she couldn't help but think of him as a sweet young thing— was dancing along next to her. She wasn't sure when they acknowledged they were dancing together, they never touched, but she felt a surge of energy and joy she hadn't felt in longer than she cared to remember.

That thought blindsided her. Her shoe went sideways as her foot continued to the floor. She stumbled straight into God-you're-hot-please-tell-me-you're-over-twenty-one's arms.

He smiled and began laughing as he held her. "Yeah," he chuckled, "you okay?"

Regaining her balance, but still in the man's arms she looked up at him. "Shit that was out loud, wasn't it?"

He nodded. "You aren't going to fall over if I let go are you?"

"Do you have to let go?"

When his eyes crinkled up with an even broader smile Saffi extricated herself from his helpful embrace. She covered her eyes, as if that gesture could hide her embarrassment. "That wasn't supposed to be out loud either."

"Maybe you should take a break, get something to drink?"

"I've had a drink. Maybe more than I realized since I'm not filtering very well."

He stood back and extended his arm indicating she should lead the way from the floor.

"You didn't tell me how old you were," she reminded him.

"I'm well over twenty-one if that's what you are concerned with."

They stopped in front of the booth where Kelly wasn't watching Saffi's drink. Kelly wasn't watching much of anything. Her eyes were closed and her face suctioned to the face of some man. It looked like she found a willing body.

"That was fast." Saffi crossed her arms and shifted her weight so her hip popped to the side.

"That your friend?" her dance partner asked.

Saffi nodded.

"Looks like she's trying to suck my cousin's appendix out through his face."

Saffi turned to him and nodded. If she put any thought into how good looking this young man was, she'd start being stupid. Well, more stupid than she already had been. It didn't matter how handsome Hugh had been, other good looking men twisted her tongue into knots. Hugh had always found it entertaining. She had always found it embarrassing.

"How's your ankle? Want to get out of here and get some fresh air, and maybe something to drink that's not going to impact your filtering system anymore?"

"That sounds like a good idea. I think they are sucking all the air out the room with that." Saffi pointed and swirled her finger around indicating the make-out session in front of them.

They stood in place and watched the kissing like a strange show on display before they both shook their heads and left.

Once out of the club, Saffi felt that same thudding in her

chest from the muffled boom of the night club. This time it didn't make her feel old, it reminded her that she was alive. Booze, dancing, not being able to form complete sentences around good looking young men, yeah, that actually felt good.

"There's a smoothie place just up the concourse, how does that sound?"

Saffi nodded.

Out from under the flashing colored lights of the club Saffi could see her companion clearly. He was younger, but not as young as she first thought. He had full lips, and his light eyes were rimmed in guy-liner. She always did appreciate when men went that extra step for clubbing. It seemed like once out of college, they stopped doing that and instead thought that dress slacks and a clean polo was dressing up for going out. Maybe it was an age thing, maybe it was a generational thing. It seemed that she used to date guys who wore makeup, and then didn't, and the only difference was age and income.

They walked in silence until they reached the smoothie stand. Saffi ordered something with blueberries and bananas, the man ordered something with heavy protein and an extra scoop of peanut butter.

"Thank you," she said as she took the smoothie. "I don't know your name. I'm Saffron."

"Oscar." He held out a large hand with long tapering fingers.

A discharge of static zapped her fingers as she reached to take his hand.

"Ow." she jumped

Oscars eyebrows bounced as he extended his hand again. "Electric."

Saffi couldn't help but notice how warm and comfortable his hand felt around hers. Time slowed, and for a second of eternity she thought there might have been something to that electric discharge between them. Something more than basic science. His eyes were mesmerizing, a pale hazel with a spot of bright blue taking up about a quarter of his left iris.

When his hand slid away from hers, time resumed normalcy. Clocks ticked, hearts beat, and Saffi ignored the attraction she felt toward the man who was out getting fresh air and a smoothie with her because his cousin was otherwise occupied.

"So that was your cousin?" Saffi asked.

They strolled down the concourse, and out onto the deck. The night was dark, practically cloudless with a glowing gibbous moon. Waves and the ship's engine created a calming background shushing.

"Yep Tyler, and your friend?"

"Kelly."

"I should probably warn you, he's..." Oscar paused.

"Only looking for a ship hook up. No worries there. That's Kelly's plan too." She didn't admit it was supposed to be her plan too, but she wasn't so sure about that now.

"And you?" he asked.

Saffi stopped and looked up at him. He was tall, but not excessively so. She didn't need to crane her neck as much as she would have if she wanted to look at Hugh. She mentally put Oscar in the six-two range.

"Never mind," he said with a chuckle, and resumed walking. His long legs ate up distance.

"Never mind what?" Saffi asked as she had to scramble after him to catch up. "What's that supposed to mean?"

"You don't strike me as the type."

"And what type is that?"

"The meaningless hook up type. There's something about you that gives me the impression you would not be the one sitting in a club somewhere playing tonsil hockey with some guy you just met."

It was a pretty slick way to turn her down before she could make any embarrassing forward plays. She hated getting discounted because of her size, and it was always her size that was the excuse. Saffron didn't look her age, and even being older than most people assumed, she had never been rejected based on her age. It always came down to the size of her ass. Body positivity be damned. There seemed to be plenty of men claiming they liked thicc, with two Cs, thighs. But they did not exist in her dating circles, or on any of those apps Kelly had her create accounts on.

"So what's giving you that impression? My ass?" She circled the area around her ample hip. "Sounds like you're saying I'm not your meaningless hook up type." She stopped with a huff. Letting her smile dissipate, she shook her head. This was stupid. That invisible confidence body-suit suddenly felt itchy. "Why'd you have to go there? I wasn't hitting on you or anything."

Any confidence, real or imaginary evaporated. She plastered a sarcastic smirk across her lips and waited.

"I did notice that, and your ass"— Oscar walked around her raking her form with his gaze. With a bite of his lower lip, he made sure she knew he was appreciating the view— "that's not a hook-up kind of ass. That's the kind of ass that demands a commitment."

Saffi bit the inside of her cheek trying to stop the blush she could feel burning. So she had been wrong, she had been the one to lob it into the booty size court. His volley had been artful. He managed to make her feel like he thought she was attractive, and yet, he still dodged that hook-up possibility.

Fine, she could live with that. If Kelly was going to spend the cruise fucking his cousin, maybe Oscar would be in need of a cruise buddy to do things with.

She dismissed it all with a shrug and continued walking as if that hiccup of miscommunication and establishment of cruise friend-zone hadn't just happened.

"We know why Kelly's on the cruise. Why are you here?" she asked.

"Family destination wedding crap." Oscar took a sip of his smoothie. "My cousin is getting married at the resort."

"Not the one Kelly is with?"

"No, not him. His sister. She didn't want a big wedding, just an ecologically unsound one."

"Oh, someone doesn't like cruise ships."

"Don't even get me started," Oscar quipped.

Saffi giggled. When was the last time she had actually giggled? They continued to stroll the decks of the ship, talking about everything from her divorce to him having previously worked in Central America— but he was an accountant now, better stability. They were both headed for the same resort in Belize. This vacation was someone else's idea. They spent hours talking about nothing.

Saffi couldn't stop a yawn from splitting her face and causing her eyes to water. "What time is it? I think my buzz wore off a few hours ago." She covered her face as another yawn took over.

"Let me walk you back to your cabin. Make sure you get in all right," Oscar offered.

"You're sweet, but no need. I've kept you out here long enough. It was lovely to meet you Oscar. Maybe we'll run into each other again."

She felt alone trekking through what felt like miles of hallway on the guest room levels without Oscar strolling by her side. He was a calming presence to her manic, broken self confidence. She scoffed at herself, she couldn't possibly miss him, she had only just met him. Inwardly she groaned. Saffi clued in that maybe, that last offer to walk her home had been a come-on.

"Oh for fuck's sake," she said out loud in reaction to her cluelessness and the bright shiny red birthday present bow stuck on her cabin door.

YOU NEED MORE LULU

Sign up for Lulu's newsletter to keep up to date with new releases and happenings. And get a free story

http://lulumsylvian.com/newsletter/

ALSO BY LULU M. SYLVIAN

Legatum

Paranormal shifter romantic suspense

The World of Wet Waterfalls and the Wildwood

Paranormal werewolves why-choose, poly-love romance

Shifter Vacation Stories

Reverse age-gap vacation romance

Second Endings

Paranormal ghost romance

Rockers

Rockstar romance, some contemporary, some paranormal

Holiday Strippers

Contemporary, paranormal, ridiculous, romance

ABOUT THE AUTHOR

 Bio-engineered to be the only redhead in a generation of blonds, Lulu feels that "aliens" may actually be the best answer for a life-time of being asked, "Where did you get that red hair from?"

She did not come into writing from years of scribbling words on paper. Her background is rooted in visual arts and making pictures. Encouraged to make those pictures out of words Lulu began writing just to see what would happen. What happened was two full-length manuscripts in three months.

Lulu cannot ride a horse, a motorcycle, spin a hula hoop, or play roller derby. But she does write steamy hot paranormal romance. She embraces the crazy that comes with that one little genetic mutation, and attempts to live up to the reputation of being a redhead that proceeds her. Lulu would like to apologize for her contribution to the hole on the ozone layer from her use of hairspray in the 1980s.

For more information, visit:
www.LuluMSylvian.com

facebook.com/lmsylvian
instagram.com/lmsylvian

www.ingramcontent.com/pod-product-compliance
Lightning Source LLC
Chambersburg PA
CBHW031257170626
46807CB00001B/193